I'd like to dedicate this book to you, my readers. I can never thank you enough for making my dream come true. Please know that I will continue to endeavor to provide you with the best stories I can. I really hope you enjoy this one.

The Woman Beneath the Stairs

Uncovering her husband's family secrets could cost her everything...

Ally's perfect marriage to Tim Hawthorne is crumbling under the weight of one trial after another. Forced to visit Tim's mother on her secluded island off the coast of Maine, Ally uncovers a sinister secret: years ago, a member of the family was the prime suspect in a young woman's disappearance from the same island. Now, history is repeating itself. Another woman has vanished without a trace. Ally digs into all the dark secrets of the Hawthorne family's past, but what she discovers may cost her more than her marriage — it may cost her life.

From multi-award-winning *Wall Street Journal* bestselling author Christopher Greyson comes a heart-pounding psychological mystery thriller that will leave you gasping for breath until the shocking conclusion.

Also by Christopher Greyson

The Girl Who Lived

One Little Lie

The Dark

Pure of Heart

The Adventures of Finn and Annie

Kiku - The Yakuza War Trilogy

The Detective Jack Stratton Mystery-Thriller Series:

And Then She Was Gone

Girl Jacked

Jack Knifed

Jacks are Wild

Jack and the Giant Killer

Data Jack

Jack of Hearts

Jack Frost

Jack of Diamonds

Captain Jack

Jack of Spades

THE WOMAN BENEATH THE STAIRS

WALL STREET JOURNAL BESTSELLING AUTHOR

CHRISTOPHER GREYSON

GREYSON MEDIA

Chapter One

"Mommy!" A terrified little girl's scream for help resonated through the screen door.

Ally jumped up.

"Mommy!!!" A maternal reaction ignited deep in Ally's chest. She rushed toward the sound, her coffee mug tumbling from her hand. She was already at the side door when it struck the kitchen floor. Yanking the door open, she dashed outside.

Through the rose bushes, Ally could see her neighbor's six-year-old daughter, Mary, lying beside a tipped-over bicycle in her driveway. A huge stray dog crouched a few yards away, ready to pounce. The little girl pulled her legs to her chest as the dog slowly circled the bike to get at Mary. It growled, barked, and opened its mouth, revealing sharp, yellowed teeth.

Ally vainly looked for something to use as a weapon before primal instinct overtook her. She charged through the rose bushes like a mother bear protecting her cub. Thorns sliced into her exposed skin. She ignored the pain as she raced to get between the predator and the girl.

The dog focused on its prey. Its jaws opened wide as it leaped at Mary.

Ally seized the beast by the back of the neck, digging her nails into its thick fur. Its jaws chomped the air as it thrashed and kicked.

Roaring louder than the dog, Ally pivoted and, using all her might, flung the creature toward the street. Dazed, it rolled across the lawn. It gave one quick glance over its shoulder and darted away, yapping with its tail between its legs.

Ally stood defiant with her hands still in tight fists as she watched the stray dog run out of sight.

A soft whimper came from behind her.

Little Mary, still shocked from the attack, lay on the ground, her knee bleeding and scuffed from her fall.

"Oh, I've got you." Ally scooped Mary up in her arms. "You're going to be okay, baby."

The little girl's eyes were still closed tight, and her lips trembled. Mary wrapped her legs around Ally's waist, burying her face in Ally's neck as she wept.

"Mommy." Mary sobbed. "Thank you."

Ally's knees buckled, and she held onto Mary tighter. Mary didn't realize who had saved her, and her words of gratitude cut Ally to her core. What she wouldn't have given to hear those words spoken, but that would never be.

The front door banged open, and Tess dashed down the steps, yanking an earbud out as she ran over. "What's the matter?"

"It was a stray dog," Ally explained.

She held onto her for a moment more before handing Mary to her mother.

"I'm never using headphones again while I do the laundry." Tess checked her daughter's injuries. "You're okay." Tess said as she tenderly brushed Mary's hair out of her face.

Ally stepped back.

"Thank you," Tess said with genuine gratitude as she smiled at Ally. "Do you want to come inside? Your hands are shaking. I could break open some wine. After all of that, you probably could use a drink."

Mary sniffled.

Ally wanted to reach out and comfort Mary but let her arm fall back at her side. "Maybe another time. I'm just glad Mary's okay."

Tess' eyes rounded in concern. "How about you? I've been meaning to come over and check on you. Tim told us about what happened. How are you coping?"

Does everybody know? She forced a smile, "Better every day."

"If you need to talk about—"

"Actually, I've got to run," Ally cut her off. Eager to avoid the subject, she started back to the house, "See ya."

When she reached the side door, Mary called out. "Thank you, Mrs. Hawthorne!"

The little girl's voice pierced her chest. "You're welcome, sweetie." Ally waved. Blinking back tears, she hurried inside.

She crossed to the sink and examined her arms. Dotted lines of blood marked the path the thorns had torn into her skin.

How can such a beautiful flower cause so much pain?

After bandaging the worst of her injuries from the thorns, she returned to the kitchen. She cleaned up the spilled coffee and inspected the dropped mug. The large, brown ceramic cup was an encouragement gift from her father. *You've got this!* was written in an embossed, gold script across the front. It looked un-damaged from the fall until she turned it over. A wide crack ran along the base. The impact on the floor had killed her favorite morning companion.

Ally's grip tightened on the handle. Her knuckles turned white, and her fist shook. She intended to toss the cup into the trash can, but the memory of Mary's cry was the spark that reignited the pain of Ally's recent loss. Her arm whipped out. The cup shot through the air and slammed into the drywall above the trash can. The handle punched into the wall, and the cup hung, suspended in the air, the phrase she once read for encouragement now mocking her.

"No, I don't got this," Ally muttered.

Ally's hand gripped the plastic spatula and thrust it into the joint compound. She slathered more white goo onto the wall, trying to cover the hole. Her anger had gotten away from her again — a sign of the inner turmoil still simmering beneath the surface. She closed her eyes and attempted to center herself amidst the chaos of emotions overtaking her body. She took a deep breath and focused on the now, and the task at hand. Behind her lay a past filled with pain, sorrow, loss, and destruction. She needed to move forward to avoid going crazy or killing someone...

In the past three months, she'd become skilled at fixing things; from cracked, slammed doors to a hole accidentally kicked in a wall during one of her 'episodes', as Tim called them. She was doing so much better now. Since she started taking new medication, Ally had done more than patch up physical walls; she was repairing the damage she'd done inside herself. She knew better than anyone that with setbacks and mistakes come consequences. As her father, a former Marine, drilled into her: "When you find yourself in a hole — quit digging and fill it in." And so, here she was, fixing her mistake.

The click of Tim's shoes against the hardwood floor in the hallway filled Ally's ears. He was home early. She hadn't planned on him seeing this. She took a deep breath and then peaked around the corner.

Tim's handsome, tall, frame was dressed in a crisp, white shirt, gray suit pants, and black Oxford dress shoes. He strolled toward the kitchen as he spoke into his cell phone. "Yes, Mother. I understand. It's not a problem. Tomorrow then." He flashed Ally a captivating smile. He was the kind of strong, under-stated man that made women swoon. He glanced at the wet drywall, raised an amused eyebrow and then held up an extended index finger before vanishing around the corner.

A mixture of emotions raced through Ally's body: confusion over what her husband had been talking about, fear of what tomorrow might bring, and a longing for his embrace.

She brushed an errant strand of hair out of her face. A damp glop of joint compound from the back of her hand stuck to her cheek. She wiped it away with a paper towel and crossed to the sink. The warm water cascaded down her hands, and she watched as each piece of mud and grime was swept away by the force before being sucked down the drain. She wished she could do the same to her feelings at that moment. Soap, water, a little hard scrubbing, and she could feel whole again.

Suddenly, Tim's powerful, gentle hands caressed her hips. He clasped her from behind and planted a kiss on her cheek. "How's the love of my life doing?" he whispered in her ear.

"It's a miracle you don't hate me."

Tim spun her around, tipping up her chin to meet his gaze. "Don't ever say that. I could never stop loving you."

"Not even after another freakout?"

Tim glanced toward the wall and shrugged. "What's that thing your father says?" He smoothed her hair. "Mess up, fess up, and then move on?"

She shrugged.

He smiled. "You did such a wonderful job repairing it. I can't even tell it was damaged."

Ally embraced him, her body trembling against his. She squeezed her eyes shut, trying to block out the memories of the past few months. He was her rock, her solid foundation in an ever-shifting world. "How did your gallery meeting go?"

"I finally sold two paintings and the horse sculpture!"

"That's wonderful." Ally raised her eyes to the ceiling and said a little prayer. They lived paycheck to paycheck, and with her not working the last three months, they were in the red. "I'm so glad."

Tim's smile faded, and he stepped back to gain space between them. Taking a deep breath, he cracked his neck from side to side, like a pole vaulter psyching himself up before a jump. "On the drive home, my mother called."

"I heard." Ally braced herself for anything. The daily drama in Tim's family seemed like a dark rollercoaster ride — you never knew when it might take a sudden drop.

"They're releasing my mother from the hospital today..."Ally listened as her admiration for her husband battled with her frustration at Tim's inability to stand up to his overbearing mother. "And she's going back to the island."

Ally forced a smile and tried to find something positive to say. "That's wonderful news. It wasn't a heart attack after all?"

Tim's face wavered between relief and ambivalence. "Her doctor and the hospital are still at odds about that. The hospital thinks it was her gallbladder. The symptoms are very similar."

Ally felt a wave of temporary relief wash over her. Her mother-in-law always seemed to be riding the hypochondria express. If she got a cold, she'd act as if she were dying and summon Tim to be at her bedside. "I'm glad she's doing better."

Tim shifted on his feet, which sent a jolt of alarm down Ally's spine. That was his tell. He was trying to work up the courage to ask Ally something.

Tim's lip curled. "About that... Dr. Bradley isn't a hundred percent positive it wasn't a heart attack, so he's going to be monitoring her closely over the next few days. Mother was hoping, if it wasn't too much of a bother, for me to come up."

Ally gulped as she tried to rein in her emotions, clicking her nails against each other in an effort to maintain control. The warning signs of her having an impending meltdown blared to life — Hot flash, check. Dry mouth, check. Tightness in chest, double-check. Ally took a deep breath and said sweetly, yet firmly, "But honey, you just went there for three weeks."

"I know." Tim rubbed the back of his neck and then shrugged. "But what can I do? She asked."

"Say no."

He hesitated before responding. "The thing is, it's not just my mother. Tom is having a lot of anxiety issues. The whole deal with Mother going into the hospital has made him very agitated."

Gently, she said, "Did your brother say that, or did that come from your mother?"

"You know you can't get a read on Tom over the phone."

"Then you should make a video call," she politely suggested.

Tim made a face. "With their internet? Not a chance."

Ally opened the cabinet to get a glass. "But I need you here."

Tim ran his hands through his dark brown hair. It needed a trim, but she liked him a little scruffy looking. His eyes met hers, and Ally saw how conflicted he was. He didn't want to leave her alone, but his family always had a way of tugging at his heartstrings. "It will only be a few days. You're doing so much better. You had a fantastic therapy appointment, right?"

Ally closed her mouth, marched over to the sink, and poured herself a glass of water. She couldn't tell Tim the truth. She'd be fine one minute, but then something would happen to set her off. Every day, there were dozens of reminders. From Mary's cry for help to a diaper commercial, it seemed she couldn't escape the pain no matter what she did.

Tim took his phone out. "There's a flight tomorrow morning that still has seats available. It'll be three or four days, tops. I promise."

Ally's shoulders slumped, betraying her disappointment. "You promised that last visit, which ended up being three weeks."

"I own that." Tim nodded rapidly. "My bad. That was all my fault. I completely see your point, but she's all alone—"

"Ha!" Ally set the glass on the counter. "Your mother isn't alone. Your cousin and her husband live with her, plus she has a bunch of servants."

"They're not servants. They're staff. And Mia and Carter are going to Italy."

"Tell them to stay. Or ask your Uncle Philip. He lives there, too."

"He's no help!"

"Why does it have to be you? Your mother has so much money she doesn't know what to do with it. She could hire a nurse."

"If it was only Mother, I wouldn't go. But Tom asked, too."

Ally's eyes narrowed, filled with suspicion. Victoria had turned the craft of the guilt trip into an art form.

He raised his hands. "I don't know if she put him up to it, but Tom did ask me."

Ally sighed. If there was one person in this world Tim could never turn down, it was his twin brother. She nodded.

Tim smiled and stepped close, setting his phone on the counter. "I appreciate you beyond words." He kissed her cheek. "Thank you for understanding."

Ally set her jaw and mustered up her courage. Taking a deep breath, she asked. "When do we leave?"

Tim shuddered like he'd stuck his finger into an electrical outlet. "We?"

Even if she were reluctant to go, she'd follow her husband and help him where she could. "I'm going with you this time." Ally's mouth had once again gone dry. "Is that a problem?"

"No, it's just that, you know...."

"No, I don't know. Can you elaborate?"

"Visiting my mother stresses *me* out. Do you want to subject yourself to that kind of environment? Especially considering everything that's happened."

"You said it would only be for a few days. I can handle that."

Tim looked like he'd swallowed a bug. He coughed and cleared his throat. "What if something comes up again? I don't want you to get stuck with me out there."

Ally grabbed him by his belt and pulled him close. "One, you are the only one I want to get stuck with." He opened his mouth to protest, and she gently touched his lips. "Two, with me there, you can keep your promise. I'm your get-out-of-jail-free card. We'll go to your mom's, make sure she and Tom are doing fine, and then we'll go. You can blame me if they try to guilt you into staying."

Tim rubbed his chin.

She didn't know what he was debating, and right now, she didn't care. "I let you go before when I wanted you here. I'm telling you that I need to be with you. I don't know if I can handle being alone right now."

Tim nodded. "Of course. That's great. Really. We'll have a wonderful time." He flashed her another dazzling smile, kissed her, and hurried out of the room.

Her initial feelings of empowerment faded as she realized what she had signed on to. Each footstep in the hallway reverberated in her ears as a migraine took hold. Visiting her mother-in-law's house held the highest spot on her 'places to avoid' list. It topped getting a root canal and colonoscopy—on the same day. But there was no avoiding it.

And where her husband went, she would follow.

Chapter Two

Ally sat on the edge of her bed, glanced at the clock, and resisted calling out to Tim to start his shower. She didn't want to nag him, but traffic to the airport was bad even this early in the morning. A moment later, the water turned on and Ally breathed easier.

She rechecked her suitcase sitting open on the bed. While she loved the privacy of Guillemot Island, if she forgot to pack something, the nearest store was a twenty-minute boat ride away — if the weather was cooperating. And with winter closing in fast, she wanted to be prepared for anything.

Tucking her pill keeper into an interior pocket, she zipped it closed and immediately opened it again. She'd never been on medication before and wasn't familiar with the rules for flying with it. Crossing to her nightstand, she removed the printout from the pharmacy, folded it, and slid it next to the pill case. She doubted there would be a problem at the airport, but with the way security was, why take chances? Just thinking about her mother-in-law stressed Ally out. If she didn't have her meds to cope, she'd go out of her mind.

Ally tried to swallow, but her mouth had gone

dry. She unclenched her fists. Her nails had dug into the skin in three places. She closed her eyes and started counting backward from twenty. Under her current condition, going to Maine was a terrible idea, but what was her alternative? The thought of staying by herself filled her with dread. And what would she do if Tim extended his stay like he did before? She had to go for the sole purpose of being there to drag Tim home.

Tim's phone buzzed on the bureau. The screen lit up, and a message appeared: NEED TO SPEAK 2 U F2F. WHEN U GET IN? MISS U BABE!

Ally picked up the phone and pressed the information button as she walked to the bathroom door. "Who do you know from 555-749-9062?"

"That's the area code for Maine," Tim called out. "Did I get a call?"

"No. It was a text." Ally read the message.

Tim laughed. "It's a wrong number. The only person who calls me babe is you."

"You don't recognize the number?"

"No. It's not for me. Are there any other messages from that number?"

Ally checked, and there weren't. "No."

"There you go."

A car horn beeped outside the house.

Ally set his phone down. "The driver is here early."

"Oh, shoot!" Tim shut the shower off. "Sorry. Can you stall for me?"

"I'll go offer him a coffee." Ally closed her suitcase, zipped it up, and carried it downstairs. She rolled it to the front door and set it on the top step as she waved to the older man parked in a mini-van in their driveway. "We'll just be a few minutes. Can I get you a coffee?"

The man powered down his window and held up a large cup. "No, thanks. Brought my own! There's some construction on the way to the airport, so I thought I'd see if we could go a little earlier. I called your husband and left a message."

"He must not have gotten it. Sorry about that. I'll let him know." Ally hurried back upstairs.

Tim stepped out of the bedroom, pulling a shirt over his wet hair. "My suitcase is already downstairs. Do you want to grab some water and a couple of muffins?"

"I already have them in my bag. You just finish getting ready."

"I need to make a pit stop, brush my teeth, and I'm good to go." Tim raced back into the bathroom and shut the door.

Ally brushed her hair back as she looked around the room to ensure they didn't forget anything. Tim's phone still sat on the bureau. She struggled to maintain her composure as she tried to reconcile what she'd been told with what she felt in her gut. Was she being paranoid, or was it the new medication? She believed Tim, but the text bothered her. Should she text something back? She could call the number and see who answered. Or she could block the caller.

It must have been a wrong number. But the area code was from Maine. She could do a reverse phone lookup on the internet. She remembered the text word for word but had already forgotten the number.

The toilet flushed, and the water in the sink turned on.

Ally took a deep breath and picked up his phone. Guilt washed over her, but she still punched in his passcode. She opened his messaging app. The text message was gone. Did he delete it?

She didn't know if there was a way to undelete a text message. She checked his other messages. There was a call an hour ago from the airport taxi, but nothing out of the ordinary. All his photos were uploaded to their joint account, so there wasn't a need to check that. She was about to search his browser history when she flicked the phone off, set it on the bureau, and marched out of the room.

Tim had never given her reason to doubt him. She wasn't going to start now. Tim was a good man. He'd never cheat.

Would he?

Chapter Three

Ally sat in the back of the taxi cab, staring at the harbor in the distance. The sky was cold and gray, and the sea matched, making it difficult to tell where the horizon met the ocean.

Tim had booked the first flight out of California, and they left their house at 4:30 that morning. Between the ride to the airport, the wait, the flight, and the ride to the coast of Northern Maine, she'd been sitting for over ten hours, and they still had a boat trip ahead of them. She flexed her aching feet, making her ankle crack. She was exhausted from the long journey, but part of her wanted to turn right around and go home. Yet she knew they couldn't go back now and steeled herself for what lay ahead.

The taxi parked at the end of a dock in front of a cute gift shop. The store was clad in faded cedar shingles and adorned in a nautical theme. Thick ropes created a pathway up a gangplank to a worn door.

"Do you mind if I run inside and grab something?" Ally called to Tim, who followed the driver to the car's trunk.

"Not at all. Take your time. I'll find out about the boat."

Ally groaned as she limped up the ramp. Her bones ached, and her feet throbbed. Despite occasionally walking up and down the aisle on the plane, she'd had a cramp in her right thigh since noon. She rubbed the spot, trying to forget her sister's ominous warning regarding the dangers of flying and blood clots.

The little bell above the door chimed as she entered. The cozy gift shop was filled with knick-knacks, making it feel like a seafaring tourist's dream store. A huge variety of souvenirs lined the shelves. Everything from T-shirts, magnets, and postcards, to model sailing ships, mermaids, and whaling memorabilia decorated every table, rack, and wall.

"Welcome to Damarbay!" In the corner, a petite older woman sat in an armchair next to the cash register, flipping through a newspaper with one hand and drinking coffee with the other. A cigarette dangled from her lips. Her wrinkled skin hung on her bones like a dehydrated prune. "You looking for anything particular?" she asked in a thick accent.

Ally smiled. "I am. Do you have any taffy?"

"We've got the best saltwater taffy on the coast. Box or bag?" She pointed with her coffee cup toward a console of candy in a rainbow of colors.

"Two assorted boxes, please. How about flowers?"

"Not this time of year. Who are they for?"

"A sick mother-in-law."

"That's the only kind of mother-in-law there is! Ha!" She laughed at her joke so hard that she started coughing. "On the off chance you like her, we've got what they call a pampering package. It's a gift set that's got a comfy throw, socks, bath stuff, tea, some candles and crap."

"Oh, I'll take that too."

The woman grinned, displaying stained, yellowed

teeth with a few missing in the back. "We don't wrap stuff, but it comes in a gift bag."

"That's perfect. I'm going to look around some more."

"Take your time. Buy the whole place if you want to. Ha!" She picked up two boxes of taffy and headed to the counter.

Ally wandered around the store. Tom loved candy, but she wanted to pick him up something else, too. Tim's brother had suffered brain damage as a boy but was highly functional. Tom was childlike, so he wouldn't enjoy something a typical thirty-eight-year-old man would want. After making a complete circle inside the shop, she was about to give up hope of finding a fitting gift when she noticed a rack of movies. Forgoing the typical adult comedies and dramas, she zeroed in on the enormous boxed set perched on top: the complete movie collection of the Marvel Avengers. It was perfect. Tom loved superheroes.

Ally clapped her hands. She picked up the heavy box and brought it over to the counter.

The clerk's eyes widened. "Did you check the price on the box? That's the whole shebang in ultra-high res. It costs two hundred and twenty-five dollars."

Ally froze. Her newfound prize suddenly lost some of its luster. She had no idea it would be so expensive. She glanced back at the display rack. They did have a few individual movies. She was about to return the collection when she thought of the first time she'd met Tom. She shook his hand and called him her hero. Tom was so happy he cried.

Ally put the boxed set on the counter.

The woman wiggled her shoulders and hummed

happily as she rang everything up. "You picked an odd time to vacation. The weather is awful. Been nothing but cold rain."

"Is the water very rough? We're going out on a boat."

"The bay is nothing but chop. You won't make it out of the harbor without barfing unless you pick up this." She set a box of motion sickness pills on the counter. "Trust me. It's either these or buy some trash bags for puking because you're gonna need 'em."

Seeing how she couldn't stomach the rides at amusement parks, the last thing she wanted was to show up at Victoria's doorstep seasick. She nodded.

The clerk tossed the pills into the bag and asked, "Where are you headed? The lighthouse?"

"Guillemot Island."

"You can't go there. It's a private island. Even if you want to, you don't want to. Haven't you heard the story?"

"No. What story?"

"I'm interested to hear this, too," Tim said, walking up behind them.

Both Ally and the clerk jumped. Because of the sound of the cash register, Ally hadn't heard the bell or Tim's approach.

The clerk set the bag on the counter and stepped back. "Nice seeing you again, Mr. Hawthorne. I, ah, thought she was, um, snooping. I wanted to shoo her away. You know, like a seagull coming around while you're eating. That's all."

From the set of his jaw, Tim wasn't happy, but he placed a gentle hand on Ally's back. "Did you get what you wanted?"

"All set."

"The boat's here. We should get going."

Ally turned to thank the clerk, but the woman hurried through an open door to a back room and disappeared.

Following Tim outside, Ally pulled the motion-sickness medicine out. "Want one?"

"I'm good. I don't think you'll need it. The harbor is like glass, and Alan said it's the same once we get past the seawall."

Ally dropped the medicine in the bag and scowled over her shoulder. "That's not what the clerk told me."

"Locals make their living off tourists. In the winter, some unscrupulous ones turn into land pirates." He wrapped his arm around her shoulder, closed one eye, and snarled. "Arrgg! Shiver me timbers, you're fairer than the finest mermaid I've ever seen."

"You have the finest booty!" Ally slipped her hand into his back pocket and squeezed.

They both laughed and strolled hand in hand down the dock. At the end was an old fishing boat, bobbing on the waves that gently lapped along the boat's sides and the dock's pilings. The hull was painted red, with black letters spelling out *The Sea Spit*. A green tarp covered the deck. The enclosed deckhouse had large windows on three sides and a small door at the front.

A beefy man with gray hair and a salt-and-pepper beard stepped out of the deckhouse. He had a stern expression but smiled when he saw Tim and Ally, revealing several deep wrinkles in the corners of his eyes. He waved and started gathering up the tarp, which covered seats on either side in the back.

"Nice to see you again, Mr. Hawthorne. Mrs." He nodded. "I kept the chairs dry for you."

"Thanks, Dennis." Tim took the shopping bag from Ally's hand and helped her into the boat.

"Will you two be staying long this time?" Dennis asked.

"No. We're only staying a few days," Ally said. "I'm glad the water isn't rough."

"You know what they say, it's always calmest before a storm. And if you ask me, a big one is coming. My left elbow's been killing me." Dennis grabbed two life jackets from a cabinet and handed them to Tim and Ally. "Sorry, but you gotta wear them. Insurance company rules. I gotta put one on too, but I don't have to tell you how important they are, do I, Mr. Hawthorne?"

Tim nodded curtly, turned his back to Dennis, and helped Ally fasten her vest.

Ally reached out and gave Tim's arm a reassuring squeeze. Her husband Tim had been a child when it happened, but he still hated when someone dredged up the accident, and she couldn't blame him. Not even their close friends knew about it in California, but in Maine, it had been front-page news, and everyone not only remembered the incident but frequently spoke about it, too.

While Dennis cast off, Tim and Ally sat in the stern. Ally pulled her jacket tighter around her to ward off the chill. With the dark skies, it felt later than three. But the harbor was calm, and the boat soon rounded the sea wall and sped across the open ocean.

As the boat sliced through the water, Ally took in the scenery around them. The rocky coastline twisted and curled behind them. The sky was a deep shade of gray. The only sound was the deep hum of the engine and the gentle splash of the water against the hull. It starkly contrasted the hustle and bustle of their life in California, and Ally was grateful for the peace and quiet. The air was salty, like the ocean, and the wind carried the scent of the sea with it. It was comforting.

Tim leaned over, his lips brushing her ear. "Having fun, babe?"

Ally turned to him, a grin spreading across her face. "Yeah. This is nice. It's so calming out here."

The boat skimmed over the water. The dot in the distance slowly spread out to reveal Guillemot Island. Greenish-gray, craggy cliffs jutted out of the ocean and rose high. As the boat turned, the Victorian mansion appeared, an enormous house of gray, stone blocks on a hill overlooking the sea. Tall chimneys rose from the roof, and twin turrets from the center of the structure. The large windows provided a regal view of the sea from any of its rooms. The pitched roof and dark hue gave it a foreboding appearance.

Dennis navigated the boat past the jagged rocks surrounding the island and into a little harbor. Slowing, they stopped at a wooden dock.

"Call me when you're ready to leave," Dennis said, throwing a rope around a piling and holding the boat in place.

"We're only staying three days," Ally said as she removed the life jacket. "Our flight is at six in the evening."

"I'll call you," Tim said, holding out both life vests. "Just in case something changes."

Ally frowned and glanced at her husband sideways before stepping over the side and onto the dock.

Once Tim removed their luggage, he waved as Dennis headed back to sea.

"We'll only stay three days," Tim said. "All I meant was if something changed with our flight."

Ally nodded, but she didn't believe him. Tim's mother was a master of manipulation; she knew exactly what to say and do to bend her son to her will. Ally took a deep breath and let it out slowly. "If something does happen to our return flight, I'll sleep on the tarmac if I have to, but we are leaving the island in three days."

"I'll keep my promise." Tim held his hand up like a Boy Scout. "Three days, and we're gone."

"I'm holding us to that schedule." Ally took out her phone and frowned. The countdown app she'd set wasn't working. "Do you have cell service?"

Tim checked his phone and shook his head. "No. They got a new tower. It more than doubled their signal." He pointed to a gigantic fake pine tree at the top of a rock outcropping. "But the weather still impacts it. It's probably a temporary thing."

Ally nodded, but a sense of dread washed over her as she looked at the house with the dark clouds circling overhead.

Tim squeezed her hand. "It's only a few days. We'll be gone before my mother has a chance to get on your nerves."

Ally wanted to say, "We're not even going to stay for coffee?" but held her tongue. She could make it that long, couldn't she? After all, no one ever died from visiting their mother-in-law.

The two made their way along a cement walkway and climbed a series of staircases carved into the slope to reach the main house. If it hadn't been in poor taste, Ally would have said something about the climb being the cause of Victoria's heart issues, but instead, huffed and puffed in silence until they finally stopped in front of the ornate wooden front doors. Worn from years of exposure to the Atlantic Ocean, the carved filigree had a magical charm.

Tim took her hand, and she realized hers was shaking. He gave it a soft squeeze. "Everything is going to be fine, honey." He rang the bell, then opened the door. "Hello?"

The grand entrance was aptly named. A marble staircase rose and branched off on either side to the second floor. The wide steps were polished to a mirror shine. The floor was marble as well but a darker shade than the stairs. An enormous chandelier hung suspended from the ceiling. Large, wooden double doors sat closed on either side of the foyer. A massive grandfather clock ticked loudly, the only sound.

As they entered, each footstep rang off the marble. The chandelier's crystal surface caught the light and refracted a rainbow across the walls and floor.

"Mother? Mia? Tom?" Tim called out.

Ally followed the scent of fresh cut flowers to a bouquet of roses and baby's breath resting on a marble table beneath an elaborate, golden framed mirror. A folded piece of paper had the word TIM written across the front.

Setting down her suitcase and shopping bag, Ally picked up the note and handed it to Tim, who read it aloud.

Tim,

Sorry, we didn't call - we couldn't. The new cell tower is on the fritz. A tech is due out later this week. Aunt Victoria wanted to celebrate, so we headed into town for dinner. Staff came to do a shop, too. You've got the place to yourself until we get back!

Mia

Ally was so mad she could spit. "It seems there's been a miracle. Your mother feels so good she's gone out for a night on the town."

Tim reread the note and froze. He cracked his neck and opened his mouth.

Ally held up her hand. "I'm too tired to hear talk about it now. I don't want to say anything because it may not come out so nicely." Ally grabbed her suitcase and picked up the shopping bag. "Are we staying in your room again?"

"Top of the stairs, second door on the right. I'm so sorry."

Ally stopped at the foot of the staircase. "This is on Victoria. This is her M.O. One minute, you're making funeral plans; the next, they're having a party." Ally turned to stare at her husband. "I'm just wondering when you're going to start understanding."

Tim crumpled the note in his hand. "I'm sorry she did this."

"This is wrong on so many levels I don't even know where to start, so I'm not going to try. I love you, but I'm exhausted. I'm going to bed."

"Do you want something to eat? Drink?"

The instant migraine growing behind her eyes drove all thoughts of food away. "No, thank you. Goodnight."

The marble railing was cool against her hand. It absorbed the heat from her palm as if it were sucking it out. "How appropriate," she muttered. The house was splendid in appearance, but it was a vampire—just like Victoria, sucking all the warmth and joy out of people, leaving them cold and empty husks.

Ally's suitcase banged off the marble, and she realized she had forgotten to pack several items. She

made a list as she headed down the hall to the bedroom — garlic, a cross, silver bullets, a wooden stake....

Chapter Four

Awakened by the morning light seeping through the curtains, Ally slipped out of bed, grabbed her clothes off the floor, and quietly went to the bathroom. With the sleeping pill she'd taken, she didn't know when Tim finally came to bed, but she didn't want to wake him.

After brushing her teeth and changing, she crept through the bedroom, quietly closing the door behind her. She went down the hallway, feeling like she'd snuck into a museum after hours. Enormous paintings in thick, dark wooden frames lined the corridor. There were several tables, each adorned with either statues, carvings, or items in glass display cases. A full suit of armor stood outside the door that, if she remembered correctly, led to the library.

With each step, her anger rose. Her mother-in-law was the queen of hypochondria. In the five years that Ally and Tim had been married, Victoria seemed to suffer every illness known to man. Of course, none of the possible abnormalities ever came to fruition. The batteries of tests always came back negative, but with each supposed illness, she would summon Dr.

Martin Bradley, her private physician. Tim said the doctor was here so often that they provided him with a room.

How much time and money had Victoria wasted? Ally tried convincing Tim that she needed a therapist, not a doctor, but he wouldn't hear of it. And, depending on the latest disorder, Tim would drop everything to be at his mother's side.

Last year, he spent the month of March because Victoria thought she had cancer. In July, it was possible COPD. And last October, it was a stroke. Tim stayed five weeks then.

It wouldn't bother Ally so much if these trips didn't strain their finances. But Tim didn't take any money from his mother, wanting to be a self-made man.

Ally stormed down the stairs and out the front door. If it weren't for her appraisal business, they'd be destitute. As an artist, he only seemed to sell pieces when his mother asked him to travel to Maine.

A cold sea breeze swept across the front yard and wrapped around her like a cool cloth on a hot day. She took a deep breath, letting the ocean air fill her lungs and chill her anger.

Tim loved being an artist, and she'd known that before marrying him. He was extremely gifted in talent but had no head for business. She was quite aware of that, too. Besides, the finances weren't the real issue. The way he dealt with his family was. By allowing himself to be sucked into his family's drama, he dragged her right along with him.

But she loved him. Adored him, really. They had a relationship that she never dreamed was possible.

"Hey!" a man shouted.

Ally turned. Marching up the walkway was a giant of a man. He was at least six foot five, with unusually long arms and legs. He was thin but broad-shouldered. Dressed in blue jeans, a dark T-shirt, and a tan work jacket, his long neck was circled with a tattoo of a three-headed dragon. The dragon on the right side of his neck was breathing fire, the flames curling up and onto his cheek, which made his scowling expression even more concerning.

"Stay right where you are," he shouted. "I want to talk to you!"

What was he doing here? This was a private island, and he certainly didn't appear like a friend of Victoria's.

Ally spun on her heels and hurried back toward the house.

"Stay!" The man yelled like he was commanding a dog.

Staying was the last thing Ally was going to do. With a glance back at him, she sprinted up the steps toward the safety of the house.

The man's boots thudded off the cement stairs behind her.

Taking the steps three at a time, she bolted up the staircase, yanked the front door open, and slammed it shut.

BANG! BANG! BANG! The man pounded on the door. "Hello? I know you saw me!"

As Ally turned the lock and stepped back to catch her breath, footsteps sounded in the foyer behind her. A man and woman appeared. He was short, with the rich tan skin and dark hair of the Middle East, while the woman was slightly taller. The man wore a pressed, long-sleeved white shirt and pleated khaki pants. She wore a simple blue dress with a white apron.

"May I help you?" the man asked in an English accent.

Bang! Bang! Bang! "Hello? Open the door!"

"I'm Ally. Tim's wife. There's a strange man outside."

"So I hear." The man walked forward. "My name is Ziad, and this is my wife, Nashwa. I'm the house steward. May I ask who this loud man is?"

Ally shrugged. "I have no idea. I went outside for a walk, and he was coming up from the docks."

"Ally?" Tim appeared bleary-eyed at the top of the steps and jogged down. "What's going on?"

"I'm trying to determine that now," Ziad said. "Someone outside is demanding entry, and I must admit I am hesitant to open the door."

Bang! Bang! Bang! "Hey, lady! Come off it! Open the door!" The man swore.

"I'll handle this, Ziad." Tim stepped forward.

"Honey." Ally placed a restraining hand on his arm. "The man is a giant and looks insane. We should call the police."

"We can't." Tim rubbed his bloodshot eyes. "The cell tower is down." He cracked his neck and motioned everyone back. "I'm just going to talk to him and figure out what's going on."

Ziad tipped his head, and Nashwa moved to the stand near the door on the far left side of the foyer.

Ally glanced around. Next to the wall was a brass cylinder holding two umbrellas and a cane. She took out the cane, gripped it in both hands like a bat, and stepped back.

Tim walked to the door. "What do you want?" he called out.

"Are you there? Can you hear me? I need your help!" The man was loud, but he stopped yelling. "Please! I'm looking for my girlfriend. She came here last night."

Tim glanced back, and everyone shrugged. "This is a private island. No one came out here last night."

"She did. I swear. Can you please open the door?"

Ally and Ziad shook their heads, but Tim unlocked the door.

As the door swung open, the mountain of a man stomped inside. His eyes were bloodshot, and he reeked of cigarettes, sweat, and a chemical odor. "Look, I just want to know where Kim is. That's all. I'm not starting any trouble and don't want the police involved."

Tim took a step back. "There is no Kim here, and I can assure you that no one came here last night."

"She did. She's here. I know it."

"How do you know it?" Victoria's voice on the second floor made them turn their heads toward her.

Victoria Hawthorne stood at the top of the stairs, regal and imposing even in her advanced years. Her hair was an elegant mix of gray and silver streaks against jet-black locks; her untouched natural beauty hadn't faded with age. Her pose was commanding—chin lifted, her back ramrod straight, shoulders slightly angled with an air of superiority that only those born into wealth can muster. Her left hand rested lightly on the marble railing like a queen gazing down at the peasants below. "I ask you again, what makes you believe your girlfriend is on my island?"

The man cleared his throat and wiped his mouth with a tattooed hand. "Kim told me that she was coming out here yesterday. She didn't come back last night."

Victoria descended the stairs as she spoke. "Why would she come here?"

"She said she had to talk to somebody."

"Who?"

The man scratched his chin. "She didn't say."

Victoria gave the man a sympathetic, tight-lipped smile. "Unfortunately for you, you have been deceived. I was home all evening, and no one came here." The man opened his mouth, but Victoria lifted a perfectly manicured long index finger. "Hold that thought." She turned to Ziad. "Please find Philip and conduct a search of the house and grounds for any possible wayward guest."

"Certainly." Ziad inclined his head and marched out of the room, Nashwa following.

"What is your name?" Victoria asked.

"Gary."

"Now, Gary, as my son mentioned, this is a private island. I have shown you the courtesy of listening to your request. If this Kim does show up, we will let her know you are looking for her. And now you need to do me a favor. Leave. I have a heart condition, and all this commotion is very upsetting."

Gary's eyes widened. "I didn't know. Like I said, I want to find Kim, but I didn't realize you've got a bad heart."

"Now that you do, it's time to go." Victoria held her hand out toward the door. "Good day."

Gary crossed the threshold. " If I don't hear from her, I'm coming back."

Tim shut and locked the door.

Ally exhaled. Despite her mother-in-law being a

hypochondriac, she had to admire the power she exuded. "That was crazy."

Victoria inclined her head. "I believe that word has been replaced with a more sympathetic term. But, yes, the poor man is delusional."

Ally wanted to point out that he appeared to be on drugs, but with her mother-in-law doing a fantastic Mother Teresa impersonation, she decided against it.

"I'm so glad you accompanied Tim on this trip." Victoria lifted her chin. "Have you injured your leg?"

Puzzled, Ally's eyebrows traveled in different directions until she realized she was still clutching the cane. "No. I took it to back up Tim. Just in case."

"Ever my son's protector. I'm sorry you weren't feeling well last night. We missed you at dinner. We went into town to pick up the ingredients so my new cook could make a celebratory meal for my son and daughter-in-law's arrival. Nashwa is Egyptian, but you wouldn't know it by how she makes her stuffed lobster."

Ally turned and stared at Tim with her mouth hanging open. "I thought they all went out to dinner on the mainland."

Victoria's lips pressed together in a thin line. "I'd never go to dinner without the two of you. You're both so thoughtful to come all this way for me. I wanted to show my appreciation, and even though I didn't feel up to it physically, it seemed appropriate to select something extra special for dinner personally."

Guilt washed over Ally. Why hadn't Tim woken her up? Ally rubbed her temples. "I apologize. I feel horrible."

Victoria took Ally's hand and smiled. "Don't. With all you've been enduring, a little miscommunication is understandable. Now let's put last night and that poor man out of our minds and enjoy your visit. I'm going to freshen up, and then I hope to see you at breakfast."

"Of course. And please accept my apologies."

"Certainly." Victoria started up the stairs. "Tim, be a dear, find your Uncle Philip and Ziad, and make sure that wretched man has departed my island."

"Yes, Mother." Tim headed for the front door, and Ally followed him outside, saying, "Oh, I feel lower than a worm. I am such an idiot. I thought that note said they were going out to dinner, not picking everything up to make one."

"I thought the same thing. I must have misread the note, too. Don't worry about it. My mother is the last person to hold a grudge."

Ally wasn't about to disagree with him after that debacle. "I do wish you had woken me up."

"I tried. You were dead to the world. But stop beating yourself up about it."

"I'm going to get her and Tom's presents and make a peace offering. Are you coming to breakfast?"

"Yes, but I better make sure that creep leaves first. Something about that guy was really weird."

"That's why I ran away. Be careful."

"I will. Save me some eggs!" Tim jogged down the path.

Ally watched him round the house and disappear from view. She glanced down at the dock.

A small gray boat with an outboard motor sat tied to the piling. Gary stood on the dock with binoculars, staring back at Ally.

Ally shuddered. She was tempted to flip him off, but angering a possible drugged-out, delusional giant wasn't the wisest course of action.

Gary lowered the binoculars. He tapped his chest

and pointed at the ground. He repeated the gesture twice more.

It took Ally a moment to figure out what he was trying to convey. She swallowed, her mouth suddenly bone dry.

Gary was letting her know that he was going to come back.

Chapter Five

Carrying the gifts she'd brought for Victoria and Tom in one hand, Ally made her way downstairs and to the dining room. After making a fool out of herself, all she wanted was to give a peace offering to her mother-in-law and then keep her head down for three days and get out of Dodge.

Ally strolled through the open double doors and into a room that always made her wonder if *Downton Abbey* had used Victoria's dining room as a model for their own. Two double doors on each exterior wall rose almost to the top of the fourteen-foot ceiling, providing a breathtaking ocean view. The two interior walls were covered in enormous paintings and a grand fireplace. A table set for eight sat atop an antique, elaborately woven gold and mauve rug, but only two people were seated.

Victoria greeted her from her place at the head of the table. "My dear Ally. It is so good to have you here. Please . . ." She magnanimously held her hand out to the chair on her right.

Tom tucked his chin to his chest and lowered his voice, creating a pitch-perfect imitation of his brother.

"Ally!" He laughed at his joke and started to rise, but Ally hurried over to him.

"Hello, my superhero!" She wrapped her arms around his neck and kissed his cheek.

The tall, handsome man smiled broadly. His resemblance to Tim was identical except for the slight droop on the left side of his face. If you didn't know him, one would think he'd had a stroke, but it was a result of oxygen deprivation to his brain.

"I brought you both a little something."

"That wasn't necessary," Victoria said.

"I'm glad she did," Tom said, eagerly peering into the bag.

"For my sweet man." Ally handed him the box of saltwater taffy, which he immediately started to open.

"Please wait until after breakfast," Victoria said.

Frowning, Tom placed the box next to his water glass.

Ally lifted the gift basket from the bag and set it on an empty corner of the table next to Victoria. "I thought you may need a little pick-me-up."

"Oh, wow." Tom pointed. "It's got a blanket, some socks, and purple ball things to play with."

"They're for a bath," Victoria explained. "And it's perfect."

"There's more in the bag," Tom said.

"That's another present for you." Ally picked up the heavy box.

"Two presents for me?" Tom grinned. His eyes widened even more when he saw the characters on the box. His hands shook with excitement. "There's so many. Captain America. Iron Man. Black Widow."

"They're movies. It's the whole collection."

"It's all of them, Mom!" Tom shouted.

"That's wonderful. Now lower your voice."

"Can I watch them now?"

"After breakfast." Victoria turned to Ally. "How thoughtful and appropriate. Did Tim inform you that we remodeled the summer kitchen into Tom's new bedroom?"

"It's huge!" Tom grinned. "And Momma put in my own movie theater. I've got a popcorn and soda machine and everything."

"Air-conditioning made the need for a summer kitchen obsolete. And Tom loves it." Victoria picked up a bell with a mahogany handle and silver cup on the end and rang it. A moment later, Ziad appeared. "Please take that up to my room and locate the others."

"Certainly." Ziad inclined his head. "Timothy and Philip should be along shortly. They wanted to wait and make sure our guest had gone far out to sea before returning."

"Was that the angry man?" Tom asked.

Ally sat in the chair beside him and placed her hand over his shaking one. "Everything's fine. He's gone. Did you hear him?"

Tom pointed at his eyes. "He's looking for the girl."

Ally pressed her lips together. Tom's command of language was childish, but he was very bright. "Did you see a girl?"

"Oh, Ally, Ally. Didn't we all experience enough drama this morning to fill the day?" Victoria waved a dismissive hand. "Tom didn't see a girl or the man for that matter. I told him about the incident when he came down for breakfast and now regret I did."

The front door banged open, and heavy boots rang off the marble in the foyer. A bear of a man ambled into the room. Short, thick, and unshaven, Victoria's brother Philip possessed none of his sister's grace, yet he still exuded power. The feeling was akin to standing too close to a wild animal. Ally was constantly on guard and wanted to leave whenever he entered a room.

Ally's father warned her that some people were like pit bulls. They smile and act all happy to see you. Day in and day out, they'd be peaches and cream until they bit your face off. He said the way to tell was to watch them when they didn't know anyone was looking.

Ally had done that with Philip. He'd been in the game room once, and his niece Mia had fallen asleep on the couch. Ally didn't care one bit for the way he eyed her. She shuddered and tried to drive the memory out of her mind.

"If anyone wanted an argument against the decriminalization of hard drugs, that fruitcake would be the poster child." Philip dragged out a chair and sat.

"The good news is that he's gone," Tim said as he strolled over to Ally, placed two reassuring hands on her shoulders, and kissed her cheek.

"That cockroach is coming back." Philip drained half his glass of orange juice. "Mark my words. That guy is riding so high on the crazy train he's convinced that his girlfriend is out here." Philip wagged his finger back and forth like a metronome. "He'll keep bouncing that idea around his little pea brain, and soon, he'll convince himself we've got her trapped out here. I'm serious." He finished his orange juice, reached across the table, and took that glass, too.

"Maybe we should call the police?" Tim suggested. "Can I use the radio on the boat?"

"Nope," Philip said. "Carter was three sheets to the wind, didn't see a rock the size of Gibraltar, and cracked the hull. Since I had to pull her out of the water and put her up on blocks, I'm giving her a high-end upgrade and gutted the dash. We've got to wait for Dennis to come back out. I'll go with him and pick up another ship-to-shore. No big deal."

Tim crossed his arms. "But if you're so sure that this guy is going to come back—"

Victoria placed her hand across her breast. "I must insist that we stop all of this nonsensical talk. I will have no more of it. I can't under my current condition."

"Speaking of your heart," Philip said, "where's your nurse?"

Victoria's eyes narrowed.

Philip dropped his elbow down on the table and raised his hand. "It's a joke to lighten things up. Relax."

A slender, older man in gray suit pants, black shoes, and a white shirt hurried into the room. His thinning gray hair was brushed back and shined like shellacked wood.

"Speak of the Devil," Philip muttered.

"My apologies. How are you feeling, Victoria?" Dr. Bradley took the seat on Victoria's left.

"Much better. Thank you, Martin." Victoria smiled. "How can I ever repay your kindness?"

Philip leaned over and whispered into Tom's ear; then Tom sat up straight and asked loudly, "By cash or check?"

Philip laughed hysterically.

Victoria's hand came down onto the table with a loud bang.

"Sorry." Philip raised his hand again. "Just making a funny."

Dr. Bradley took Victoria's wrist, placing his fingers on her pulse. He glanced at Philip. "Your sister is currently wearing a heart monitor. I've asked you repeatedly not to upset her."

"It was a joke." Philip's hand tightened around the empty orange juice glass.

Victoria's eyes blazed. She and her brother stared at each other as an uncomfortable silence descended.

Philip looked away. "You know what? I want to make sure that Gary guy kept going." He stood, almost knocking over his chair in the process.

"I'll have Nashwa bring a plate down to your house," Victoria said.

"Lovely." Philip marched out of the room.

"I wish you wouldn't let him bother you," Dr. Bradley said. "Your pulse is elevated."

"I am grateful to have one." Victoria covered his hand with her own.

The sound of approaching footsteps made Ally glance toward the door. A couple in their forties strolled into the room, hand in hand. Mia was Tim's cousin, her mother being Victoria's sister, who passed away years ago. Carter was Mia's husband. Tim playfully referred to them as the sponges because their livelihood existed from the generosity of Victoria.

"I am so sorry we overslept." Mia's voice was light and bright, matching her pixie-like frame.

"We seemed to have overindulged in celebrating the prodigal's return," Carter added, holding the chair out for his wife.

"I don't recall a time when you two needed an excuse for overindulgence," Victoria said.

Carter laughed like she'd just said the funniest thing he'd ever heard. He laughed so hard that Tom joined in, which spread all around the table, stopping back at Victoria, who sat stone-faced.

Nashwa wheeled a cart into the room, followed by her husband carrying a water pitcher. While Ziad refilled their glasses, Nashwa set plates in front of each quest.

"This smells fabulous," Victoria said. "What have you graced us with this morning?"

Nashwa stood tall, but her chin dipped slightly, and she stared at the floor. From the glow of her cheeks, she was embarrassed by the attention. "Baked eggs with spinach, mushrooms, goat cheese, and chorizo. Accompanied by honey pancakes with sweet dukkha, apple and pear compote."

Carter shoveled a forkful into his mouth, then moaned and shuddered. "These are to die for."

Tom chuckled and imitated Carter's moaning.

Ally took a bite and immediately wanted to scarf down the entire plate. "Wow! This is fabulous."

"You've outdone yourself, Nashwa," Victoria said.

Nashwa smiled. "Please let me know if you'd like anything else," she said, then hurried out of the room.

"I'll be having seconds!" Carter called after her.

"Me, too!" Tom yelled.

"No, you will not," Victoria said. "We all need to watch how much we eat and drink." She raised an eyebrow at Mia and Carter.

"It really is important," Dr. Bradley added. "If you like, Victoria, I can review some menu ideas with Nashwa."

"Not on your life." Victoria wet her lips. "I believe in portion control, not bland rabbit food."

"Healthy food doesn't have to be bland." Dr. Bentley sipped his coffee. "That's why I wanted all of you to try Leonardo's last night."

"I can't believe it was closed," Carter said. "Ow!"

Mia glared at her husband.

Ally struggled to swallow the bite of pancake in her mouth. She sat processing Dr. Bradley's words. They *had* gone to the mainland to go out to dinner! Her mother-in-law lied about going into town to get the ingredients for a special meal to share with Tim and her. The restaurant was closed, so they were forced to change plans. Her father, who cautioned her about lying, always backed up what he told her with a Bible verse: Whatever you have said in the dark will be heard in the light, and what you have whispered behind closed doors will be shouted from the house-tops for all to hear! And now that Dr. Bradley and Carter had brought Victoria's lie to light, Ally was getting ready to do some shouting.

Tim placed a restraining hand on her arm.

Ally turned to stare at her mother-in-law, but Victoria focused on the doctor.

"How long will I need to wear this heart monitor?" Victoria asked. "When you check the readings, the results from this morning will be off the chart."

"Are you having any symptoms now?" Dr. Bradley angled his chair.

"A little shortness of breath." Victoria placed her hand over her heart and leaned back in her chair. "But I'm sure it's nothing to worry about."

"Nonsense." Dr. Bradley stood. "You need to lay down. I should have insisted upon it earlier."

Ally had a stranglehold on her cloth napkin. She twisted it between her fists and watched her opportunity to confront her mother-in-law about her outright deception slip away. But how could she say anything now that Victoria had played her "I have a bad heart card"? It was like having diplomatic immunity — she was untouchable.

Victoria's eyelids fluttered. "I apologize everyone,

but perhaps I do need a moment's respite. I hope you understand."

"Of course, Mother," Tim said. "Can I do anything for you?"

"No, my sweet boy. Thank you all." Victoria held onto the table with one hand while Dr. Bradley supported her other arm.

Together, they slowly left the room.

Ally balled her napkin up and dropped it onto her plate. "I'm going for a walk."

"Would you like some company?" Tim offered.

"No, thank you, honey. I think it would be best if I went alone." Ally marched out of the room. She was so angry she didn't get her coat as she stormed from the house.

The gray sky was dark, and whitecaps danced in the sea. Her arms rigid and hands clenched into fists, she headed in the opposite direction of the dock. A walking path circled the island, and it was the perfect place for her to offload her indignation and feelings of betrayal.

With her mood darker than the sea, she broke into a jog.

As Ally ran, the rhythmic pounding of her feet on the path and the salty air helped to clear her mind. She knew she needed to talk to Tim about his mother's lie, but she wasn't sure how to approach the subject.

The path split, the left side leading to one of the two guest houses on the island. They were cottages, really, but very nice. One was specifically for guests, while the other was used full-time by Philip.

Philip was an odd character. Thrice divorced, he now acted more like the gardener and maintenance man than a socialite. Tim said he'd squandered his inheritance and was now happy to call the island home due to legal issues and warrants elsewhere. She suspected it was more of a gilded cage and served more as a place of banishment than a refuge.

She rounded the island's far end and continued until she saw the covered boathouse. She slowed to a walk and took a deep breath. The sea stretched out to her right, endless and unyielding.

The double doors of the boathouse were open, but the family's boat was outside. It sat out of the water up on boat stands. A freshly sanded patch on the hull stood out.

"Ally?"

She turned to see Tim jogging toward her. His face was etched with concern. "Are you okay? I didn't want to leave you alone for too long."

"I'm fine. Just needed to clear my head." She paused, then took the plunge. "Tim, I need to talk to you about something."

"Sure, anything. What's on your mind?"

Ally took a deep breath. "Your mother lied to us. She didn't go into town to get ingredients. They were all going out to dinner. It just happened that the restaurant was closed, so they changed their plans."

"I know. But it's not a complete lie. They did bring back stuff for dinner—"

"Your mother said they'd never go into town for dinner without us. You heard Dr. Bradley. That was exactly why they went to town."

"Technically, Dr. Bradley didn't say dinner either. Maybe he meant they would go in for lunch and return for supper?"

"That is such garbage. He might not have used the word dinner, but he said last night. No one eats lunch at night. I can't even believe you're trying to justify it. Your mother lied, but you don't want to own up to it."

"What do you want me to do? Call her out?"

"YES! She lied to our faces."

"I'm not going to give her a heart attack."

Ally kicked a rock off the path. It bounced, rolled down the slope, and plunked into the water. "She doesn't even have a heart condition. You said it yourself, it was a gallbladder attack."

"It may have been. But right now, she's wearing a heart monitor so they can be sure."

"A lot of good that will do since she doesn't have a heart to monitor!" Ally instantly regretted her words. "Sorry." She kicked another rock. It rolled down the hill and struck the sole of a sandal floating in the water. The sandal rolled over, revealing bright red fabric.

"That was a little harsh," Tim said.

"Look!" Ally thrust out her hand, pointing.

Tim glanced over. "It's just an old shoe."

Ally grabbed hold of a twisted tree trunk and started down the bank. "It's not old."

"Careful. Even if it isn't, it's trash. Leave it alone."

Ally bent over, waiting for the next wave to push the sandal closer. The tide rose, and she snatched up her prize. Turning it over in her hands, she examined its condition. "It is new. It's not worn, and the color isn't faded."

Tim shrugged as he helped her up the bank. "I don't get why you're making such a big deal out of it."

"What if Gary isn't nuts? What if this belongs to Kim?"

Tim chuckled. "Is crazy contagious? You're jumping to a lot of conclusions. If his girlfriend is on the island, why did she lose her shoe?"

Ally thought for a moment as she held the dripping sandal. "I don't know."

"It could be anybody's. For all we know, it's one of Mia's."

"Why would her shoe be in the ocean?"

Tim shrugged again. "Do me a favor, and don't bring it up. You saw how bothered my mother was by this morning already."

Ally bit her tongue. There'd be no living with Victoria now that she could shield herself from everything with the magical words — I have a heart condition. "Fine. But three days, Tim. Seriously. I think I will go out of my mind if we stay longer."

Tim took her by the hand. "Absolutely. Three more days and you'll hear"—he cupped his hand to his mouth and pretended to be a wrestling announcer—" Tim and Ally have left the island!"

Ally laughed and leaned into him as they strolled back to the house. As they went, she glanced down at the sandal in her hand. The material was a shiny cherry red. All except for three dark spots on the side of the strap.

"What's wrong?" Tim asked.

"Nothing," Ally said. She didn't want to get into another argument about jumping to conclusions because now, she not only thought this could be the missing girlfriend's shoe, but memories of forensic shows played in her mind, and she wondered if those dark spots were bloodstains — and that sounded crazy even to her.

Chapter Six

After spending a whole day on the island and having an agonizing family dinner, Ally strolled through the quiet library, searching for something to read. She desperately needed something to take her mind off Gary and his supposed missing girlfriend. Without the internet, she needed to go to some old-school entertainment, but the truth was, she loved physical books.

The shelves circling the large room were full of works ranging from classical literature and the arts to her favorite mysteries and thrillers. The library had a faint scent of paper and leather. A pleasant aroma filled her nose and made her wonder just how long it had been since she had fallen into the pure bliss of words on the page.

Bright lights reflected off the darkened windows. In the distance outside, the moon occasionally peeked through the cloudy sky, making the ocean sparkle momentarily.

Settling on *The Big Sleep* by Raymond Chandler, she carried her find to the oversized chair in the corner. Turning on the table lamp, she tucked her legs underneath her and flipped open the book.

The door to the hallway whipped open. "There you are!" Mia hurried over. "We've been waiting for you."

"What? Me?"

"Tim's watching one of those movies you got for Tom, and Uncle Philip is still sore about Auntie giving him a hard time. We need a third for hearts."

"I'd love to, but I'm reading."

Mia glanced down at the page. "It's page one! You must have just started, or it isn't a good book. Come on. Please do me a favor. If you don't come, I either have to shoot pool or play pinochle, and I can't stand pinochle. It's Carter's night to pick, and he said if there were three of us, he'd play hearts, but there aren't, so I'm begging."

Ally grinned. Despite Mia's erratic behavior and rapid-fire speech, she cared for Tim's cousin. She closed the book and nodded.

"You're the best!" Mia squealed, grabbing Ally by the hand and leading her to the game room like she feared Ally would change her mind and run away. "We're so glad you're here. Winter is always such a bore. We should go somewhere warm. You and Tim should come with us! It would be a blast."

Two doors down, light streamed onto the hallway carpet. The game room was very well-lit. The vaulted ceiling was painted with a mural of foxes playing cards. A large chandelier hung over the middle of the room, a fireplace stood in the corner opposite the door, and a pool table lay in the center. Oil paintings lined the wooden walls, each one depicting a sporting event. A long bar with a marble top ran along the left-hand wall. Further on sat a mahogany table covered with green felt, a deck of cards resting on it. The tall, straight-backed, briarwood chairs had been polished to a shine. Plush rugs covered sections of the wood floor.

"Oh, good, you found her. Where was she hiding?" Carter asked from behind the bar.

"In the library, reading!" Mia chuckled as she dragged Ally over to the card table. She said to Ally, "There'll be plenty of time to do that on the plane. Tonight, we need to catch up."

"In honor of our third being a bibliophile, I will make her my famous Hawthorne Daiquiri. Light rum, fresh lime, and grapefruit juice with a dash of maraschino liqueur."

"I better not," Ally said. The truth was, she'd love a drink, but with her antidepressant medicine, she shouldn't. Ally sat bolt upright. Had she taken her medicine last night? She'd been so upset she remembered taking the sleeping pill but nothing after that. She'd have to check her pill keeper when she went to bed.

"In that case, I'll make you a virgin version. They're spectacular and still taste like you're being naughty. In fact, that's what I named them." Carter winked. "The Naughty Virgin Daiquiri."

Mia clapped. "I'll have the Hawthorne!" She reached across the table and grabbed Ally's hand. "I haven't told you how sorry I am. How are you getting along?"

"Each day is a little better."

"That's the attitude!" Carter called over. "Mia and I can't have children. The fault's on my end, though. Just remember, the fun is in the attempt! Try, try, try again!"

Mia rolled her eyes. "Do be quiet. Tim was so excited. I heard he made a double crib."

"Oh, that's right, you were expecting twins,"

Carter said, bringing the drinks. "Twins run in the Hawthorne line."

"You know that Victoria and Philip are fraternal twins," Mia said.

Ally's mouth fell open. "I didn't."

Carter started choking on his daiquiri. "Neither did I. How can that be possible? That old buzzard has to be ten years older."

"He isn't." Mia leaned in and whispered. "It's all the drinking and smoking. Victoria once told me that Philip started drinking whiskey when he was fourteen and carried a silver pint in his coat while still in boarding school."

"It shows." Carter sipped his daiquiri. "I swear his liver must be pickled. I've never seen a man drink so much."

"I don't mean to pry, and I'm not trying to pressure you," Mia said. "I only bring it up in case you and Tim are going to try again."

"Adopt!" Carter said. "That or settle on a dog. The payoff on a puppy comes around much faster, too. Speaking of which, do you know how much dog lovers spend on their fur babies?"

Ally shrugged.

Carter continued, "A ridiculous amount of money, but I intend to tap that gold mine. My new line of gourmet dog treats will be the hottest thing on the market. I can let you in on the ground floor for a minimal investment."

Ally blew a raspberry. "We don't have enough to invest in a nice vacation. What about Victoria?"

Carter eyed Mia, who set her elbow on the table and pointed at him. "Talk to her yourself. I asked, and I quote, 'unless that scatterbrained husband of yours takes the time to present to me an actual business plan, I will not lose another cent on one of his get-rich-quick schemes.'"

"It's not a scheme," Carter huffed. "It's a can't-miss way to make money quickly. Very entrepreneurial. Who needs a plan for something so guaranteed?"

Ally held up the deck of cards and interrupted, "What game are we playing? Hearts?"

They played three quick games, with Carter winning every one. "I am on fire!" He stood and danced a little jig. "Who wants another refill?"

Both Mia and Ally raised their hands.

Ally smiled. She'd already had two, but they were so good. Even though the drink didn't contain alcohol, she felt like she had a little buzz. "You make a good naughty virgin." Once the words were out of her mouth, she blushed.

Mia laughed and gave Ally's arm a light squeeze. "It's so nice to have another girl around!"

Ally shuffled the cards. "Why didn't you ask Victoria or Dr. Bradley to play?"

Carter lined the glasses up and began to pour the drinks. "I think the good doctor is too busy giving Auntie another thorough examination."

Ally laughed.

Mia glared.

"I'm joking!" Carter laughed a little too hard and too long for Ally to believe him.

Mia seized her arm. "Please don't repeat that. Carter didn't mean it. It's the booze and his little brain talking. You know how stupid he can be."

"I am an idiot. I can bring in a host of witnesses who will attest to that fact." Carter nodded rapidly. His hands shook as he continued to talk and finish the drinks. "That was a line I shouldn't have crossed. And it is not true. Not at all."

"What isn't true?" Tim asked as he strolled into the room.

Everyone froze. Carter looked desperately at Mia, who gazed pleadingly at Ally.

"Is your Uncle Philip your mother's twin?" Ally asked.

"Of course he is. You didn't know that?"

"She did!" Carter blurted out. "I was the stupid one. That's what I meant when I said it wasn't true. I couldn't believe it. Your mother looks so young. Healthy. Radiant. And Philip is ... not."

"I can't argue with that." Tim walked over to the table and kissed the top of Ally's head. "How are you doing?"

"Carter's won every game, but I'm having a wonderful time."

Tim reached down, picked up her glass, and smelled it. "What are you drinking?"

"It's a virgin daiquiri."

Tim took a sip, and his eyes narrowed. He glared at Carter. "You put booze in this?"

Carter cringed. "I did no such thing."

Tim marched over to the bar and stared at the bottles Carter used to make the drinks.

"I made her a virgin Hawthorne Daiquiri, and I did not use rum!" Carter stepped back and crossed his arms.

Tim snatched the bottle of maraschino liqueur off the bar.

"That's not real booze. It's for flavoring," Carter said. "I demand an apology!"

Tim pointed at the label. "It's thirty-two percent

alcohol. She is on antidepressants. You can't mix those with alcohol. You're a moron."

Carter leaned forward and read the bottle. "Oh, I am a moron." He turned to Ally. "I'm so sorry. I had no idea you were taking medication. And I swear I thought it was a flavored syrup."

"It's all right, Carter." Ally stood, her cheeks burning with embarrassment. "Thank you for the game." She picked up her book and nodded to Mia.

"Don't you want to finish your hand?" Mia asked.

"Actually, I'm still wiped out from the flight. I'm going to call it an early night."

"I'll walk you up to bed," Tim offered.

Ally's steely gaze cut him off. "I'm fine. Why don't you go back to watching a movie with your brother?"

Tim's eyes searched hers. She knew he wanted to talk and probably had no idea why she was upset with him, but now wasn't the time. "Okay. I'll be up in a little bit." He leaned slightly in for a kiss and thought better of it. "Night. Love you."

Ally made her way out into the hall and toward her room. Tears sprang up in her eyes. She didn't have anything against taking medicine to ease her depression, but the last person she wanted to know about it was Victoria. The topic had come up one Christmas and her mother-in-law had gotten up on her soapbox and declared that anyone who didn't have the internal fortitude to rise above their situation without medication was a weak, vile creature who should be locked away for a time to make them change.

Why did Tim open his stupid mouth? Now that Carter and Mia knew, Victoria would too. Gossip to that trio was the fourth food group.

Ally sniffed, wiped her eyes, and opened the bedroom door. Victoria remodeled the room since their last visit. A mahogany sleigh bed with a red, silk coverlet embroidered with miniature roses sat in the middle of the far wall. On the left was the entrance to the bathroom, a tall antique dresser, and two matching night tables on either side of the bed. On the right were two large windows and a red velvet chair with a matching ottoman with a glass of water on the side table. Maroon curtains hung over the windows, but moonlight and a few stars managed to peek through. The long window seat had soft blankets in masculine tones strewn across it.

Setting her book on the night table, Ally headed for the bathroom.

After a long, hot shower, she ran the faucet in the bowl sink and scrubbed her teeth and gums. Even with brushing her teeth, she could still taste the daiquiri. That wasn't the problem. She wanted several more—but this time with rum.

The water in the sink wasn't draining. That was the main reason Ally didn't care for bowl sinks. It had something to do with air pressure. She wasn't exactly sure what caused it, but it was a simple fix.

Turning her toothbrush upside down and using the butt end, she swirled the water in the sink, creating a giant whirlpool. She watched the spiral slowly be sucked down the drain.

The pipes rattled and clanked.

"Hello?" someone whispered.

Ally jumped back. Her heart thumped in her chest like a poorly loaded washing machine. She was sure where the voice came from, but that wasn't possible. She stepped forward and peered down the sink, inclining her ear toward the drain.

The pipes rattled and shook.

The noise was as faint as a whisper in the wind. "Please."

Ally gasped and shook her head. Did she really hear something? Could it be that missing girl?

"Hello?" Ally whispered back. "Kim?"

The shower head dripped slowly and steadily, like the ticking of a grandfather clock.

Sweat beaded Ally's brow. She brushed it aside with shaking hands, but it felt like she'd just gotten out of the shower. She opened her mouth, but no words escaped. She tried to swallow, but her throat was so tight and dry she couldn't breathe. Maybe it was the heat trapped in the bathroom?

She opened the door and hurried as far away as possible, stopping at the windows. She felt dizzy. A hot shower didn't cause this. She was having a panic attack.

She was hearing voices again. She hurried over to the dresser and began yanking the doors open. She'd heard the whispers before — right after she'd lost the twins. Her therapist convinced her it was a dream, but she was certainly awake now!

With each drawer she opened, Ally's panic rose. Where was her medicine? She'd opened all the drawers, but her white pill keeper wasn't there.

She searched the nightstands and the bathroom and then dragged her suitcase from the closet. Nothing.

How could that be? She'd taken her medicine last night, hadn't she?

Ally pressed the palms of her hands against the sides of her head. Did she forget to pack it?

Ally swore and slammed the suitcase closed.

Now what would she do? This house was a petri dish for anxiety and depression. She only had to make it two more days, but she was already starting to lose it.

Marching to the dresser, she took out her phone and swore again. She couldn't call her therapist. The stupid cell tower was down. Taking a deep breath, she walked over to the chair in the corner, pulled the curtain back, and sat.

She was making much ado about nothing. She hadn't heard a voice. That was simply an old house's pipes creaking and groaning, nothing more. She had forgotten her medicine, but that wasn't the end of the world either. The last thing she wanted to do was freak out.

Her phone beeped.

She glanced down. Three bars! It was working. Ally searched her contacts, found the number for her therapist, and dialed. The line rang four times and went to voicemail.

"You don't know how sorry I am that I missed you! It's Ally. I'm here on the island and just realized I forgot my med—"

Her phone beeped, and a triangle with an exclamation mark appeared. No service.

"Crud." Ally sat there staring at the dark screen, hoping whatever magic fixed the cell tower would do it again.

A muffled beep sounded from the dresser.

Tim's phone! Maybe he has a signal. Ally dashed over.

Unlocking Tim's phone, Ally frowned. He didn't have a signal. But he did have twenty-four new emails. The emails were either from people interested in Tim's artwork or spam. She checked his text messages, but there were no new ones. The memory of the one he received in California cut her again.

Are you coming back soon? Miss you, babe!

Ally slumped down on the bed. The screen flashed a low-power warning and shut off. She stared at her reflection. All of the stress was getting to her. And now there wasn't a way to get any medicine to cope with it.

Ally rose, put the phones back in the dresser, and hurried to bed. Two more nights. That was all. Two more, and they'd be away from here.

The pipes in the bathroom rattled and clanked.

Ally pulled the blanket over her head. She was catastrophizing. She fixated on the worst possible outcome and treated it as real, even when it was not. Tim said it was a wrong number, and he'd never given her a reason to doubt him. It had to be a coincidence. And old houses make noises. It was just the pipes. That's all— just the pipes.

Or was it?

Chapter Seven

As soon as the sky lightened, Ally slipped out of the bedroom with her book cradled under one arm. She passed down the hallway, stopping at the top of the stairs to stare out the grand window in the foyer. She would have loved seeing a glorious sunrise over the ocean, but dark clouds blotted the sky. Even the choppy sea seemed upset as the waves splashed against the rocks, churning a grayish-green foam. It wouldn't matter if a hurricane was raging in two days. She'd get on that boat and off this island.

She quickly stopped in the kitchen and grabbed a protein bar, an apple, and a water bottle. Today, she wanted to hide, so she left a note for Tim saying she was going on a hike to explore the island. Returning to the foyer, she grabbed her jacket.

Footsteps sounded in the downstairs hallway.

Ally slipped out the front door and quietly closed it before anyone saw her. The wind had picked up, and the salty air on her cheeks widened her eyes and invigorated her. She took her time strolling along the path.

Seabirds cawed, and waves crashed onto the rocks, sending magnificent plumes of spray high into the air. She'd never been to Ireland but imagined it would be similar. She loved the ocean from a distance. It held so much beauty and mystery, but the power and danger it wielded could not be forgotten. In some ways, it was similar to riding a horse. They were both wild and untamed, so she had to constantly retain her diligence, making it difficult to relax and enjoy the ride.

She rounded a corner and stopped. Staring down at a little inlet, she marveled at the still waters, shielded from the open ocean. The rocks curved around like a person laying their forearm on a table and protecting something in the curve of their hand. But on the other side of the natural harbor, the ocean roared.

Her eyes widened in understanding. This must be where it happened. She'd never asked Tim specifics about the incident, but she'd pieced together story fragments over the years.

Tim had been ten or eleven and was collecting crabs. He'd gone too close to the opening, and a rogue wave grabbed him, dragging him to the open ocean. Tom valiantly dove in and swam after his brother.

Ally shivered. Tom had saved Tim's life but at such a high cost to himself.

Why Victoria chose to stay on this island was beyond her. Soon after Tim and Tom were born, their father also drowned. Tim mentioned it when they first started dating. But the only thing he'd said was that he was four years old when his father drowned. That was all. With it being such a personal thing, Ally had waited patiently for him to discuss his feelings about it later, but they never came. Eventually, it became so awkward that she decided to hold off, but when she'd gotten pregnant, she saw her opportunity to help her husband deal with the grief of his past. She thought offering to name one of the twins after his father would spur a discussion, but she miscarried before that could happen.

A couple of guillemots raced across the sand of a dune to her right, disappearing into the pinweed and beach grass. Ally took a deep breath and continued walking, a sense of unease creeping up on her. As she rounded a bend, she noticed a boat moored down at the dock. A man in a dark coat was securing it in place. A black mariner's cap with a thin bill was pulled down on his head, obscuring his face.

She paused, considering turning back, but her curiosity won out. Slowly, she walked toward the man, trying not to make too much noise.

The man deftly lashed the rope to the piling, then stood and gazed up at the house. The man didn't move or acknowledge her presence.

Ally glanced at the red and black boat and read the name, *The Sea Spit*.

Dennis suddenly turned and faced her. His expression was stern and serious. "Morning, Mrs. Hawthorne," he said in a deep voice. "You're up and about early."

"I thought I'd get some exercise before reading." She held up her book. "Are you picking someone up? Or did you bring a technician out?" she asked hopefully.

"What was that?"

"The cell tower isn't working. They're expecting a technician to come and fix it. I was wondering if that's why you're here."

"No, ma'am." Dennis took a deep breath and stared down at his feet. "I'm not sure how much I can say, and the truth is, I don't know any particulars. Perhaps you should head up to the house."

"Why? Is something wrong? Who did you bring?"

"I really can't be getting involved. It's not my place. If you go back home, I'm sure they'll fill you in." He nodded, stepped over the side of the boat, and disappeared into the boathouse.

Ally's pounding heartbeat made her temples throb. This was precisely the type of stress she did not need! Gripping her book tightly, she jogged up the stairs to the mansion. With each step, she felt a growing desire to turn around, dash back to *The Sea Spit*, and beg Dennis to take her to the mainland.

Yanking open the front doors, she saw the foyer was empty. But voices came from the sitting room on the right.

Ally hurried over and stopped in the open doorway. The sitting room was filled with people, two she didn't recognize.

The hexagonal room formed the base of the central tower of the house. With a sixteen-foot vaulted ceiling and huge windows on every exterior wall, it was well-lit even on a day like today. Several chairs and loveseats circled the room, facing the middle. Tim, Tom, Victoria, Dr. Bradley, Mia, Carter, Ziad, and Nashwa sat while a man in a dark gray suit, a uniformed police officer, and Gary stood before the fireplace. Tim sat beside his mother, looking tense.

"Tim, what's going on?" Ally asked, her anxiety rising.

Tim crossed over to her, his expression softening. "Ally, Uncle Philip went to find you. We need to talk."

"Hold on a second, Mr. Hawthorne," said the man in the suit, who, with his receding gray hair, looked to be in his late fifties. "It would be best if I speak to all of you simultaneously." Deep wrinkles appeared as his expression hardened. He spoke with an air of authority, and considering he was built like a linebacker with broad shoulders and a thick neck, people listened.

"Oh, please don't be so dramatic, Frank." Victoria waved a dismissive hand. "Philip isn't here now. Do you expect all of us to wait until he stumbles back now that my wayward daughter-in-law decided to return? Besides, we all know what this is about." She cast a disdainful glance at Gary. "This man stormed into my home yesterday with his outlandish accusations. You're not taking him seriously, are you?"

"Kim did come here," Gary said. "I tried to tell you, but you wouldn't listen. And now I can prove it."

Frank raised his hand and stuck his finger under Gary's nose. "I told you to keep your mouth shut."

Frank was three inches shorter than Gary, but the sight of the gold detective badge on Frank's belt made Gary close his mouth.

Ally followed Tim back over to the couch, feeling the weight of the strangers' eyes on her. She sat, taking his hand, feeling the warmth of his skin.

"We need to take every report seriously, and we now have a witness," Frank said.

"Who?" Victoria asked.

"I'm not at liberty to say, but I believe that Kimberly Hill came out to the island two nights ago and is now missing."

"The shoe!" Ally blurted out. "What kind of shoes was Kim wearing?"

Everyone turned and stared.

"What do shoes have to do with anything?" Frank asked.

"I found one near the dock. I left it out by the front steps. Maybe it's hers?"

Victoria pinched the bridge of her nose. "And now the paranoid conspiracy theories start. Why don't you ask Mia about her footwear? She sheds her garments whenever she and Carter decide to procreate, and seeing how that happens with a frequency that would make a rabbit jealous —"

"Auntie!" Mia sat bolt upright. Her cheeks glowed.

"I'm simply being factual," Victoria continued. "And you can't deny it's true. Yesterday, Tom found your brassiere in the corner pocket of the billiard table. This whole thing is nonsense."

"It isn't!" Gary said.

Victoria slowly rose. Her withering scowl forced Gary into silence. "My point is that if you are convinced this girl came here two nights ago, please scour the island. Search the house. Leave no stone unturned, as the cliché goes. I will not have another pall of speculation and innuendo descend on this family!"

Frank swallowed and nodded. "Thank you for understanding, ma'am."

"All you needed to do was ask, Detective."

"I asked, and you said no," Gary said.

"You asked if your girlfriend had come to my home. I stand by my word and say again that no one came here that night. But if you had asked me politely to search my house, I guarantee you that I would have most assuredly refused. Would you allow a drug-addicted vagabond to wander all over your home?"

Gary's eyebrows knit together, clearly confused.

The police officer—his name tag read Scott Davis —stepped forward. The bright-eyed, clean-shaven man looked fresh out of the military with his buzz-cut hair, pulled-back shoulders, and lifted chin. "Excuse me, miss. You mentioned something about a shoe?"

"Don't answer that," Frank said, turning to Gary. "What kind of shoes was Kimberly wearing the night she came here?"

Gary scratched the stubble on his chin. He made a face and shook his head. "I got no idea. She's got dozens of them."

Victoria crossed her arms. "Oh, what my lawyers would do to a witness of his intellect and memory in a court of law."

"You said you saw her that night. What was she wearing?" Frank asked.

"A red dress. I thought it was too cold, but she said she wanted to wear it."

Frank stared at Ally. "Let's see that shoe, Mrs. Hawthorne. The rest of you stay here for a minute."

Tim rose and took Ally's hand. "I go with my wife."

"Fine. But the rest of you stay here."

The three of them crossed the foyer and stepped outside. Ally looked over the edge of the steps where she'd left the shoe, but it was gone. "I left it right here." She glanced over the other side, but it wasn't there either. "It was a new red sandal. I found it in the water near the dock."

"It was new?" Frank asked.

"Yes."

"I don't like disagreeing with my wife, but it didn't appear new. It was stained," Tim said.

"But that could have been blood," Ally said.

Tim rolled his eyes, and Frank put his hands on his hips.

Ally's back stiffened in her defense. "It was

stained in three places on the strap. They were dark stains," Ally said.

"And why do you think it could have been blood? Are you in law enforcement?"

Ally shook her head. "I'm a real estate appraiser."

Frank crossed his arms. "Are you one of those CSI mystery buffs?"

Tim nodded.

"I am not," Ally said.

"You're reading *The Big Sleep* right now. It's a mystery," Tim said.

"That's not the same as being a mystery buff."

"Whether you like mysteries or not is irrelevant," Frank said. "What I want to know is what happened to that shoe! Do either of you have any idea where it could have gone?"

Ally and Tim both shook their heads.

The three returned to the sitting room.

"Kim's shoes were red," Gary announced. "I know because she was wearing a red dress."

"Not to call your fashion sense into question," Victoria said, "but have you considered she may have opted for a complementary color? Where is this shoe?"

"It wasn't there," Frank said, exchanging a look with Scott. "Did anyone else see it? It was next to the front steps."

"You left trash on my doorstep?" Victoria reeled back as if Ally had defecated on the lawn.

"I thought it was evidence," Ally said.

"Mystery buff," Tim whispered.

Ally wanted to hit him.

"I did not see any footwear," Nashwa said.

"Nor I." Ziad raised his hand, and Nashwa pulled it down.

Everyone else in the room denied seeing the shoe, too.

"That leaves Philip," Frank said. "Where is he?"

"I doubt my brother will come back. Unlike me, he is not fond of law enforcement," Victoria said.

"If you knew he wouldn't return, why did you send him to look for Ally?" Frank asked.

"Because he is my brother." Victoria smiled. "Let's simplify all of this. As I mentioned, I have a heart condition and was recently released from the hospital. Dr. Bradley can reaffirm that, and his word is beyond reproach. So, search the house and the island. I give you permission. Maybe you will find this girl walking along the beach and having a grand time. Take the day, but I promise you this, Frank. Once you are certain she is not here, I want this matter put to rest. I do not want another circus. Do you understand me, or should I call the mayor now?"

"That won't be necessary, Mrs. Hawthorne." Frank took a deep breath. "This is a simple missing person case. I don't want this to get out of hand either. So, in light of previous events, I only brought Officer Davis with me."

"Which is woefully inadequate to conduct a thorough search." She pointed at Gary. "I insist that man stays with you. The rest, besides myself and Dr. Bradley, will help."

"I'm not tramping around outside." Carter sat up.

Mia grabbed his wrist. She must have dug her nails into his arm from the pained expression dawning on his face.

Carter gritted his teeth. "On second thought, we would love to wander around on a cold, drizzly day searching for figments of people's imaginations."

"Okay." Frank checked his watch. "Officer Davis

will be in charge of the group outdoors. If you see something, don't touch it. Call him over. Do not touch it. Tim, do you mind showing me around the house?"

"Not at all." Tim stood, and so did Ally. "My wife stays with me." He turned to his brother. "I'm going to be busy for a little while, buddy. Can you start the next movie without me?"

Tom shook his head. "I'll wait. I'll go play pinball."

"All right. I'll be there as soon as I can."

While everyone besides Victoria and Dr. Bradley filed out of the room, Ally's mind raced. What did Victoria mean by another circus? What happened before, and why had Tim never mentioned it?

Chapter Eight

Ally stood beside Tim in the foyer while he explained the house's layout to the detective. Questions fluttered in her mind like the guillemots outside the windows, darting out of sight only to reappear moments later.

"I haven't formally introduced myself," Frank held out a beefy hand. "Detective Frank Burgess."

"Ally Hawthorne."

"I also didn't get a chance to ask you directly, where were you two nights ago?"

"Here. Tim and I flew in from California. We took *The Sea Spit* over with Dennis. After we arrived, I didn't see anyone. All of the family and staff had gone ashore."

"So it was just you and your husband on the island?"

"For only a little while," Tim interjected. "Everyone came back soon after we arrived."

Frank rubbed the end of his nose with his thumb and index finger. "If you don't mind letting your wife answer, I'd appreciate that, Mr. Hawthorne. What time did everyone return, miss?"

"I don't know. I was exhausted from the trip and went straight to bed."

"You didn't come down for the dinner party Mrs. Hawthorne was having? Wasn't the meal made especially for you?"

Ally wanted to point out that that was a lie but kept silent. That indiscretion was between her and her mother-in-law, not the police. "I'd taken a sleeping pill and don't honestly remember my husband waking me up."

Tim crossed his arms. "I thought we were supposed to be searching for this alleged missing woman, not grilling my wife about her sleeping habits."

"I'm only trying to establish a timeline."

"For what?" Tim asked, the muscles in his forearms tightening. "All you know is that some crackpot said his girlfriend may have come to the island. I know you said you have a witness, but I've seen enough TV shows to know that's a bunch of bunk, or else you would have said who he is and what he saw."

"Unfortunately, it isn't hoo-ha, Tim. Dennis said he ferried a girl out here two nights ago. She said she was going to see a friend on the island. When Dennis offered to wait, she told him there was no need."

Ally stiffened when she remembered the text message to Tim. "What is this woman's full name?"

"Kimberly Wilson. Have you ever heard of her?"

Both Tim and Ally shook their heads.

"Kimberly worked for your mother. She cleaned the house. Still doesn't ring a bell?"

"Was she one of the cleaning crew that comes in every two weeks?" Tim asked, and Frank nodded. "Then I've probably seen her, but while they were here, everyone tended to leave and get out of their way. Do you have a picture?"

Frank pulled out his phone, pressed a few buttons, and held it out for Tim and then Ally to see the photograph of a beautiful young woman in her early twenties with long, chestnut hair that cascaded down her back in waves. Her lips were full, and her skin was tanned, giving her a glowing complexion.

"I don't know her," Ally said, returning the phone to Frank.

"What about you, Tim?" Frank asked, still holding the phone out for Tim to see.

Tim shook his head, but there was a haunted look in his eyes that Ally couldn't ignore. "I've never seen her before, but she looks familiar."

Frank scowled. "Those are mutually exclusive statements. You've either never seen her, or she looks familiar. Which one?"

"I don't remember specifically seeing her, but there's something familiar about her face. Maybe I ran into her, taking Tom inland? But I don't know her."

"Well, then, we have our work cut out for us," Frank said, slipping his phone back into his pocket. "Let's search the house, and then I'll check how they're doing outside."

Ally's mind raced with questions. Who was Kimberly Wilson, and did she come to the island? Was it she who sent the text messages to Tim, and it wasn't a wrong number like he told her?

"I apologize," Ally said. "I haven't had breakfast and feel a little light-headed."

Tim moved closer. "Are you all right? Do you want to lie down?"

"No. No. Let me grab something to eat, and I'll catch up with you."

While Frank and Tim continued down the hallway, Ally headed for the kitchen. She needed to clear her head and piece together everything that had happened since getting to the island.

The kitchen was empty, and she crossed to the fridge to grab some orange juice. Tim was right about one thing, she begrudgingly admitted. She was a mystery buff. She loved to read them and binge-watched shows, both fictional and real-life police dramas. Something was wrong about all of this, what though, she couldn't put her finger on. She needed to talk to Tim.

"Hey!" Philip said as he stomped into the kitchen. He was sweating. "Have you been here the whole time? I went all around the stupid island looking for you."

"I'm sorry. I ran into Dennis at the dock, and he told me I should get to the house. I must have just missed you."

"And Vicky didn't send nobody to get me? Are you serious?"

"She told the police that you weren't very fond of law enforcement and probably wouldn't come back. She said that's why she asked you to go find me."

Philip chuckled as he opened the fridge and took out a beer. "You want one?"

Ally wanted to point out that it wasn't even nine in the morning, but instead, she lifted her orange juice. "I have a drink, thanks."

"Haven't you ever heard of a beermosa?"

"Is that a real thing?"

"Yeah. Try it." He marched over, grabbed her glass, and before she could protest, he poured half the beer in. "Go on, drink."

With the large man looming over her, Ally felt compelled to take a sip at least. To her surprise, it was drinkable.

"I told you it was good." Philip grinned, downed half of the beer in a gulp, then set the empty bottle next to the sink. "I spotted the rookie cop outside with everybody except you, your husband, and the detective. Are they looking inside?"

Ally nodded. "What happened before?" The words tumbled out of her mouth without the permission of her brain.

Philip eyed her suspiciously as he returned to the fridge for another beer. "That's a pretty loaded question. You want to narrow it down to a date or give me a clue what you're talking about?"

She took another swig of the beermosa to build up her courage. "The detective used terms like 'in light of previous events' and that he wanted to avoid the 'circus' that happened before. What event was he referring to?"

Philip removed the cap on his beer bottle and leaned against the counter. The corner of his mouth ticked up in a slight smirk. "Tim never told you about any of that? Nothing at all?"

Ally shook her head.

Philip sipped his beer and then wiped his lips with the back of his hand. He set his bottle on the counter, picked up a dishcloth, and used it to blot the sweat from his forehead. "And you're not the kind of wife who goes digging into his past? They got the internet now. You could google it."

"I never felt the need," Ally said.

"Are you sure you want to ask me instead of my dear nephew?"

Ally set her glass down on the table so hard some sloshed out and splashed her hand. "Right now, Tim is giving a detective a tour of this house. My husband is many things but lacks your experience of dealing with the police. I don't know what to do, but as his uncle and with your background, I thought I should speak with you."

Philip crossed his arms. "So you're asking for my advice? If that's the case, I'd play it just like my sister is doing it. If you kick the cops out, they'll think Tim had something to do with this missing girl. But if you let them look around, they'll leave when they find nothing."

"Why would the police think my husband had anything to do with this girl?"

Philip sipped his beer and stared at her like they were playing cards, wondering what kind of hand she held. "Because something did happen before. It was a long time ago when Tim was still just a kid. I don't know how old he was, but he'd just gotten his license. The whole story is kinda like an STD type of thing. You think you got rid of the problem, but every once in a while, you start to itch, and there it is again."

Ally felt her disgust, fear, and frustration rising. She drank half her beermosa. "What happened?"

"You're putting me in a tough spot. Don't you want Timmy to tell you?"

"Don't belittle him. I'm asking you."

Philip stuck his tongue in his cheek, then turned and spit into the sink. "When Tim was in school, a girl went missing. The police questioned Tim about it."

Ally's stomach soured. "Why? Did she go to Tim's school?"

"No. She wasn't even from around here. Her parents got divorced, and she'd come and spend summer here with her father."

Ally relaxed a little. "But if she didn't go to school with Tim, why did the police question him?"

"They dated. Her name was Jane something.

Nice kid. Cute with a sweet figure. Don't go getting upset, it was a lightbulb relationship. On and off. Off and on. That kind of thing."

"What happened to Jane? Did they ever find her?"

"No. But the thing is, her home life in both places was in the toilet. Her mother was a druggie who died, so Jane lived with her grandmother. Her father remarried. Jane was a third wheel in two houses. She ran away a couple of times before. She dumped Tim cold one summer. He hadn't seen her in almost a year when the police showed up asking about her. The thing is, someone said they saw her taking a boat over here. Later, the witness said he was mistaken, but the damage was done. The rumors took off like wildfire. Rich boy, poor hot girl. Locals still think something happened, but it's all bull. You know your husband. Do you think he could kill someone?"

"No!" Ally rested her elbow on the table and tried to calm her breathing. "This whole thing is ridiculous."

"That's what I figure, too. If you ask me, and you did, that Gary guy is looking for a shakedown with a big payday. He's lying and hoping my sister will buy him off to avoid bad press."

"What do we do?"

"Nothing. Let the cops do their thing, and then I'll do mine."

"Which is?"

Philip flashed a crooked grin. "Gary and I will have a little tête-à-tête. I'll slip him some cash and convince him that this is a one-time shop."

"Has this happened before?"

"Something similar, so don't worry about it. My nephew is the artsy type. He's too sensitive to smack a girl around. He didn't do anything to Jane or this Kim if she really exists."

Footsteps sounded on the cellar stairs.

Philip hurried to the fridge, grabbed two beers, and dashed out the door.

The cellar door opened. Tim and Frank strolled into the kitchen.

"I thought you were going to grab something to eat and come looking for us?" Frank said.

"I was about to." Ally stood and smiled.

"Did I hear the door?" Frank asked. "Did Philip come back?"

"No." Ally blurted out, unsure of her sudden want to protect Tim's uncle. "It's just me in here."

Frank stepped closer to the table. He bent down and smelled her glass. His nose wrinkled. "Do you normally drink this early in the morning, Mrs. Hawthorne?"

Tim's eyebrows knit together.

"What? I didn't ... Oh, I had a bit of a migraine, so I decided to try a natural cure. It's called a beermosa. I only had one."

"Only one?"

Ally followed Frank's gaze to the sink and the two empty beer bottles on the counter. Ally bit her lip, and the words of Sir Walter Scott echoed in her head. *Oh, what a tangled web we weave when first we practice to deceive.*

"Would you please excuse us for a moment, Frank?" Tim smiled, but from the way the veins on the sides of his head pulsed, he was livid.

"I'll go check on Scott," Frank said.

Tim waited until Frank had left the room, and they'd heard the front door close. "What are you thinking drinking again!"

"Don't shout at me. Give me a second to explain. I was getting breakfast when your Uncle Philip came into the kitchen."

Tim exhaled and leaned against the counter. "If Philip came in, I'm surprised there aren't more beers around. Why did you lie to the police?"

"Don't say it like that!"

"But you did. And now Frank thinks you're a drunk." Tim picked up an empty bottle and gazed at it like he wished it were full. "I'm sorry I snapped. I need to tell you something." He set the bottle down and looked out at the yard. "I don't even know where to begin."

Ally sat down.

"There was this girl I dated in high school. We were about as serious as two teenagers can be. She didn't live here. It was a split-home situation, so she only came around in the summer and some holidays. The summer of my junior year, she dumped me over the phone. No explanation. No second chance. Nothing. A year later, Frank shows up looking for her — here."

Tim turned to face her. His eyes were watery and distant. She wanted to go to him. Comfort him. But she needed the truth more.

"I swear I never saw her after she dumped me. I even thought about going to Arizona to talk to her, but I didn't. And she never came out here. But someone, I don't know, claimed they saw Jane take a boat to the island. That was her name, Jane Nelson."

Ally sat with her hands in her lap, her heart pounding. "That sounds exactly like what's happening right now."

"I know. I know." Tim's lips pressed together in a mashed line. His knuckles turned white as his hands gripped the edge of the countertop. "But someone tried to do something like this before. It turned out to be some PR stunt for a movie. It was one of those lost video type of things. Uncle Philip straightened him out."

"Why didn't you tell me?"

Tim stared at his feet. "Did you really want to hear that there was a girl I loved so much that when she left, I almost lost my mind? It was my junior year. I went crazy. I probably had some kind of mental breakdown. When the police showed up, do you know what my first thought was? I was happy Jane was back. I wanted to talk to her so badly. She never told me why she ended things, and I needed to know. It was like reading a mystery, and the last pages are missing."

Ally sat there trying to process everything. Current events clashed with the jealousy building inside her. She always assumed Tim had relationships before her but never imagined he'd fallen in love so deeply with someone.

Tim placed both hands on the sides of his head and swept his hair back. "Because I smiled, the police suspected me. It wasn't because I'm some sicko who thought something happened to her. I believed I'd have a chance to talk to her, but I never did."

"Did they ever find her?"

Tim shook his head. "Then the witness recanted. I don't know exactly what happened, but the police cleared me and closed the case. That didn't matter because I still became the freak show in town. People whispered. My friend's parents stopped letting me come over. That's why I moved as far away as I could."

"Alaska would have been further."

Tim glared and then smiled.

Ally rushed over and wrapped her arms around his waist. "I understand, but you should have told me."

Tim kissed the top of her head and nodded. "I can't believe it's happening again. But I promise you, Ally. I had nothing to do with this. I've never even seen the woman."

Ally rested her head against his chest and closed her eyes. Despite the text message and his past, she believed him. But that didn't matter. The real question was, did the police?

Chapter Nine

Ally charged upstairs while Tim and Frank finished searching the house. She hurried into the bedroom and tore through her suitcase, carry-on, purse, and all of Tim's luggage in a vain search for her pill case. She took three deep breaths to calm her breathing, but it wasn't working. Her pulse raced, and her mouth tasted foul.

Remembering the beermosa, she walked into the bathroom and brushed her teeth. Now was the worst time for a panic attack. How would it look if she fell apart with a detective here? The police would leave soon, and she'd have time to think. She had to keep it together until then.

She shut the water off. The pipes rattled and clanked, but she didn't hear any voices. That was an improvement. After drying her hands, she returned to the bedroom, removed their phones from the dresser, and plugged them in. When the cell tower came on, the first thing she was going to do was call a lawyer for advice.

How could everything have gone wrong so fast?

Ally's knees wobbled, and she sat on the bed. If anyone knew the answer to that question, she did.

Five months ago, her life was perfect. She loved her husband, her job, and her home. She was busy decorating the nursery, happier than she'd ever been, when the first sharp pain stabbed her stomach. Even though it was her first pregnancy, she sensed something was horribly wrong.

Tim swept her into his arms and carried her to the car. They broke several laws on the way to the emergency room, but in less than an hour, she went from being a pregnant mother to grieving the loss of two babies.

The doctors had their theories of what medically happened, but Ally blamed herself regardless of what they said. Tears streamed down her cheeks. She was their mother. She was supposed to nurture and protect them. She failed before they drew their first breath.

A little boy and girl. They'd named them James and Jenna.

Ally slumped down on the comforter and wept bitter tears. Why? The question haunted her for months. Depression. Therapy. Medicine. The cycle began. She'd feel better for a few days or perhaps even a week, and something would happen. She would hear a child laugh or see a toy. Her hand would cradle her stomach, and the rage would come.

But not today. Today, all of her anger had vanished. She felt empty. Everything good in her seemed to be missing. She laid her head on the pillow, the tears running over her cheeks and wetting the fabric.

Tim swore he had nothing to do with this, but if that was true, why were the police here? Were they simply doing their due diligence and checking things out? If they didn't find Kim, would they walk away, or was this the beginning of some circus, like Victoria said?

Ally curled into a fetal position and cried until she fell asleep.

———————

Muffled shouts made Ally open her eyes. She sat bolt upright, brushing her matted hair off her face. How long had she been asleep?

She slid out of bed and opened the door.

Downstairs, people shouted and yelled. She recognized Tim's voice. She rushed down the hallway and descended the staircase.

"Don't be ridiculous, Frank," Victoria said. "Under no circumstances are you taking my son to the police station."

The ground shifted underneath Ally's feet. She grabbed the doorframe to keep from falling over. "What? Tim, what's going on?"

Tim held both his arms out in frustration. "They searched the island and the house and found nothing. So now, they're asking me to go with them for more questioning."

"I'm not asking," Frank said. "Besides, you would be more comfortable answering questions back at the station than here."

"We'll see about that!" Victoria took out her cell phone and grimaced. "That useless cell tower." She raised her hand over her head and shattered the phone against the marble floor.

"You need to calm down, Mother." Tim placed a restraining hand on her arm.

Victoria seethed. Her teeth were clenched, and her lips twisted in a snarl. Her arm trembled.

"Dr. Bradley!" Tim called. "Come here now."

"I will not have it, Frank." Victoria continued, "I'm warning you. I'll sue the department and you personally. Do you understand me?"

"I'm just doing my job. Right now, it's only questions."

"You know what will happen if you bring Tim into the police station. It will be all over town by morning."

Dr. Bradley rushed into the room.

"Where have you been?" Victoria snapped.

"I apologize." Dr. Bradley wrapped one arm around her waist. "Why don't you come to the couch and sit down."

"No!" Victoria stuck a trembling finger in Frank's face. "Your search turned up nothing. We've cooperated with everything you've asked. Give me one reason you want my son to go with you."

Frank turned to Tim. "Do you want me to say this in front of your mother and wife?"

"I have nothing to hide. Say it," Tim said.

"You've lied to me since I came to this island." Frank took out his phone. "You swore you've never seen Kimberly Hill."

"He didn't say that." Ally stood beside Tim and held his hand. "Tim admitted that he may have seen her if she worked at the house. He didn't know her name, and you can't blame him for that. The cleaners only come every two weeks. He doesn't even live here. I wouldn't expect him to recognize her, nor should you."

Frank nodded. "I'd agree with you if it weren't for this." He held up his phone. On the screen was a photograph someone had taken while standing on the street looking into a Chinese restaurant. Tim sat at a table with a white tablecloth and candles. Kimberly Hill sat across from him, holding his hand. "Can you explain this picture, Mr. Hawthorne? That is you, correct?"

Ally felt like she'd been punched in the face. She blinked rapidly as her brain flung excuses into the air. Maybe the picture was photoshopped? Or did someone use AI to generate it? That was easy to do nowadays. It wasn't real. She didn't want it to be. It couldn't be!

Tim's mouth hung open. He shook his head like he was trying to clear water from his ears. "Wait a second! This is some kind of setup. I remember her now. That was a couple of months ago. I took Tom out for lunch and a movie on the mainland. He went to the bathroom, and this woman walking by the table suddenly sat in his seat. She tells me she read about Tom saving my life. The whole thing was odd and embarrassing."

"Why are you holding hands with a stranger?" Frank said.

Ally resisted the urge to cross her arms but also wanted to know the answer.

"I wasn't!" Tim pointed at the picture. "Look at it. Her hand is covering mine. She said something about my being a sweet man, squeezed my hand, and left. The whole thing happened in less than two minutes."

"Wait a second!" Ally eyed the phone screen. "You're asking the wrong question, Detective. Don't you think it's strange that someone happened to take a picture standing on the sidewalk at this exact moment?"

"Ha!" Victoria added. "My daughter-in-law should take your job when it soon becomes available. It would be best if you were investigating whoever gave you that picture. They are the ones behind this blackmail scheme."

Frank swiped his finger across the phone, pulling up another photograph, a wide-angle view of the original picture. Two people, whose faces were blurred out, took selfies outside the restaurant. "This is the original. We've disguised the people's faces for privacy, but the guy in the picture knows Gary. After he took the picture, he recognized Gary's girlfriend and took a close-up because he thought Kim was cheating on Gary."

"What does Kim have to say about this?" Dr. Bradley asked.

Victoria cringed. "She's missing, so I doubt she has anything to say, Martin."

Frank placed his hands on his hips and leveled his gaze on Tim. "And your story is that some random woman, who turns out not to be random at all since you know her, decided to hold your hand in a restaurant?"

"I don't know that woman!"

The front door opened, and Nashwa, Ziad, Carter, Mia, and Officer Scott entered.

"Still no sign of her, sir," Scott said.

"And where is the Neanderthal?" Victoria asked.

"Philip went back to his cottage." Carter grinned. "But if you meant the other one, I have no idea."

"I can't find him either, sir," Scott said.

Nashwa and Ziad headed for the kitchen while Carter and Mia went upstairs.

Victoria pinned the young policeman in place with a withering gaze. "Are you saying that I now have a drug addict wandering my island unattended?"

"I, uh, guess so," Scott said.

Victoria marched over to stand toe-to-toe with

Frank. "When I allowed you unfettered access to my home, my one request was for you to keep that mongrel on a leash."

"Gary probably headed down to the dock," Frank said.

"Your job may hang on that fact, so let me recommend you make certain of that — now," Victoria said.

Frank pointed at Scott. "Head to the docks and tell Dennis I'll be coming down in a few minutes."

"Alone," Victoria added. "My son will not be accompanying you without a lawyer."

"Is that really how you want this to go down?" Frank asked Tim. "Right now, you're not under arrest. But I do need to ask you to accompany me to the station for some further questions without your mother and wife present. Will you agree to that?"

Ally squeezed Tim's hand and shook her head.

"You know what?" Tim pulled his hand free. "I will. And while I'm there, give me a lie detector test. I had nothing to do with this."

"Don't be a braggadocio jackass," Victoria said. "Wait until I reach my lawyer. Ziad!" Victoria called out. "Ziad!"

Ziad rushed in from the kitchen. "Yes, ma'am?"

"Run and get my brother. I know you must be exhausted, but please make haste."

Ziad nodded and raced out of the house.

"You should listen to your son. If he comes with me, we can keep this out of the papers for now."

"Are you threatening me with going to the media?" Victoria's voice rose. She shoved Dr. Bradley's arm away. "Let me remind you how you got that shiny golden trinket on your belt. And don't forget, the one who giveth can also taketh away."

"I have to do my job. If it isn't me, someone else

will. Look, Tim's suggestion of a lie detector would go a long way. If he's not hiding anything, why not take the test?"

"Because they're not reliable." Ally grabbed Tim's hand and tried to get him to listen. "They can give false positives. What would happen if he failed the test?"

"There would be chum in the water," Victoria said. "And all the sharks would come to feed."

"Exactly!" Ally said.

"That will happen if I don't do anything, too." Tim held his wife's hand and stared into her eyes. "I can't go through all that again. I know I didn't have anything to do with this, but this time, I'll prove it."

The front door opened, and Scott ran in. He gulped for air and put his hands on his knees as he tried to catch his breath. "Gone." He panted.

"Gary's gone?" Frank asked.

Scott shook his head and then nodded.

Victoria took Tim's other hand. "Do you want to place your trust in these Keystone Cops? This police officer doesn't even know yes from no."

Scott straightened up. "There's no sign of them. I can't find Gary, but the boat and Dennis are gone, too."

Frank rushed out the door, and Ally, Tim, and Scott followed him to the dock. Ally held the railing as she rushed down the slippery steps. A misting rain was falling, and the cement was slick. Her eyes search the dock, the harbor, and the horizon. There wasn't any sign of the boat or the men.

Frank took out his phone and swore. "Tell me you have a shortwave radio on the island."

"It's broken," Tim said. "Philip was going to hitch a ride later with Dennis to get another one on shore."

Ally started breathing easier. She didn't understand why until she realized Tim couldn't go to the police station now.

Scott cleared his throat. "During my previous search of the island, I saw another boat, sir. Down that path."

Frank turned to Tim. "Can you give us a ride to the mainland?"

"It's not operational. It's being repaired. Carter hit a rock, so Uncle Philip is giving it an overhaul. That's why he pitched the old radio."

Frank turned and stared in the direction of the mainland. "Then we're trapped here."

Ally crossed her arms as relief washed over her. Dennis's disappearance bought them some time. Victoria would contact her lawyers, and they would straighten this whole mess out.

"I'm sure the police will come and give you two a lift once you don't report back in," Tim said.

Frank shook his head. "I told you I wanted to keep this off the radar to avoid another zoo. So I didn't tell anyone where we were going. No one knows we're stuck out here."

Chapter Ten

Ally sat on the chair in the corner of the bedroom, watching the sunset. The evening sky, smears of gray and black, resembled an abstract painting. Considering the incomprehensible events of the day, it was only fitting to end it on a muddy note.

Tim continued to pace in front of the bed. Occasionally, he'd mutter something or move his lips, but he'd yet to tell her why he dragged her in here.

The clock on the wall ticked loudly as it counted down the seconds. There was a sense of anticipation in the air like whatever Tim would say next would shift her life in a different course.

"How can this be happening again? I swear to you, I've never had an affair. Not with Kim and not with anyone. Nothing. I've never even had an emotional internet fling or whatever they call them. I'm telling you the truth."

Ally closed her eyes. This wasn't about what Tim told her but the things that had gone unsaid. He'd left a whole chapter of his life hidden from her. And now, she wanted full disclosure.

"You know all my passwords. You have access to

my phone and computer. We have a joint bank account. I don't keep anything from you!"

"What about Jane?"

"That's different, Ally. It was high school and my first love kind of thing. I fell hard, and I fell deep, and she just left. I thought she ran away. She couldn't stand her parents, and I didn't blame her. She'd run away before. She even asked me to go with her once. I thought she was kidding, and I told her no. When I realized she was serious, she said she changed her mind. That was right before she dumped me. I figured she went through with it, and I hoped she started over someplace nice. She wanted to go into nursing. She had it all planned out."

"Didn't you ever try to find out what happened to her?"

"No, but out of respect for her. When she dumped me, she said she never wanted to see me again — ever. The police even said they thought she had run away. The only people that believed something bad happened to her were the kooks and the money chasers."

Ally chewed on that for a minute, and it did make sense. He hadn't seen Jane Nelson for a year, and she wasn't his girlfriend anymore. And the only witness changed his story. What else would Tim do but try to go on with his life?

"That explains the past, but what about the present? The police have a photograph of you with the missing girl." Ally's tone rose along with her anger. "How could you not recognize Kim from the picture Frank showed you? If someone approached me in a restaurant and held my hand, I'd remember their face!"

She expected him to yell back, but Tim's voice

was slightly above a whisper when he spoke. "Would you, if you couldn't look them in the eye? Do you have any idea how much it kills me when people talk about Tom? I can't stand being around him."

"What? Why? Tom is the sweetest man I've ever met."

"Yes, but ... I mean, you should have known him before I did that to him." Tim's hands clenched into fists at his side. When Ally opened her mouth, he held up his hand. "We were twins, but it was like he was my big brother. He was so smart. He always knew what to do and watched out for me."

"You're not to blame."

Tim scoffed. "People who don't understand say that. My mother. My teachers. Even Tom. But everything that happened was my fault. Mine. Tom will never get married. Or have a job or kids. All because of me."

"He saved your life."

"He should have let me die. That's what I think every time I come here. But he's why I can't stay away. I owe him. So yeah, I took him to that restaurant in town with the worst Chinese food I've ever eaten because he loves it. Tom went to the bathroom, and that woman came over. She sits down and starts by saying, 'I want to let you know that what you're doing for your brother is so special.'" Tears welled up in his eyes. "Do you know how many people say that to me? Everywhere I go with him, people look at him with pity and at me like I'm a saint. And they're all so wrong. They treat me like the hero, but Tom is the real hero. I breeze into town, take him to a movie and a few restaurants, and then return to my life. So no, I didn't get a good look at her because I was too busy staring at the FLOOR!" he shouted.

Ally inhaled and sat there while he cried. Tim's uncle Philip was right about one thing. Tim was a sensitive man. But that wasn't a flaw. It was another reason she loved him.

"I want to believe you," Ally said.

"Why don't you?"

"Do you remember that text message you received before we left California? I've been thinking about it. Even if the sender deleted the message, I don't think it would get removed from your phone."

"I never even saw that message. So, if you're asking me if I deleted a message I didn't know I got, the answer is NO! Why are you obsessing about a wrong number?"

"I'm not fixated on it. The cell tower came back on for a minute and —"

"Did you call for a boat when you had a signal?"

"No. I tried to call my ..." Ally's voice trailed off, and she looked at the floor. As the silence grew, she rubbed her trembling right hand with her left.

"You said you tried to call someone. Who?"

"Don't make this about me. I didn't know the cell tower would go right back down again."

"I'm not making it about you, but you're accusing me of deleting a text message I haven't seen, and now you won't tell me who you called."

"Don't you think it's too much of a coincidence that you got a message from a woman saying that she missed you and hoped you're coming back soon, and now a woman came out here to see you?"

"It doesn't sound good, but I don't know her or what happened to the text message. But only you and I can access my phone." Tim's eyes narrowed. "Level with me. You said no more secrets, and I swear I'm being honest. It's time for some reciprocity. Who did you try to call?"

Ally stood up straighter. "My therapist."

Tim stood there waiting for her to continue, and when she didn't, he started rubbing the back of his neck and pacing again. "Instead of calling for a boat, you called your therapist?"

"I was having a panic attack. You told Carter and Mia that I'm taking meds when you promised you wouldn't."

"Hold on! You were drinking, and that's the last thing you should be doing with that medicine."

"I didn't take my medicine, so it doesn't matter."

"You didn't take your meds? Your prescription medication?"

"I forgot them. That's why I tried to call my therapist so she could get me an emergency refill."

"That won't do you much good if we don't have a boat to get to the pharmacy!"

"Don't yell at me!" Ally shouted. "I was freaking out, okay. I just brushed my teeth and shut the water off ..."

Tim's eyes rounded in concern.

Ally turned away. "Don't look at me like that."

"This is serious." Tim moved in front of her but didn't touch her. "You shut the water off, and what?" He waited for her to fill in the blank. When she didn't, he said, "You heard voices again?"

"I told you I was having a panic attack."

Tim gently took her hand. "It's okay. We got this. We got through this before, not with all this other stuff going on, but we can get through this." He exhaled and ran his hands down his face. "Let's go talk to Dr. Bradley. He might have something he can give you."

"I don't want everyone to know I'm taking meds."

"Since I said something to Carter, everyone knows now. I'm sorry."

Ally swore.

"Look at me." Tim angled himself so she was staring into his eyes. "I'm sorry about all of this. Our coming here and not telling you about Jane. Everything. But I promise I'll sort it all out. We need to stick together. That's what we do. We're a team." He held up his fist, and she bumped it.

"I'm not crazy," Ally said.

"I think I may be," Tim smiled and kissed her. "But the doctor said you shouldn't stop your medicine cold turkey, right?"

Ally nodded. "You know that's the least of our problems?"

"One by one, we'll fix the others. Uncle Philip is putting the motor back into the boat today. Then he can go for help."

"How long will that take?"

"He said a day or two tops. The boat doesn't need the electronics. He can find the mainland with his eyes closed."

Someone knocked on the door. "Tim?" Tom called out. "Momma wants to see you. She's in the sitting room."

Tim took a deep breath and opened the door. "Hey, buddy. How are you doing?"

"Fine. Momma wants to see you now."

Tim held his hand out to Ally.

Tom moved in between them. "Momma said she wanted to talk to you, and I want to tell Ally about Iron Man."

"Give us one second," Ally said.

"I'll be back in a minute, or meet me there. Either way."

Tom stepped further into the room. "I just watched another Iron Man. That's the one when his girlfriend comes over."

As Tom continued speaking, Ally realized the one person in the house she could count on to tell her the truth was standing right before her.

"I'm so glad you like the movies," Ally said, moving to the doorway and making sure Tim was out of earshot.

"I love them all. Thank you again. There are so many of them. Tim told me to watch them in the order on the box. That's what I'm doing. I start on the left and go right." Tim explained why he liked Captain America, and Ally let him talk.

"That's wonderful. I thought they'd be perfect. I have a question for you. Do you remember a friend of Tim's named Jane?"

Tom moved toward the door, but Ally blocked his way.

"You do remember her?"

He nodded. "But I don't like talking about her. I'm not supposed to."

"Who said you're not supposed to?"

"I don't like talking about her." He shifted his weight from one foot to the other. "It makes me sad. Tim!" He called out.

"It's okay, Tom. I don't want you to be sad. I was only wondering when the last time you saw Jane was?"

Tom closed his eyes and stuck his fingers in his ears. "TIM!" Tom shouted.

"We're coming now!" Ally quickly added and

lightly touched Tom's arm. She forced a smile on her face. "Let's go!"

"Yeah!" Tom grinned and followed her into the hallway.

Ally exhaled as she hurried to keep up with Tom's long strides. Asking him proved to be a dead end. But there was always Carter and Mia. And they loved to talk.

She followed Tom down the stairs to the sitting room. Victoria sat in a chair at a small table facing Tim.

Without saying a word, Tom left and headed to the kitchen.

Victoria glanced toward the door and gave Ally a Mona Lisa smile. That was another thing about her mother-in-law that drove Ally up a wall — she could never tell what Victoria was thinking.

Tim stood, whispered something to his mother, then strode to Ally. "My mother was just explaining that she had Ziad prepare guest rooms for Frank and the police officer. Uncle Philip thinks the boat will be ready tomorrow. See? Everything is going to be fine." He took a deep breath. "My mother wants to talk to you for a minute." He kissed her cheek and whispered, "It's all good. Really."

Feeling like a child headed to the principal's office and running down a mental list of everything they had done wrong in the last week, Ally crossed the room and sat.

"The first thing I want to say is I apologize that Tim broke your confidence, but under the circumstances, I think his doing that is for the best. And there's no shame in taking antidepressants."

Ally pursed her lips and tilted her head to the side. "I thought you disapproved of people taking anti-anxiety medication. You said that people who took them were weak."

"Nonsense. You certainly misunderstood me. I disapprove of people who abuse them or don't realize that they are a tool to be used to ascertain the cause of the problem. One must commit to self-reflection if one truly wants to get better, not just mask the symptoms with a pill. I've been on them many different times. After the death of Tim's father and then the incident with Tom, to name two."

Ally drummed her fingers on the arm of the chair. There was no way she could have gotten her mother-in-law's view so wrong. Had Victoria lied in the past and hid the fact that she'd taken medication, or was she gaslighting Ally now?

Victoria continued. "I spoke with Dr. Bradley, and while he didn't have any, he did say this sleeping aid"— she handed Ally a plastic pill bottle — "can be taken with any of the antidepressants that are on their way."

Ally's brow knit together. "On their way?"

Mia hurried into the room carrying a small box.

"I called a different kind of pharmacist." Victoria grinned.

"I'm so sorry you're not feeling up to snuff." Mia set a box the size of a briefcase on the coffee table. "I wasn't sure what you were taking, so I brought the whole shebang. I've got Amitriptyline, Effexor, Lexapro, which is an Escitalopram and gives you that good serotonin, Paxil, Remeron, and Trintellix. If none of those are a match, I can ask Carter. He's got some."

"I'm taking Effexor XR."

"I've got the low dose at 37.5 mg. I also have the

make you smile full octane version. 225 mg. That's the max."

"I think I was taking 150 mg."

Mia leaned forward and winked. "With everything going on, I'd put the pedal to the metal and go with the max, but that's just me."

"Under the circumstances, I'll take your advice. Thank you."

Mia gave Ally the bottle, wrapped her arms around her neck, and hugged her. "Don't ever think that you can't talk to us. We're family. And in this family, we stick together."

Victoria nodded. "That is the Hawthorne creed. Family above all else."

Ally swallowed. In the years she'd known Victoria, she'd never felt welcome. And now that she did, she wasn't sure that was a good thing.

Chapter Eleven

Ally awoke feeling better than she had in months. Not only did she sleep peacefully and without nightmares, but today, the cloud of depression that normally swooped in as soon as she opened her eyes failed to cast its shadows over her soul.

She took a deep breath and stretched like a cat in the sun. The bed was warm, and the sheets soft. Wrapping herself up in the comforter, she rolled over.

Tim was already up and gone. The sun had risen but did little to brighten the dark, overcast day. She still smiled and marveled at how good she felt. When she returned to California, she'd have to talk to her therapist about increasing her dosage. Or was something else responsible for her mood? With everything happening lately, she should be hiding under the covers. But this adversity had once again brought her and Tim closer, and now even her mother-in-law was being nice!

She closed her eyes and said a quick prayer of thanksgiving. Victoria treating her like a human was indeed a miracle.

After using the bathroom, she dressed and headed

out of the room. She padded downstairs, trying not to make any noise. The house was still and quiet as if holding its breath in anticipation of something. She shook her head, trying to eliminate the dread coming over her.

Reaching the foyer, the marble beneath her feet felt anchored to the world's core. Solid and unmoving, the stone connected her to the earth, and grounding was good.

Ally slipped into the kitchen.

Nashwa was putting things away in the refrigerator. "Good morning! Would you like some breakfast?" she asked, stopping her work. "It's labneh and pickled cherry toast."

"No, thank you. I wanted to take a walk around the island."

"Today?" Nashwa wrinkled her nose as she glanced outside at the overcast sky. "There are some umbrellas in the foyer. It looks like rain."

"Thanks, I will." Ally crossed to the refrigerator. "You've probably heard this a thousand times, but you're an artist with food. The honey pancakes you made were unbelievable. I could eat them all day."

"If you prefer, I could make those again in addition to the labneh and toast."

"Oh, no. I'm sure the toast is fantastic, too. Maybe I'll have some when I come back." Ally grabbed a water bottle, but when she shut the refrigerator, she stared at Nashwa's reflection in the stainless steel.

Nashwa stood with her arms crossed, and her eyes rolled toward the ceiling. Her lips moved, and she rocked back and forth slightly. Ally had no idea what Nashwa was saying, but the cook was mocking her.

Ally clutched her water bottle tightly and headed

to the front door. Eager to leave the room, she didn't look back.

Had she said something to offend Nashwa? She replayed the conversation in her head and didn't think she had. What she should have done was turn around and confront her. That was the correct way of handling that situation. Firm but without anger. It had to be miscommunication, right?

Ally opened the front door, and the happiness she'd been feeling fled toward the sea. The dark clouds threatened rain. She selected the smallest umbrella, a little black one that was only as big as the water bottle. With the push of a button, it would pop out and expand, but wrapped up, it was easy to carry.

She stepped outside, grateful the rain was holding off. She rechecked both sides of the steps for the missing sandal, but there was no sign of it.

Deciding to head in the opposite direction today, Ally headed along the walkway and down the steep wooden steps toward the path far below. The worn stairs were slick with dew. She held onto the metal railing until her feet crunched the path's gravel.

As she followed the trail, a sense of peace again washed over her. The sound of the tide lapping against the rocks and the smell of ocean air, fresh from the impending rain, enveloped her senses. Ally's thoughts wandered as she took in the scenery. She thought about Tim and how much she loved him. He was her rock, her haven amid all the chaos in her life. And with all that was happening, she still clung to him. There had to be some other explanation for this missing girl. If there was one person in this world she could trust, it was her husband.

He must be at the boat helping his uncle prepare it for sea. She hoped Philip could. He had been an engineer once with a massive company in Europe. He was only thirty then, but his shady dealings were already legendary. Tim only knew a few details, but Philip had tried to start his own company using his current employer's list of clients. Lawsuits, bankruptcy, and a divorce followed. Instead of humbling Philip, he kept trying one get-rich-quick scheme after another, leaving more lawsuits, bankruptcies, ex-wives, and several criminal convictions in his wake.

The trail dipped down and split. To the right was the beach. While she'd love to walk along the seashore, the overnight rain would have saturated the beach. The thought of sinking in sand dampened that appeal.

Ally opted for the path on the left. It meandered around until she approached the inlet where the accident had occurred. At the crest of the hill, an old cement bench overlooked the ocean. It was so covered in moss Ally hadn't noticed it yesterday. Ally could never sit there, even if it was dry.

Pulling up the collar of her jacket, she started to turn when something in the water caught her attention. Being from California, she was used to seeing large sea lions and seals. They'd become so numerous they were now a nuisance. But something was wrong with the one floating in the inlet. It was covered in seaweed, and its fin dragged alongside its body.

Ally slowed to a stop. Her breath caught in her throat. It wasn't a seal in the water, and that wasn't a fin. It was an arm. She opened her mouth to scream, but nothing came out. She stepped forward. No. No. What was she doing? She should run and get help.

The body bobbed in the water, the waves pushing it toward the shore. Like a large piece of driftwood, it lifted on a little wave and rolled over. The greenish-pale skin of a face slowly turned toward her.

The umbrella and water bottle tumbled from her trembling hands. Ally shrieked. Her sneakers kicked sand and gravel into the air as she raced down the path. Over and over, she screamed.

Ally's heart pounded as she sprinted toward the boathouse. Men ran toward her, but her focus was on her Tim, running the fastest out in front. She slid to a stop.

He grabbed her in his strong arms. "What's wrong?" Tim asked, his voice soft and calming.

Ally could barely speak, gasping for air between sobs. "There's a body in the water," she managed to choke out, her hands shaking violently. "I saw it ... it was a person, and they're dead."

"Where?"

"In the inlet."

Tim's face paled.

Philip, Frank, and Scott stopped behind Tim and exchanged concerned glances.

"Stay here," Tim said to Ally.

"Hold on." Frank stepped forward and motioned for Scott. "I need to ask her some questions. Who is it?"

Ally stood frozen to the spot. Her mind raced, replaying the image of the floating body again and again. "I don't know." She clung to Tim's jacket.

"Where is this inlet?" Frank asked.

Philip started walking. "I'll show you."

Frank stood his ground. "I apologize, Mrs. Hawthorne. But if you can, it would be helpful if you came along."

Ally nodded. "I'll show you." If it wasn't for Tim's

arm wrapped around her waist supporting her, she would have fallen going back down the path.

A light rain fell as she and the men continued. Once they rounded the curve, the inlet came into view. Philip had stopped and peered into the sea. "I don't see anything," Philip said. "Where was it?"

"Past the middle, closer to the right-hand side and the shore. There was seaweed all over it." Ally's stomach soured.

Tim held onto her while Frank, Scott, and Philip climbed down the rocks.

After a moment, Scott pointed. "There is something over there. Down to your right, sir. Closer to shore."

"I see it," Philip muttered. "It's a body, all right." He moved forward.

"Don't touch it!" Frank called out as he scrambled over the rocks, slipping as he went. "We need to photograph it." He stopped and took out his phone. He looked up and scanned the surface. "Where did it go?"

"It went under," Philip said.

"What?" Frank hurried to the edge of the rocks, the waves lapping at his feet as he peered at the sea. "Where exactly did you see it?"

"Right there," Philip pointed to a spot a few feet away.

Frank handed Scott his phone and then glared at Philip. "Why didn't you grab it before it sank?"

"Because you told me not to, Columbo." Philip shot back.

"There it is again!" Scott shouted.

A small wave lifted the corpse and pushed it against the rocks. Scott took a picture while Frank leaned forward.

Frank slipped and slid up to his waist in the sea. Philip seized the collar of Frank's jacket and held on.

"Pull me up!" Frank yelled.

"I will," Philip said, a hint of amusement in his voice. "Grab ahold of the corpse first. You don't want to lose him again, do you?"

Frank reached into the water and managed to get hold of the sleeve of a blue jacket. Philip pulled Frank, who held onto the body, dragging them both up onto the rocks.

"Don't just stand there. Give me a hand, Scott!" Frank said.

The rookie slid down the slope, stopping inches above the water.

The three men carried the body above the high-tide mark.

Tim was pale, and his entire frame trembled. His eyes were dark and had a faraway look to them.

"We don't have to stay here, honey." Ally squeezed his hand.

"I'm all right. I can do this. It's not Tom. Tom's fine. It's not Tom."

Ally wrapped a protective arm around his waist and managed to get him to look toward the boathouse instead of the inlet.

The body was covered in seaweed, and Ally couldn't see who it was.

Philip crouched down and stared at the dead man's face. "Looks like we've got to get that boat running. It's Dennis, and seeing how he's dead, I don't think he's giving us a lift."

"This is not the place for your kind of humor," Frank snapped.

Philip stood nose to nose with the detective. "Seeing how this is my island, I'd say that any place on it is the place for my kind of humor. Besides, Dennis doesn't mind." He looked down at the corpse. "Do you, Dennis?"

Scott's complexion had turned a light green. He handed Frank back his phone.

"I need to clear this area now," Frank said. "Scott, return to the house and get Dr. Bradley. Philip, do you have a cart or wheelbarrow?"

"If you're thinking about moving the body, I've got a flat cart for cleaning up branches. It can navigate the path."

"That would be perfect. Could you please go get it?"

Philip snapped his fingers and pointed at Scott. "Hey, rookie! The cart is in the back of the house near the air-conditioners. When you get Martin, grab the cart too."

Scott looked at Frank, who nodded. The young police officer frowned and then jogged down the path toward the house.

"What are you going to do with ... him?" The words tumbled from Ally's mouth.

"We need to get him out of the elements," Frank said, peering up at the sky. "We'll take him back to the house. I need to treat this area as a crime scene. You and Tim should return to the house. Please tell everyone else to stay away from this area."

"A crime scene?" Tim said. "You don't think this was deliberate, do you?"

"I'm not saying anything right now." Frank wiped the rain from his face. "This is standard procedure."

Philip scoffed. "You and I know Dennis wouldn't leave you high and dry and sail off without you. That walking meth lab Gary had something to do with it."

"We can't go jumping to conclusions. It may have been natural causes or some kind of accident."

"Natural causes? What do you think? Did Dennis decide to take a swim in the healing waters off the coast of Maine in the winter with all his clothes on? He was murdered, and that freak Gary did it."

Chapter Twelve

Ally paced the sitting room floor while Victoria gazed out the window, drinking some amber alcohol from a short-stemmed snifter. Ally had discovered the name of the glass on one of those antique shows she watched. It was an odd name for a glass, and it stuck in her head. They were for brown liquors. She figured Victoria was the type that would only drink cognac or brandy from the proper vessel. She doubted she'd drink whiskey. Then again, there was bourbon.

Ally would like to drink anything straight from the bottle, but now that she was taking her medicine, she wouldn't. She already felt like a wayward astronaut tumbling through space. Getting drunk was the last thing she needed. Still, the draw of drinking herself into oblivion was powerful. She'd love to forget all about finding Dennis' body, the missing woman, possible affairs, and past mysteries.

Victoria had grown silent and seemed deep in thought as she stared out the window.

The rain beating against the glass gave Ally a strange sense of comfort. Even though her mind raced, she found the steady rhythm of the rain soothing. Although it was early afternoon, the clouds had grown so thick it was nearly dark outside. Ally took a few deep breaths, trying to relax her mind and body as she continued to pace.

"Will you please stop running in circles before you wear out my Persian carpet?" Victoria said without turning around.

Ally stepped off the rug and onto the marble but kept walking.

"You do behave like a petulant child at times."

"Excuse me?" Ally stopped.

"Apology accepted. Now come. Sit and let us discuss this rationally." Victoria moved over to the small table with two chairs beside the window.

Ally stopped pacing, her eyes fixed on Victoria as she took another sip from the snifter. "Why did you call me here, Victoria?" she asked, her voice shaky.

A wry smile dawned on Victoria's lips. "Don't be so nervous, dear. I needed someone to talk to. Someone who understands me. Someone who cares for my son almost as much as I do."

Ally clasped her hands together in a vain effort to keep them from shaking as she spoke. "What are we going to do? That detective thinks Tim had something to do with that girl's disappearance. And now Dennis is dead."

"We'll deal with it. We always do."

Ally shook her head, her voice rising. "How, Victoria? This isn't something you can make go away."

"I would not be so hasty to limit what I can do." Victoria sipped her drink, and the aroma of brandy wafted across the table. "Dennis was a scared little man. It is quite possible that he panicked and left on his own. Fear and rushing are two things that can turn deadly on the open sea. He may have slipped and fallen overboard or had some type of medical issue brought on by his anxiety."

"But will the police believe that? Your brother thought that Dennis may have been murdered."

"Philip has loved drama since he was in diapers. He should have gone into the theater. I'm certain that isn't the case." Victoria swirled her glass and stared into the dark whirlpool of liquid. "It is fortunate that Dr. Bradley is witnessing the initial examination. Martin is a pillar in the community. His opinion will carry a great deal of weight."

"If Dr. Bradley believes it was murder, what then?"

Victoria gazed at Ally like she was studying a painting. Their eyes locked until Ally looked away.

"Martin will not reach that conclusion."

Ally stared down at her trembling hands. Victoria couldn't know that, but she sounded so sure Ally wanted to believe her. However, Dr. Bradley was still conducting the examination. And unless she told him what conclusion to reach ...

"While Dennis's death is a tragedy, we shouldn't dwell on it. My brother is expediting the repair of the boat, and once he escorts the police off my island, these incidents will soon be forgotten."

Ally wanted to run out of the room, rip open the front door, and scream at the sky. It hadn't been more than a few hours, and Victoria wanted to put a man's death behind them. Did Dennis have a family? He had to have people who cared about him. Even if he didn't, a man lost his life. He deserved someone looking into how he died.

"Now, about this missing girl," Victoria continued. "I don't think she exists. I believe that Gary was just another con artist who cooked up some half-baked scheme to make some quick money by black-mailing me."

Ally crossed her arms. Part of what Victoria said made sense, but something about her theory bothered her. "If Gary is a con artist, why would he bring the police out here?"

"Did Gary bring them, or did the police come here on their own? You heard Frank say it yourself — Gary only wanted to file a police report, but Frank decided to keep it hush-hush, so he bundled Gary up and ferried him straight out to the island. If Frank permitted Gary to file the report, Gary would not have brought the police with him. With that paper in hand, Gary would have arrived on my doorstep and dangled it in my face. Then he would have said that he can make the whole thing go away for the right price."

Ally thought about it for a moment. "That makes sense. You think like a detective."

Victoria shook her head. " I think like a criminal. So you see, my dear, sometimes the simplest conclusion is the truth. Most likely, what happened is Gary realized he had overplayed his con. Gary had Dennis bring him back to the mainland. Dennis dropped him off, immediately turned around, and attempted to return to the island. On the way, an accident or medical emergency happened to the poor man. Either way, this whole sordid affair is almost over." She smiled and sipped her brandy.

"But what about the police? They're going to keep looking for Kim."

"I don't believe the woman is missing at all. There is a Kimberly Hall. Most likely, she worked for the cleaning company I hired. She may even be the girl-friend of the grifter. However, if the police ever locate

Gary, they will discover she was in cahoots with him. But Tim has nothing to concern himself with, and therefore, neither do you."

Ally leaned forward in her chair. "No offense, Victoria, but these are serious charges. How can you toss them off and say there's nothing to worry about?"

"Look at the facts, child. Our accuser has vanished, and since there is no official report, the police have no reason to keep looking into this matter. As Hercule Poirot would say, 'The case, it is closed.'" Victoria raised her snifter in toast and finished the contents.

Footsteps sounded in the foyer. Dr. Bradley hurried into the room but stopped on the threshold when he noticed Ally.

Victoria slid her chair back and stood. She motioned Dr. Bradley to the oversized leather chair. "Oh, Martin, you look terrible. Come in, and let me fix you a drink."

"Make it a double." Martin crossed the room and slumped into the chair. He rested his elbow on the armrest and his forehead between his index finger and thumb. His skin was pale, and his hand trembled. "What a wretched experience. I'm a doctor, not a coroner."

Ally closed her mouth, doubting either one would understand the *Star Trek* reference if she pointed it out.

Victoria poured him a large snifter of brandy and brought it over to him. "Drink this, and I'll have Nashwa make you something to eat."

Dr. Bradley shook his head. "I don't even want to think about food. Since I have testified in medical proceedings in court before, Frank requested that I act as a witness while they videotaped the body of a man I spoke with yesterday. It was quite unnerving." He took a long gulp of brandy and made a face.

Victoria squatted next to his chair, her hand tenderly stroking his arm. "I'm so sorry you had to endure all of that. Let's be grateful the matter is concluded."

"It's not." Dr. Bradley took another sip. " Frank wants me to write something, including my thoughts regarding the visible injuries."

"And in your professional opinion, Dennis's death was accidental," Victoria said.

Dr. Bradley took a long sip, thought for a moment, and took another. "How can I say that? I don't know. It's not my area of expertise. I'm not the coroner."

Victoria held his hand and squeezed it until he met her gaze. "Were there any external wounds to his body? Besides superficial scratches caused by the sea and the rocks?"

"He did have a bump on his head."

"I knew it!" Victoria smiled and placed a hand on his knee. "I was certain that you would discover the truth, Martin. Dennis must have bumped his head and fallen into the sea. A regrettable, accidental tragedy."

Ally sat in her chair, staring down at her hands. Victoria's version of events was possible, but considering Gary was missing, as well as Dennis's boat, what were the odds of it being an accident?

"In light of those facts," Victoria continued, "in your professional opinion as a doctor, Dennis's death was the result of an accident, and you saw nothing to indicate otherwise."

Dr. Bradley opened his mouth.

Victoria slightly crooked an eyebrow. If she had punched him in the throat, it would have produced a similar reaction — his eyes bulged, he coughed, and fought to catch his breath. Once he'd done so, he drained his glass and rose, exhaling loudly. "I'm going to take a long shower and write the report. In my professional opinion as a doctor, Dennis's death was the result of an accident, and I saw nothing to indicate otherwise."

Victoria touched the small of his back and whispered something that brought a broad smile to his face.

As Dr. Bradley exited the room, Ally snapped her fingers. "Wait a minute, Victoria. I don't think it was an accident. Dennis wasn't wearing a life preserver. He said he had to wear one when he took us to the island due to the new insurance regulations." Ally hurried to catch Dr. Bradley, but Victoria grabbed her arm.

Victoria's smile faded. "Perhaps Dennis forgot. Or maybe he only wore his life jacket because you and Tim were in the boat. Dennis was an old salt of the sea, and some habits are hard to change. Or you are mistaken. Either way, it is an irrelevant tidbit."

Ally shifted uncomfortably. "I'm not going to lie."

"No one is asking you to." Victoria released Ally's arm. "But you need to realize something. In this world, there are all sorts of groups and people. One of those delineations is the haves and have-nots. Some people hate and resent us solely because we are a family with means. They will stop at nothing to tear us down for no more reason, to gloat when the mighty have been brought low."

Victoria touched Ally's shoulder tenderly, and her tone softened. "Listen to me. You and I love this family too much to see innuendos and lies tear it apart. But if we keep a united front, everything will work out. I assure you. All you need to do is say nothing and let me handle everything."

Victoria nodded, and, like some Jedi mind trick, Ally found herself nodding along with her. Her mother-in-law smiled and strolled out of the room.

Ally retreated as far away as she could go. Standing in the corner, she stared at the heavy rain, the large drops pinging off the windows. She leaned against the window frame, unsure of everything and everyone — even herself. Dozens of questions splashed off her mind like the rain against the glass. Before she could even think of an answer to one, several more questions took its place.

Ally slumped forward. Her breath fogged up the pane, but the onslaught of rain and questions continued. Lightning flashed and thunder boomed. Clamping her eyes closed, Ally covered her ears but couldn't drown out the noise. It only grew louder. A massive clap of thunder was so loud it sounded like a roar and made the window shake.

This wasn't over, Ally was sure of it. Victoria may think she controls the world, but it isn't true — the Devil rules the earth, prowling the land like a roaring lion, seeking whom he can devour.

Chapter Thirteen

Ally stood next to the fireplace in the sitting room. The cheery fire did little to brighten her mood. She rubbed the side of her throbbing head, debating about checking with her new pharmacist, Mia, to see if she had anything for a migraine. The aroma from Nashwa's dinner cooking made Ally's stomach grumble. She hadn't eaten all day and was starving. But how could she think about food with all that was happening?

Frank and Scott had returned to the inlet to take additional photographs. Tim, Philip, Carter, and Ziad were fixing the boat. Victoria was off somewhere with Dr. Bradley, and Tom watched a movie.

The front door banged open. Frank and Scott's voices echoed in the foyer. Frank said something about the bathroom, and a moment later, Scott entered the sitting room.

The tips of the poor man's ear were cherry red, and so was his nose.

"You must be freezing," Ally said, grabbing a chair and placing it in front of the fire. "Sit down and warm up before dinner."

"Thank you." Scott hurried over. "The temperature dropped twenty degrees." He blew on his hands and held them out toward the fire. "I don't know if I've ever been so cold. Arizona, this is not."

"Is that where you're from?" Ally asked, setting another chair down beside his.

Scott nodded. "I didn't want to work border patrol, and I'd never seen snow. I'm starting to rethink my decision."

"The summers are beautiful. Winters have a unique charm. People refer to it as an acquired taste."

Scott chuckled. "It doesn't taste so good right now. Maybe snow will be better than freezing rain." His eyes traveled around the room. "I don't understand why you don't live someplace warm if you have all this money. Like the Mediterranean. Somewhere tropical."

"To each his own."

"You're out in California, right?"

"The northern part of the state."

Scott pulled the chair closer to the fire. "Is it a house like this?"

Ally laughed. "No, it's a three-bedroom ranch. We converted one of the bedrooms to my office and the garage into Tim's workshop."

"Why are you doing that? Is Tim just pretending so he can pull off the poor artist thing?"

Ally's mouth pinched. "No. We're not rich."

Scott's left eyebrow lifted high, and he cocked his head to the side. "You guys are loaded. You've got a private island, a mansion, servants ..." He ticked off each one on his fingers.

"Victoria has those things, we don't." Ally crossed her legs and then her arms. "Tim doesn't want to live off his mother's money."

Scott did a triple-take so quickly that Ally was

surprised he didn't give himself whiplash. "Are you serious? You are serious." His mouth fell open, and he sat there blinking. "Your husband is either one noble guy or the world's biggest fool." Scott stuck his hands beneath his armpits. "Boy, I don't think I'd be able to do that."

Ally nodded. She doubted she would either.

"Isn't some of the money his?" Scott continued. "His father died, right? Didn't he leave him a pile of cash?"

"Tim's father left everything to Victoria. Tim could ask for it, but he doesn't want to."

"What do you want?"

Ally took a deep breath. The truth was that she'd thought about that money often. She and Tim struggled financially at different times, and his refusal to ask his mother for help had caused some cracks in the marriage that they still worked on to heal. "It would be nice if she'd at least offer to pay for Tim's travel expenses to come out here."

Frank hurried into the room, grabbed a chair, and pulled it before the fire. "I still can't feel my toes." He thrust his legs out. "A cold front must have swept down from Canada."

Scott breathed into his hands. "Are you sure it wasn't from the Arctic Circle?"

"Wait until January. It gets way colder than this," Frank said.

"Is it too late to put in for a transfer?" Scott asked.

Nashwa entered the room carrying a tray with three large steaming drinks. The scent of apple cider, cinnamon, nutmeg, and other spices filled the air. "Mrs. Hawthorne thought you needed to warm up. I brought one for you, too." She smiled at Ally.

"Thank you so much." Ally took the warm glass and inhaled deeply. She took a sip. "It's so creamy!"

"Does this have alcohol in it?" Frank asked.

"You're tasting the butter." Nashwa smiled. "That's the secret. It will warm you up in time for dinner."

Scott downed half the drink and let out a satisfied groan. "I think it's already working."

"Did you happen to see any boats when you were on the shore?" Ally asked hopefully.

Frank shook his head, pressing both hands to the warm glass's sides. "And I doubt any will be out in this weather. Have you seen Dr. Bradley?"

"Not since this afternoon. The task you assigned him left him a bit squeamish. I think he's lying down. Did you find anything at the inlet?"

Scott shook his head, and Frank loudly cleared his throat.

"We can't comment regarding an active investigation," Frank said.

"Of course, sorry," Ally said.

Nashwa returned with another tray and three more drinks.

"You're a lifesaver," Scott said, finishing his first drink and taking another off the tray.

"This is delicious," Ally said. "I'll have to get the recipe for Christmas."

"I'm so glad you like it." The color rose in Nashwa's cheeks. She hurried out of the room.

Ally swallowed. Scott's lifesaver comment hit a nerve. It wasn't right to say nothing. "Dennis wasn't wearing a life preserver when we found him," Ally pointed out.

"You noticed that?" Frank nodded approvingly. "You are a mystery buff. I picked up on that, too."

"He was wearing one when he ferried us over. We all did," Scott said.

Frank glanced at his partner and gave the slightest shake of his head. "I do have a question for you, Mrs. Hawthorne." Frank turned in his chair to face her.

Ally sipped her drink. The warmth in her stomach spread throughout her body. The warm glow from the drink eased her anxiety, and she shrugged. "Ask away." She took another big sip.

"Did your husband ever mention Kimberly Hill?"

"Nope. Never."

"And you hadn't seen anything to give the impression he may have been spending time with someone else?"

"You mean having an affair? No. Tim wasn't, and there were no clues because it didn't happen. Tim's a faithful husband."

"There were no charges on credit cards you didn't recognize? No phone calls or text messages from unknown numbers?"

Ally hesitated. She'd seen enough crime shows to know Frank could get access to Tim's messages — even if they were deleted. "I don't think there are any messages in his phone from an unknown number. But I'm pretty sure he gets spam calls like anyone else."

Frank finished his drink and set the empty glass down on the table. "Let me level with you, Mrs. Hawthorne. I've been doing this job for close to thirty years. Do you know what experts call terms like, "I think" and, "I'm pretty sure"? They refer to them as deceptive phrases. People use them when they're hiding the truth, if not outright lying."

"I would be very careful with your accusations against my daughter-in-law, Frank," Victoria said as she marched into the room.

Frank exhaled and stood up. "We were having a private conversation."

"This is my home." Victoria kept walking until she stopped just outside Frank's personal space. "Therefore, nothing is private to me."

"This is official police business."

"And I have done everything to cooperate. But I'm putting an end to this witch hunt you've lodged against my son."

"I don't have any axe to grind against Tim. I like him. But I have a job to do. Tim was having an affair —"

Victoria raised her slender arm and held up her index finger. "Careful, Frank. An alleged affair. The only proof you have of a supposed dalliance is a photograph that appears to be suspiciously staged. As far as I am concerned, all matters relating to my son are finished. I allowed you into my home and can throw you out of it, too. And if you think it was cold this afternoon, try spending the night on the beach."

Frank bristled. "You wouldn't."

"I most certainly would. I understand you must deal with Dennis' accidental demise, but any other matter is finished. Is that understood?"

"Finished?" Frank's voice lowered to a deep rumble. "In a pig's eye, it is. I've got a report regarding a missing girl I'm investigating."

Victoria's eyes blazed. "You have no report because none was ever filed, was it?"

"Only because I talked Gary out of doing it."

"May I quote you on that in court?"

Ally gasped. Victoria was going for the jugular.

The veins in Frank's neck rose like a garden hose filling up with water. "Here I try to do you a favor so this doesn't end up splashed all over the front page, and you threaten me!"

"No one has threatened anyone and lower your voice. There is no report to follow up on, and Gary is gone, I suspect, for good. Therefore, there is no case. Am I incorrect?"

Ally stood rooted to her chair. She was both in awe and shocked. Victoria had no fear of anyone. In so many ways, Ally yearned to be like her.

But Frank wasn't finished. "There was a witness to Kimberly Hall coming here."

"And that witness is now dead." Victoria smiled triumphantly. "Don't look so shocked that I figured out it was Dennis. Who else would it be? Besides, Dennis accused my son before. Seeing how he recanted that testimony, don't you think he would have changed his story if he had lived?"

"We both know why Dennis changed his story before. He always regretted doing that."

"So you say. Either way, he's dead, and you have nothing. Therefore, the matter is finished. Shall we go to dinner? Nashwa has made a Beef Wellington to die for."

Ally closed one eye. The warm feeling in her stomach continued to grow. If she didn't know better, she'd say she had a really, good buzz going on.

Frank rubbed the end of his nose. "I can't let this go, Victoria, not again. I'm going to keep looking into this."

"Really? On a professional level?"

"Of course. That's what I'm doing now."

"You are? So both you and this police officer are currently on duty?"

"Yes." Frank cocked an eyebrow.

Victoria pressed her lips together and slowly,

slightly shook her head. "I'm so disappointed in the two of you. You say you're on duty, but you both have been drinking. I can smell it on your breath. Dr. Bradley!" Victoria called out.

Frank snatched his glass from the floor beside his chair. He sniffed it, and his eyes widened. "I asked Nashwa if it had alcohol in it! She said it was butter!"

"It does have butter. It's hot, buttered apple cider. I understand that you both were cold from being outside, but I think it's shameful to think you added alcohol to it."

"We didn't add it! Your cook did!"

"You have a choice to make, Frank. Do you want to throw your career away on the word of a missing druggie? Wouldn't you rather sit down for a warm dinner with a friend? Make your decision, or I'll have to ask Martin if, in his professional opinion, the two law enforcement officers in my sitting room are under the influence."

Ally's hand covered her mouth. Victoria had slipped all of them a mickey — including herself. The buzz she felt wasn't from spices or warm butter. It was booze.

Footsteps sounded in the foyer.

Victoria folded her hands in front of her. "It is my understanding that your daughter has applied to Cornell. Are you aware that the business classes are held in Hawthorne Hall? A recommendation from the right family would ensure she can attend." She turned to Scott. "And you, Officer Davis. Your stellar police work here should be rewarded. I will have to speak with the Chief and see that happens."

Scott hung his head and stared at his feet.

Dr. Bradley hurried into the room. "Did you call me Victoria?"

Victoria raised an eyebrow. "Well, Frank? Scott? Will you be joining us for dinner?"

Scott raised his eyes and looked at Frank.

Frank nodded, and the two men left the room without saying a word.

Dr. Bradley clasped his hands together. "I've been smelling that delightful aroma for the past hour. I'm starved."

"Wait until you taste Nashwa's Beef Wellington," Victoria said. "Why don't you all head in while I speak with my daughter-in-law."

Ally stood and crossed her arms while waiting for the others to leave the room.

"Do get that cross look off your face," Victoria said. "Having a couple of glasses of rum is a small price for dislodging your husband from that situation."

"I'm taking antidepressants! I shouldn't drink."

"You shouldn't make it a regular habit, but ..."

"I shouldn't have had any," Ally fired back.

"The horse is already out of the barn. Lesson learned and all that. Let's put this dreadful ordeal behind us and enjoy the meal."

Ally stared at her mother-in-law in disbelief. A man lay dead in the garage. She'd just blackmailed two law enforcement officers into dropping a case after serving them spiked drinks, and now she wanted to have a nice meal?

Victoria took Ally by the arm and led her out of the room.

Ally's lips pressed together. She'd changed her mind. She didn't want to be anything like Victoria.

Chapter Fourteen

Ally sat at the little table in the bedroom, staring out the window at the darkness. Having endured the most uncomfortable dinner she'd ever attended, Ally listened to the sound of the running shower, eager for Tim to finish so they could discuss how to deal with their mess.

Things were looking better in a legal sense, but morally, Ally felt like she was in the gutter. A man was dead, and a woman missing. Ally couldn't simply look the other way — not if she ever wanted to sleep again. She knew it wouldn't matter how many antidepressants she took. If she tried to bury the truth, it would be like sticking toxic waste in a barrel, dumping it into a hole, and covering it up. Sooner or later, the barrel would rust, and the contents would ooze and slowly poison Ally from the inside.

No. She had to tell someone. If Frank wouldn't listen, she'd find someone who would, once she got off the island. As she sat there, lost in thought, Ally heard the sound of the shower shutting off and the bathroom door creaking open. She looked over to see Tim emerging from the steam-filled room, a towel wrapped around his waist.

"Hey," he said, running a hand through his damp hair. "You okay?"

Ally sighed. "No, Tim. I'm not okay. There's a dead man and a missing woman, and we're somehow wrapped up in it all. And I can't ignore it and pretend everything's fine."

"I know," Tim said, pulling on a pair of jeans. "Believe me, I'm struggling with it too. But what can we do? Until Philip gets that motor going, we're stuck here."

"What your mother did isn't right, Tim," Ally said, placing her book on the small table.

"I didn't have anything to do with it."

"I know, but you need to speak with her. I can't stop thinking about Scott. You should have seen the look on his face. What kind of police officer do you think he will turn out to be?"

"So you want me to go and convince them to keep investigating me because my mother spiked their drinks?"

"And mine. But it's not just that. She blackmailed and bribed them, and she's done it before from the sound of things."

"My mother handles every situation with a carrot and a stick. She'll dangle money underneath someone's nose. That's the carrot. If they don't take it, she hits them with the stick."

"It's not funny."

"I'm not trying to be. That's how she operates. I feel like I grew up in the Mafia."

Ally thought for a moment. "Did you know that Dennis was the person who originally saw Jane come to this island?"

Tim sat down on the bed. "Dennis? No. The police would only say that *someone* saw Jane come out here. Later, they changed their story."

"Because your mother paid him off."

Tim ran his hand through his damp hair. "That's what she does, but it doesn't mean Jane came here."

"You won't know that unless you ask her." Ally's frustration rose.

Tim exhaled and stood back up. "I must have asked her a dozen times over the last twenty years. Do you think I don't know how my family operates? That's just one of many reasons that I moved so far away. If she can't buy someone, she threatens them. My mother didn't pay for the library in town because she likes to read, or cares about literacy. She did it because she wanted to expand the boat dock and needed people in power to look the other way."

Ally folded her hands in her lap. "You never mentioned any of this. And you always do what your mother asks."

"That's not entirely true." He picked up the towel off the floor and held it in both hands. "But I'm guilty of abusing the system, too. Look at my life. An artist of my caliber should be begging for change during the day, yet we live in a nice house with a pool in California."

"You're doing great. And with my appraisal work, we have what we need."

"Why do you think I do so well? Who do you think buys my pieces?"

Ally stood up. She was very defensive of her husband, even if his current antagonist was himself. "Your works sell all over the world."

"Due in large part to my mother. Behind the scenes, she twists people's arms into purchasing my pieces.

Deep down, I knew, but I didn't want to admit it to myself. I've tried not to be a sponge, but the truth hurts. I saw a list that Ziad left out for an upcoming party. Three of the people who purchased my latest pieces are on it." The pained expression in his eyes pricked her heart.

"Your work is fantastic. So what if some of your mother's friends bought it? I'm sure she brags about you. Of course, they'd go and check it out."

"Only none of them mentioned knowing my mother when they came to the gallery." Tim tenderly stroked her cheek. "I'm going down for a drink. Do you want a bottle of water?"

"No thanks. I'm going to take a shower."

Tim handed her his damp towel and kissed her cheek as she passed him. "Sorry again about my mother spiking your drink."

"Like you said, you didn't do it." Ally walked into the bathroom and closed the door.

Ally grabbed the edge of the countertop and hung her head. She was the one in therapy, but despite all her pleadings, Tim wouldn't consider it. He should. It would help him to unpack his unspoken anger at his mother and to work through his guilt and self-loathing.

She looked up at herself in the mirror. A tear rolled down her cheek as she thought about how the situation had only grown worse the more often Tim came here. Now she understood why. This environment was slowly sucking him dry. This wasn't Tim — the strong, honorable man she loved — it was a hollow shell of who he used to be.

Turning on the shower, Ally stepped inside and let the hot droplets fall onto her skin, washing away her tears and carrying away her worries. All she could do now was stand beneath the falling water and pray that Tim would find peace soon.

The shower never reached the temperature she sought. She wanted the water so hot it was almost unbearable, but it barely rose high enough to produce a good steam. As she shut the water off, the pipes clanked and rattled.

Somewhere, far off, she heard a woman softly crying.

Ally grabbed the edge of the tub and sank to her knees. She covered her mouth with both of her hands to keep from screaming. Was this real, or was her mind again playing tricks on her?

She inclined her ear to the drain and listened.

Water dripped off her and the showerhead. Each plunk had a slightly different tone, depending on the height it fell from.

"Hello?" The whispered cry was so faint Ally wasn't sure she heard it.

She held her breath and strained to drown out all other sounds, including the pounding of her heart.

"Help me. Please."

Ally wiped the water from her eyes and stared at the drain in disbelief. The voice was louder this time, and there was no denying it was a female's.

"Hello?" Ally whispered back.

"Is someone there? Can you hear me?"

Ally placed her hand against her mouth and took a deep breath, ready to call out.

The bathroom door whipped open.

Ally screamed.

Tim stumbled backward, took two long steps, and knelt beside the tub. "Are you okay? Did you fall? Are you hurt?" His hands slipped on her wet skin as he grabbed hold of her.

Ally gasped for breath and a suitable answer. Her eyes searched his, but warning bells flashed in her mind. The woman was real. Kim must be here, in this house. Gary was being honest when he said Kim came out to the island. Dennis had seen Kim, too. And if they were telling the truth, was Tim the person who was lying?

"The drain was clogged." Ally blurted out.

Tim laughed so hard he fell backward and landed on his butt. He leaned against the wall, letting his hand rest on the floor on either side of him. "I thought you were hurt. I should have known you'd be cleaning. You are too special."

Ally stood up and grabbed the towel. "You scared the life out of me." She avoided his eyes as she stepped over him and onto the bath mat. She hated lying to him but didn't know who she should trust — including herself. Considering her past, she needed to be sure the voice wasn't only in her head.

Tim scrambled to his feet and hugged her.

"You're going to get yourself all wet," Ally protested.

"I don't care." He kissed her. Long, hard, and in a way they hadn't done for months. "I was going to play cards with Carter and Mia, but if you'd rather ..." He wiggled his eyebrows.

Ally pressed her lips together and shook her head. She couldn't make love to Tim now. Not without finding out if the voice was real. If his story was true or not. "How about after your game? I wanted to head to the library and get a different book."

The disappointment on Tim's face was evident, but he'd been so understanding about their sex life, or lack of it, since the miscarriage. "Great! I'll beat the pants off them and then come back and do the same to you!" He gave her another kiss and squeeze. "I love you, Ally."

"Love you, too. Don't drink too much. You know how it affects you later."

Tim made a face and rolled his eyes. "It doesn't, but I won't." He hurried out of the bathroom, and a moment later, the hallway door closed shut.

Ally quickly dried off and got dressed. She rushed back to the tub and listened at the drain. Water dripped off the shower head and landed cold on her neck. Her skin pricked, and she shivered.

"Hello?" she softly called out.

Silence.

"If you can hear me, I'm coming to look for you."

Chapter Fifteen

Ally closed the bedroom door behind her and stood in the hallway, listening. Laughter echoed out of the game room. To avoid being seen, she headed to the right and the staircase on that side of the building. The carpeting muffled the sounds of her steps as she descended to the first floor.

The door at the bottom of the stairs creaked as she opened it. Another door to her right led outside, and the hallway began on her left. She debated about trying to reach the cellar through the bulkhead in the back of the house, but there was a high probability it was locked. And considering the amount of noise the door she just opened made, people might hear her getting in that way.

No. Going down the cellar stairs in the kitchen was still the wisest choice.

The first door to her left opened, and Ziad appeared. "Oh, Mrs. Hawthorne. I heard someone and thought you might be my wife coming to get me."

"Sorry. I was, ah, stretching my legs." She smiled, trying not to cringe at her excuse.

Ziad glanced down the empty hallway and

pursed his lips together. "Do you have a moment?" He stepped out of the way and held out his hand, encouraging her to enter the room.

Ally nodded and stepped inside a small study. The room made one feel they were in a captain's quarters aboard a ship. It was done in dark wood, and the shelves were all exposed. The decorations were mostly brass — a telescope, a sextant, and a bell. The other shelves were lined with books, the large volumes stacked alphabetically. The top shelf had a large globe made of wood and metal. A map was tacked to the wall, and she assumed the pushpins dotting it indicated all the places someone had traveled.

Despite the dark decor, the room was cozy and inviting. The couch and chairs were all soft leather, the desk was antique, and the polished mahogany was worn smooth. One could imagine the years of hands that had touched it, adding a patina of oil that was etched into the grain.

Ziad closed the door behind them. "Thank you for speaking with me, and I hope I am not overstepping in doing so. But I wanted to tell you something about your husband, Tim."

Unsure, Ally braced herself for anything. "Go ahead," was all she managed to say.

"My wife and I have been employed in the house for only a little while. In that time, your husband visited often."

Ally swallowed. She wanted to add "too often," but instead crossed her arms and waited for him to continue.

"I've been employed as the house steward for many people in many countries. It is a position I like, and it enables me to meet many different personalities. I've found your husband particularly fascinating to watch, and now that I've heard what the police are saying about him, I felt the need to speak with you."

Ally held her breath.

"I don't believe a word of their accusations." Ziad smiled.

Ally exhaled.

"Your husband is one of the few persons who treat others with respect. I'm referring not only to myself and my wife, but also to everyone. He invited me to accompany him and Tom so often to the mainland and the movies that I finally accepted. The person he is here is the same as he behaved there. He is gracious and kind almost to a fault."

Ally smiled politely. "Thank you for saying that."

"Do you know what Tim's favorite subject to discuss is?"

"Art?"

"You. You were born and raised in Wamego, Kansas, home of the Wizard of Oz Museum. Your favorite color is green, movie is *Casablanca*, and food is Chicken Marsala. And if Tim is to be believed, which I do, you are the best wife and friend he could have."

The hot glow in her chest rose to her cheeks. "Did Tim say all of that?"

"And more. I hope I haven't overstepped, but I wanted you to know."

"Thank you, Ziad. It means a lot to me."

"I better get back to Nashwa." He checked his watch and grimaced. "She wants to watch TV before bed. *Downton Abbey*, a little ironic." He opened the door and hurried down the hallway.

Ally stood with her arms still crossed, staring out the doorway. She inhaled and gave herself a much-needed hug. Tim meant the world to her, and it felt wonderful to hear it was reciprocated, but the fresh doubts in her mind about her husband scattered Ziad's words. She still had to discover the truth — whether it exonerated Tim or added to her fears.

Walking toward the hallway, she noticed a huge portrait hanging on the wall at the end of the study. A tall man crouched on the rocks along the ocean's edge in the middle of two boys who leaned lovingly against his shoulders.

She recognized Tim's father from photographs, but looking at the painting was different. Seeing him life-size made Tim's father a bit more real in a way. The painting itself was breathtaking. The artist somehow perfectly captured the joy and love in those three faces.

Ally gasped when she read the signature. Timothy Hawthorne. He'd never told her he created this piece, nor was the painting in his portfolio, even though it was his finest work.

She gazed at the happy expression on the young boy's face, and her chest tightened. Tim couldn't have had anything to do with Kim's disappearance. But the only way to prove that was to continue her search and find the girl.

Closing the door to the study behind her, she continued counting the doors as she went. Four doors down, she stopped at the room directly underneath hers and listened. Music, explosions, and gunfire sounded from the other side. It was Tom's new bedroom.

Ally bit her lip. He must be watching one of the superhero movies she'd given him. A pang of guilt washed over her. So far this trip, besides at meals, she hadn't spent time with her brother-in-law. You couldn't blame her with everything going on. Still, Tom didn't know that. She'd have to do better.

In an old house like this, it would be typical for noise to travel up and through the holes cut in the floor for the pipes. And if the sound wasn't coming from Tom's bedroom, that only left one place — the basement.

Ally crept down the hallway and through the foyer. The lights in the kitchen were on, but the room was empty. Making her way to the cellar door, she opened it and flicked on the light. Standing at the top of the stairs and peering down at the rock walls below, her feet felt rooted in cement. In every horror movie she'd ever seen, going down into the cellar never ended well.

Staring into the dimly lit basement, she remembered the first time she'd heard the other voices. She'd been in the shower then, too. Those voices ended up being in her head, but the real problem came when she started speaking with them. Was that what was happening now? Was this the beginning of another breakdown?

Taking a deep breath, Ally started down the stairs. She didn't care if everyone, including herself, believed she was crazy. If some poor girl was trapped down here, she needed to help.

The steps were wide and thick. A dank smell tickled her nose. As she descended, the odor only intensified. It was a mix of mildew and damp earth. She grimaced and peered around. The walls were stone, and the low ceiling made her feel claustrophobic. Boxes were scattered about, some with old newspapers and magazines dating back to the 1980s. The shelves were filled with cardboard boxes and stacks of firewood. A large oil stain marked the spot of the old tank and furnace. The modern furnace and water heater gleamed in the light cast from the bare bulbs.

Heading roughly in the direction of her room on the second floor, Ally made her way around a pile of plastic boxes stacked against a support pillar. She stopped and listened. The silence was so deep when she exhaled it was loud. No sounds seeped down from above.

"Hello?" Her voice echoed off the walls, making her sound small and feeble.

Silence.

Ally glanced back at the stairs. She was getting closer to the spot beneath her room. She moved closer to the far wall. The corner of the house bumped out here. Four large stacks of window screens lay against the wall. The top of a tall door was visible behind the stack on the right, where the wall jutted out.

Glancing up and then back at the kitchen stairs, Ally's brow knit together. This was the spot. She was beneath Tom's bedroom, and her room was above that.

Quietly moving the screens blocking the door, she opened it. It creaked and groaned, revealing stairs leading up. Puzzled for a moment, she stared up the steps. The muffled sounds of explosions and gunfire filtered down.

Ally quietly closed the door. The staircase must have been for the summer kitchen. They left it when they renovated Tom's room. But why would the summer kitchen have stairs in the first place? Her eyes widened. She hurried back to the stack of screens, leaning against the wall of the stairs. One by one, she lifted them away until a small door appeared. It was metal and only a little taller than her five-foot-five frame. Ally stood there staring at the entrance to the old wine cellar. Victoria had built a new one upstairs years ago, and this was abandoned.

The metal handle was cool to the touch but turned easily in her hand. Her eyes widened as soft light seeped out. On the inside, a wall sconce next to the door cast a light no brighter than a candle. The ten-by-ten room stood empty of wine, the wooded racks now bare. All of it had been relocated to the modern, temperature-controlled winery off the kitchen.

Something in the shadows in the back of the room moved.

Ally stepped inside, her eyes adjusting to the darkness.

A small, receded alcove sat in the middle of the back wall. Wooden benches lined the sides of it. A water spigot jutted out from between the bricks. Crouched in the corner was a person.

"I'm sorry for whatever I did. Please let me go." The whisper sounded like it came from a woman.

Ally crept closer. She turned on the old light switch on the wall in the middle of the room.

The woman in the corner shielded her eyes. Metal clinked, and the light gleamed off the shackles on her wrists. Her pretty face was dirty, and a line of dried blood caked the left side of her head. Her red dress and bare feet were spotted with mud.

"Kim?"

Kim nodded. She tried to put her hands together, but the chains securing her to the wall were too short to allow that. They were only long enough for her to remain seated on the bench. Her mouth twisted in a pained grimace, and tears rolled down her cheeks. "I didn't know. I'm so sorry. Please. I'll stay away. I won't tell anyone."

"I'm not going to hurt you. I've been looking for you."

"Ally? You're Ally, right?"

Ally's heart raced as she heard her name from the stranger's lips. She froze. How could Kim know her name? Fear and confusion swirled inside her as she tried to decide how to respond. She wanted to run away, but something held her in place. Her mind raced with questions, but she knew the only way to get answers was to stay put.

The chains rattled as Kim leaned forward. "I got your message. That's why I came to talk to him. I swear I came to break things off. I had no idea he was married."

"You didn't know who was married? How do you know my name?"

Kimberly's lips mashed together. She raised her shoulder and tucked her chin to her chest as if expecting Ally to strike her.

"You were having an affair with my husband?" The words ripped a hole in Ally's soul.

Kim sobbed and nodded. "But I didn't know. He didn't wear a ring and said he was single." Kim slowly raised her head, and she met Ally's gaze. "My friend knows I came here. He'll go to the police if I don't come back. I told him to do that, and he will."

The echo of the chain clinking bounced off the walls. Ally spun around, gazing through the doorway and back into the cellar, expecting someone to rush into the room at any moment. Shaking her head clear, Ally hurried over to Kim.

Kim scooted away, but the chains only permitted her to move a few inches. They pulled tight as Kim pressed her back against the brick wall. "Please don't hit me again."

"I didn't hit you. I swear. What happened?"

"I was almost to the front door. I stopped to think about what I would say and heard someone. I started to turn, but something hit my head. I woke up in here."

"Who did this to you?"

"I don't know. I've been trapped down here. You're the first person who's come."

"I have to get you out." Ally grabbed Kim's shackle.

Kim searched Ally's eyes and mumbled something, but Ally didn't understand what she said because of her sobbing. The shackles holding Kim were new and made of steel. There was a place for a key and no way to open it without one.

"Call the police!" Kim begged. "Not the local police. It has to be the state police."

"Gary went to the local police to report you missing. They're here now."

Kim's eyes widened in horror. "No. Oh, that idiot. I told him not to do that. Tim's mother bought off the local cops. Who's here? Who came?"

"A detective and a police officer. He's a rookie. His name's Scott Davis."

"I don't know him. What about the detective?"

"Frank Burgess."

Kim sobbed and hung her head. "He's in on it. He covers for the family. They paid him off before. I'm such an idiot. I knew a rich guy falling for someone like me was too good to be true. Call the state police. Please!"

"I can't." Ally vainly tugged on the chain. "The cell tower is down."

Sobs racked Kim's slender frame. Tears rolled down her cheeks. "Where's Gary?"

Ally's eyes went wide. She had thought Gary had killed Dennis, but Gary was really Kim's boyfriend. Had whoever murdered Dennis also killed Gary?

"Where's Gary?" Kim asked again.

Ally gently touched her shoulder. "I'm going to get help."

"Don't leave me! Please don't leave me!"

"I'm going to get something to get you out of these chains. I promise I'll be back as soon as I can."

"You're lying," Kimberly cried. "You hit me, didn't you? Please let me go."

"I didn't hurt you. I'm going to help you. You need to be quiet and wait for me, okay?"

Kimberly nodded, but from the way she cowered in the corner, it was obvious she didn't believe Ally.

Ally hurried to the door. As she slowly closed it, Kimberly's sobs stabbed her heart. The metal clicked shut.

Ally scanned the handle. There was no way to lock the door. How could she prevent whoever chained Kim up inside from hurting her if they came back? She couldn't. But she could hide the fact that she'd found Kim. Quickly moving the screens back into place, Ally hid any evidence of her finding the door. She raced for the kitchen stairs and skidded to a stop. There was no one she could trust. She couldn't let anyone know what she'd discovered.

Scanning the shelves for tools, Ally found none. She opened a few boxes and peered inside. They were filled with different holiday decorations and summer items.

Ally took a deep breath and slowly released it. Where would they keep tools? The boathouse! Uncle Philip was fixing the boat. There had to be some tool there that Ally could use to free Kim from her shackles.

Forcing herself to slow down, Ally crept upstairs. She didn't know who was responsible for hurting Kim and chaining her up, but if they were willing to do that, they were capable of anything — even murder.

Chapter Sixteen

Ally waited at the top of the stairs, listening. The kitchen was quiet. Far away, laughter echoed into the foyer from the game room.

Her mouth was dry, sweat rolled down her back, and her knees shook. She grabbed the railing to keep from falling. Her mind reeled. Tim lied. He did have an affair. His mistress, the missing woman, was real and locked in the basement. Someone in this house, most likely her husband, was responsible for putting her there.

Her Marine father's voice echoed in her mind, "There's a time to think and a time to act. Think later, get moving, and leave before someone finds you!"

It was too risky to go out the front of the house or grab her jacket. She slipped out the back door of the kitchen and into the night. Freezing wind gusts stung her exposed skin, but at least it had stopped raining.

What she wouldn't give for her father to be here now. But he and Mom were someplace in Florida living the RV life. Even in his sixties, he would know what to do and get it done. She couldn't think of anyone better than her father to be beside her.

Tim had betrayed her, and his family would side

with him. Seeing how Dr. Bradley and Victoria appeared to be more than friends, Ally couldn't turn to him. Both Frank and Scott folded when Victoria offered them bribes. That left only Ziad and Nashwa, but they both worked for Victoria.

Ally was on her own.

Shivering, she hurried down the dark walkway toward the boathouse. She needed to find bolt cutters or a saw — anything to get Kim out of that room and someplace safe.

It was so dark that making her way along the path was slow, but her eyes slowly adjusted as she continued. In the distance, waves slammed against the rocks, and the wind made the trees groan as their branches rubbed together. Some small creature scurried to her right. Its yellowish eyes met hers before it disappeared into the brush.

A faint light glowed in the window as she approached the boathouse. The hairs on her neck stood on end. Was someone inside? Philip had been working on repairing the boat all day. Was he still at it?

She tiptoed closer but stumbled on a loose stone. The clatter of the rock echoed above the rumble of the sea and wind.

Ally crouched down, darted off the path, and watched the door. Her heart raced as she waited, the seconds slowly ticking by. No one came, and she heard nothing from inside.

Taking a deep breath, Ally snuck forward and peeked in the window. The house looked deserted at first, even of the boat. Glancing around the corner, she saw the boat on its stands. A large blue tarp covered the stern. Sticking out from underneath was the shiny metal propellor of the recently installed motor.

Her hope of getting help shifted to panic. When whoever kidnapped Kim realized the boat was repaired and help was on the way, what would they do to their captive?

Ally pushed open the door to the boathouse. She cautiously closed the door behind her. The room was large, with gray walls, a cement floor, and a roof of wood slats. Circling the room and lining the walls were benches, cabinets, and equipment. The counter in the center was cluttered with tools, a well-used power drill, and a portable battery-powered saw. Sanders, wrenches, and pliers lay about, but none seemed useful for freeing Kim.

Moving to a workbench, she grabbed an old-fashioned saw with a wooden handle and a long triangular blade. The teeth on it were spaced far apart. She remembered watching her grandfather build her tree fort with one. Realizing it was a wood saw, she set it down.

Ally grabbed a flat screwdriver and stuck it in her pocket. She hadn't checked the end of the chain connecting Kim to the wall. Maybe it was screwed in? Moving a canvas tarp aside, her eyes lit up. She grabbed the hacksaw and held it up like a trophy.

Gravel crunched outside.

Ally ducked down, trying to make herself as small as possible. Her breath came in short, shallow puffs. She tried to calm down and take deep breaths, but her vision grew hazy. She was having a panic attack.

Breathe! Breathe!

Outside, next to the boat, someone hummed a tune.

Ally covered her mouth and backed up into the shadows. The tingling in her chest spread to her fingers. Even her toes went numb. She couldn't faint now! If someone came in the front door, there was no way out. She was trapped. They'd find her.

Footsteps sounded again, but this time, they were going away. The person wasn't heading to the house. They were walking toward the interior of the island.

Why? It didn't matter, as long as they were leaving!

Ally crept toward the door. After waiting another minute, she slipped outside and silently walked along the edge of the path toward the house. Once she'd gone a little further, she broke into a jog. The wind had picked up, but she didn't notice the cold.

Taking two steps at a time, she crested the hill and dashed across the front yard, carefully keeping to the shadows. By the time she reached the kitchen door, she was panting for air. The light in the kitchen was now off. Peering through the window, she scanned the empty room. Satisfied no one was inside, she grabbed the handle, but it wouldn't turn. Ally swore and tried again, but it didn't budge. It must have locked behind her when she went out.

Now what was she going to do? The bulkhead!

Crouching low, she circled by the kitchen, sitting room, and sunroom until she reached the cellar bulkhead. She grabbed the metal handle and strained, but the doors were locked.

Ally had no choice but to head to the front of the house. Not wanting to explain the hacksaw if someone saw her, she pulled up her shirt and tucked the saw into the rear waistband of her jeans, the handle pressing against her back. As uncomfortable as it was, at least it was hidden.

She quietly climbed the front steps and tried the door. It was also locked. Ally bit her lip. Now what? She couldn't ring the stupid doorbell without alerting everyone to what she was doing.

The handle turned, and the door swung open. Ziad stared at her with one eyebrow arched high. "Are you okay, Mrs. Hawthorne? What are you doing out here without a jacket?"

Ally opened and closed her mouth, then decided to partially tell the truth. "I was in the kitchen and thought I heard something outside. The door locked behind me."

"I apologize." Ziad stepped out of the way and let her inside. "With everything that's happened, I wanted to ensure the whole house is secure. I must have locked you out. I'm so sorry."

"No worries. I'm glad you sealed us up. It makes me feel safer."

"You and my wife both prefer having a bubble of security." Ziad nodded. "Can I get you anything?"

"No, thank you. I feel like a snack, so I think I'll raid the refrigerator."

"Would you like me to get something for you?"

"Oh, no. I'm not even sure what I want. I'll forage around like a squirrel in the nut shop."

Ziad smiled. "Good night, Mrs. Hawthorne."

"'Night." Ally made a quick stop in the hallway bathroom. Setting the hacksaw on the sink, she pulled the hand towel off the rack. She rubbed her face and arms to get some heat back into her extremities. Turning the hot water on, she warmed her fingers and splashed some on her face.

After drying off, she put the hacksaw behind her back, pulled her shirt over it, and checked herself in the mirror. There was a little bulge, but it was only noticeable if you were looking for it. Her eyes shined brightly as she stared at her reflection.

"You got this. Go get Kim out of there."

Ally headed straight for the kitchen. She heard

people in the game room. To judge from how loud they laughed, they were still going strong. Leaving the kitchen light off, Ally crossed the room and stopped at the refrigerator. Kim had to have been in the cellar for days. Ally opened it, grabbed two bottles of water, a wrapped package of prosciutto, and a small Tupperware container of tortellini, then headed toward the cellar stairs.

The overhead light clicked on. Ally jumped and spun around.

Victoria stood in the doorway.

"I, uh ..." Ally glanced down at the food in her hands, and her mind went blank.

"Great minds think alike," Victoria smiled as she headed to the fridge. "I need a little something too."

Ally exhaled.

"Please," Victoria held her hand out to the kitchen table. "Join me."

Oh, no. Not now. Why couldn't my mother-in-law get the munchies and just go back to her room?

Ally walked over to the table, pulled out the chair, and hesitated as the metal saw blade pressed against the skin of her back.

"I'm more of an ice cream snacker." Victoria opened the freezer. "I have some stracciatella gelato from Bergamo in northern Italy. It is pure bliss!" Victoria noticed Ally hovering above the seat and raised an eyebrow.

Ally sat, the blade of the hacksaw digging into her flesh. She grimaced but channeled the pain into a smile. "That sounds fabulous. But I'm good. Maybe I'll try some later."

Victoria glanced at the small pile of food sitting in front of Ally. "That is a bountiful snack."

"I didn't know what I was craving, so I grabbed an assortment."

"Craving? Interesting choice of words. Is there something I should know?"

The pregnancy innuendo landed like an arrow through Ally's chest straight into her heart. Memories flooded her mind — eating peanut butter and bananas, picking out cribs, and staring at the ultrasound pictures.

"Oh, boy!" Tom yelled from the doorway. "I was coming to get some ice cream too!"

Victoria frowned. "It's too late for that. Please go back to bed."

Tom made a face and opened the freezer. "It's not too late if you're having some. And you're eating out of the carton. You said that was gross."

"I'm the only one who eats this gelato." Victoria ate a spoonful.

"No." Tom grabbed an ice cream sandwich and unwrapped it. "Carter does, too. He eats out of the carton like you."

Victoria made a face. "Please tell me you're joking."

Tom shook his head. "I'm gonna watch *Guardians of the Galaxy*." He rushed over to the table, wrapped his arms around Ally, and kissed her cheek. "Thank you again, Ally!" He gave her a big squeeze.

The hacksaw dug deeper into her back.

"Night, night." Tom waved as he hurried out of the room.

"It looks like both of my boys prefer you over me." Victoria placed the cover back on the ice cream. "I've suddenly lost my appetite. I'll follow my son's example and head off to bed."

"Good night." Ally stayed sitting despite the blades of metal pressed against her skin.

Victoria eyed the food piled in front of her. "Bon appétit." She set the ice cream container in the sink and strolled out of the kitchen.

Ally waited until Victoria was well up the stairs before she reached back and removed the saw. The tips of her fingers were smeared with blood. It wasn't much, but it certainly hurt. She glanced down at the thin blade of the saw in her hands. Would it be strong enough to saw through the thick shackles?

Chapter Seventeen

Ally quietly closed the cellar door and hurried down the stairs. She crossed the basement, setting the food and water bottle on the floor. After moving the stack of screens, she gathered her supplies in her arms and opened the wine cellar door.

Ally ground her teeth when she realized her mistake. She'd left the main light on. If the kidnapper had returned, they would have known someone else had been there. "It's me, Ally," she whispered.

Kim's chain clinked as she leaned forward. "You came back?" Tears rolled down her cheeks. "I thought I may have dreamed you."

Ally set the food on the bench and pointed at the closest light in the ceiling. "I forgot to shut that off. Did anyone come in?"

"No one. Is that food? Can I please have a drink? I'm so thirsty."

Ally opened the water bottle and gave it to Kim. She drank like she'd just crossed the desert. Water poured down her chin.

"Small sips," Ally said.

Kim gasped for air. "Thank you. Thank you so much."

"Give me your right hand." Ally picked up the saw.

"Can I have some food?"

Ally ripped the top off the Tupperware and handed Kim the fork. It was awkward with her left hand shackled, but Kim dug into the tortellini.

Ally examined the shackles. The metal band encircling Kim's wrist had two hinges and a key lock. Each hinge was over an inch and a half long and would take forever to cut through. But did she need to do that?

"The weakest link," Ally muttered and grabbed the chain.

It was hard going to get the cut started. The blade kept sliding on the metal link, but once she etched the surface, a groove took shape. Soon, tiny silver flecks began falling on the bench.

"It's working!" Kim cried. "It's working!"

"Shh." Ally grabbed some prosciutto and handed it to Kim. Ally seized the chain tightly and sped up. With each forward thrust, more sparkles fell, and the saw blade sunk lower. Her arm was beginning to tire when she broke through the link.

Kim clamped her hand over her mouth. Her eyes were shiny with tears and hope.

Ally seized the screwdriver and stuck it between the chain link. With Kim bracing her arm and Ally pushing as hard as she could, the metal twisted. The chain landed on the bench with a loud thud.

Ally's eyes darted to the closed door. Sweat poured down her face. She grabbed her shirt and mopped her brow.

Kim wrapped her arm around Ally's shoulder, burying her face in her neck, and sobbed.

Ally stroked her back. "Keep it together. One more to go."

"I'm so sorry about Tim. I had no idea he was still married. He said you divorced him."

Ally shook her head and continued to saw. Tears now filled her eyes.

"He said you left him like Jane. You just walked out of his life and didn't look back."

"He talked about Jane? Jane Nelson?"

Kim nodded. "She's the girl who went missing. He said you both broke his heart. When I asked where you went, he laughed and said you were probably hanging out with Jane in his mother's basement. I couldn't believe he could joke about something like that. He said it was gallows humor. I had to look up what that meant."

Silver shavings sparkled as they floated onto the bench. The saw blade slowly cut deeper into the metal.

"I'm sorry about what happened to you," Kim said. "With the twins."

Ally froze. Her chest hurt so badly she couldn't move. "He told you about that?"

She nodded. "He said that made you go crazy, and that's why you ran away. But then he said ..."

"What did he say?"

"He said neither of you got very far and laughed again. I told him I didn't like those jokes, so he stopped. He was really sorry afterward."

Ally gritted her teeth and kept at it. Wait until she got ahold of Tim. He'd be really sorry then.

"Do you know what happened to Jane?" Kim asked. "Did he tell you?"

"He never mentioned her before we came here. I didn't know anything about her."

"Are you kidding me? It was a huge story here. It's like an urban legend now. They say she never left the island. People think she's buried out here somewhere."

Ally's shoulders shook as she started to cry again, but she didn't stop sawing, even when the tears fell freely. It was too much. All of the pain of Tim's betrayal crushed down on her. The muscles in her arm felt like they were on fire, but she kept at it. Push. Pull. Push. Pull. *Snap*.

The blade broke into three pieces.

Kim froze.

Ally grabbed the longest piece. The metal burned her fingertips, and she dropped it. The blade had been six inches long, but now the longest piece was little more than three and bent at almost a right angle.

"What are we going to do?" Kim's body trembled.

Ally stared at the groove in the link. She had cut a little past the halfway point. "Maybe I cut far enough through." She picked up the screwdriver.

They pushed, pulled, and tried everything, but the metal refused to bend.

"Wait a second. I have another idea," Ally said, picking up the longest length of the blade. She laid it on the bench and did her best to flatten out the bends and twists.

Ally grabbed the chain and, holding the broken blade between her fingertips, started to saw. The blade moved a little and then caught. Her fingers slipped off. She started again and again, but it was hopeless.

"Were there more blades where you found the saw?" Kim asked.

"I don't know. I didn't look." Ally had no idea how

late it was. She'd been down there for what felt like hours, but how much time had gone by?

Ally set the piece of the saw blade against the floor and used her foot to press down on it. "If I can flatten it out a little—"

Metal snapped underneath her shoe. The broken blade snapped in half again.

Kim buried her face in her hands.

"Don't give up." Ally stood. "I'll go back and see if there's another one. If I find one, you'll be out of here in ten minutes."

"Don't go. Please don't go."

"I'll be right back." Ally gathered everything except a broken piece of the saw blade, which she held out to Kim. "Try to saw with this while I'm gone." She then held up the screwdriver. "If someone comes back before me, pretend you're chained up and use it. Okay?"

Kim sobbed but nodded.

Ally hid the screwdriver behind Kim, then hurried over to the light and shut it off. Darkness blanketed the back half of the wine cellar.

Kim whimpered.

Carrying out the food, water, and broken saw, Ally slipped back into the cellar and shut the door. She dumped the items in her arms into a box and closed the lid. After putting the screens back in place, she hurried for the stairs.

The kitchen was dark and deserted. The house was quiet. Ally snuck over to the door leading outside and unlocked it. She slowly opened it and stepped out.

A cold rain fell, and the wind howled as she raced back to the boathouse. The icy droplets stung her exposed skin and quickly sucked the warmth out of her.

But she wasn't going to melt or freeze to death. She needed to find another saw or blade — anything to get through that last chain link.

As she made her way to the boathouse, she tried to keep her thoughts positive, but the darkness, cold, and rain leached away her hope. What if she couldn't find another blade? What if she had to leave Kim there? The thought made her stomach twist into a knot. No. She had to succeed.

Ally slowed down as she approached the boathouse. She crept out of the shadows and peered through the window. The room was empty. She slipped inside, shivering and soaked to the bone. She searched through the toolboxes, but there were no more saw blades. She shoved at the toolbox in frustration. Her mind raced, trying to come up with a plan.

She rechecked the toolboxes and workbench but found nothing else that would be useful. She was about to give up when she remembered the boat outside. Uncle Philip may have left more tools out there. There had to be something that could help.

Ally ran through the rain towards the boat. The sky over the horizon started to lighten. Had she been at it all night? Panic seized her.

Nearing the boat's bow, she noticed a dark blue plastic tarp covering two sawhorses with a sheet of plywood across them to form a makeshift table. She yanked off the tarp and scanned the tools underneath. In the middle of the pile was a sixteen-inch hacksaw with a thicker blade than the last one. She seized it off the table, looked up, and gasped.

The boat's bow had been patched and sanded, but someone had smashed a jagged three-foot hole through the side.

Why? Who? Is whoever did it still here?

Ally scurried back into the shadows of the boathouse and listened, scanning the darkness for any sign of the saboteur. Rain pinged off the roof, and the wind howled, but she didn't hear anyone. Someone had scuttled the boat. Someone didn't want them getting help. She needed to get back to Kim.

Plunging headlong down the path, Ally raced back to the house. The gravel kicked up beneath her feet, and branches tore at her clothes and skin, but she pushed herself to go even faster. Taking the stairs three at a time, she dashed around back and slid to a stop. She slowly opened the door and slipped inside.

Catching her breath, she scanned the room. The kitchen was empty. She froze. Light from the open cellar door spilled into the kitchen. There was a noise on the stairs. Someone was in the basement. The kidnapper was heading down to get Kim! Ally had to do something now.

She rushed forward, holding up the saw, but it was a feeble weapon.

Detective Frank Burgess stood on the top step. His hair and jacket were soaked with rain. He gasped and stepped into the kitchen. "Mrs. Hawthorne? Are you all right? Was that you outside?"

"It was you! You did all of this. Stop right where you are!"

Frank pursed his lips. "What was me?"

"Stop!" Ally stepped back as Frank continued to walk forward. "I'm warning you."

"Calm down, Mrs. Hawthorne. You're not making any sense."

"Why were you going into the cellar? Why are you all wet?"

"I heard someone outside. I thought it was Gary, but it must have been you."

Ally shook her head. "If you heard someone out-side, why were you going down into the basement?"

"Put down the saw, Ally. You're not making sense."

"HELP!" Ally screamed, raising the saw higher. "HELP!"

Footsteps sounded in the foyer. Scott rushed into the room, dressed only in his boxers and carrying a gun.

"Drop the saw!" Scott ordered.

Ally shook her head. "You need to listen to me, Scott. I found Kim. She said Frank was in on it. She said the family paid him off."

Scott's eyes narrowed, and he glared at the detective.

"Don't look at me like that, son. She's crazy."

"I am not. Kim will swear to it."

"Where is she?" Scott asked.

Ally shook her head. "Not until Frank gives you his gun. We can't trust him."

"Can't trust me?" Frank shouted. "You're the one who's nuts!"

"Do it, sir. I want your gun," Scott said.

Frank's face turned a splotchy red. His lips mashed into a line. "That's not gonna happen."

"Give me your sidearm, sir, and we can hear what she has to say."

Frank exhaled and nodded. He slowly raised his hands. "I'm going to take out my gun with my left hand and put it on the counter." Frank did as he'd promised, then took two steps back.

Scott walked forward and grabbed Frank's gun.

Ally glanced toward the foyer. Why didn't the others come?

"They're probably sleeping off hangovers," Frank

said, answering her unasked question. "I've given him my gun. Can you put the saw down now?"

Ally lowered the hacksaw and moved to stand beside Scott.

"Where is Kim?" Scott asked.

"Aren't you going to cuff him?"

"I have the situation under control. Where is Kim?"

Ally shook her head. "Not until he's cuffed."

Scott held out his hand. "Give me the saw."

Ally's eyes widened, and she stepped back. "Do you not believe me, or are you in on it too?"

"I just made my superior officer hand over his gun," Scott said. "I believe you, but I can't risk letting you hurt him."

Ally thought about it and set the saw on the counter.

"Where is Kim?" Frank asked.

"You know where she is. You're the one who put her there. That's why you were going to the basement."

Frank lowered his voice. "Listen to me, Mrs. Hawthorne. I know all of this has been very stressful for everyone. We're going to get Dr. Bradley and have him give you something—"

"I'm not having an episode. I found Kim. She's chained up downstairs. I cut through one of the chains, but the blade broke. I had to get another." She reached for the saw, but Scott had removed it from the counter. She cast a puzzled glance at him.

"I'm not the bad guy, Mrs. Hawthorne," Frank said. "But there's isn't anyone in the cellar. I wasn't going down the steps. I was coming back up. I checked everywhere. The only difference is, when I first checked down there, your husband didn't tell me about an old wine closet underneath the other stairs."

"You went inside?" Ally gasped.

"It's empty."

The words slammed into the side of Ally's head like a punch. She staggered sideways and then grabbed hold of the counter to steady herself.

Frank reached out for her arm.

Ally knocked his hand away and darted past him.

They called after her, but Ally thundered down the stairs and raced across the basement. The screens had been moved out of the way of the wine closet. The door stood partially open.

Ally stopped in the doorway. The room was deserted. She walked forward, her legs shaking.

The alcove in the back was empty. Kim was gone.

Ally kept going. She stared at the deserted bench, blinking rapidly. The bolts screwed into the bricks that held the chains were still there, but the chains were gone. There wasn't any sign of the food or broken saw. Even the metal filings had disappeared.

How?

Footsteps sounded behind her.

"Kim was here. She was chained to that wall."

Frank moved up to her left while Scott approached on the right.

Scott shined his flashlight into the empty alcove.

Frank's voice was soft as he spoke. "Mrs. Hawthorne. There is no woman here. Why don't we all go upstairs and see the doctor?"

Ally opened her mouth, but no words came out. She couldn't breathe. The room spun, and everything went black.

Chapter Eighteen

"Mommy!" A little girl's voice called out.

"It's us, Mommy!" A boy giggled.

Both children laughed, and Ally smiled as she stood in the shower and stared at the water slowly swirling down the drain.

She lay down in the bottom of the bathtub. The water from the shower caught her hair and pushed it over the drain. It was warm, but still, she shivered.

"Are you okay?" the little girl asked.

Ally didn't want to frighten them by telling them how she really felt. "Mommy's fine. I'm just sleepy."

"Then go to bed, silly." The boy's voice was bright and playful. She could picture him covering his mouth with his hands as he giggled.

Ally lay there, the water slowly rising. It was more than simply being tired. She hadn't slept for days. Every time she tried to close her eyes, her hands would move to her flat stomach, and she wanted to scream.

She licked her lips. The water had risen to her mouth, but she didn't care. Maybe she'd get rest then. And she could be with her babies.

"Get up, Mommy," the little girl called out.

"Please get up," the boy chimed in.

The water covered her nose. It was warm and peaceful.

"Ally?" Tim shouted from somewhere inside the house.

She'd miss him, but what good was she to him like this? It was better if she fell asleep, just for a minute.

The bathroom door splintered and blasted inward. The handle hit the tile and shattered the square.

Strong arms lifted her up and out of the tub. She wasn't breathing but wasn't scared.

"Please, God! Please, God!" Tim cried over and over again ...

———

Ally stirred, her eyes fluttering open and then shut. She was in bed, still fully clothed, but something felt strange. Like trying to peer through a dense fog, her mind was muddled, and she couldn't think clearly. She forced her eyes open, but her eyelids drooped. A sense of dread swept over her. She attempted to lift her arm, but it seemed like some invisible force weighed it down. Panic set in as she realized that she couldn't get up.

Footsteps to her right made her slowly turn her head.

Tim sat on the edge of the bed, his eyebrows knit together, concern etched across his face.

Ally gasped. She wanted to run or slap him. She'd prefer both, but neither was an option without being in control of her body.

Not only had he betrayed her, but he might have been the monster who kidnapped Kim.

"Did you do it?" The words tumbled out of Ally's mouth.

Tim squeezed her hand. "It's okay, babe. I'm here."

Ally stared into his eyes. She loved her husband so deeply that, at times, it hurt, but she couldn't ignore the words of the woman beneath the stairs. "Did you do it, Tim?" she said again.

Tim leaned forward, puzzled. "Did I do what?"

"I spoke with Kim. She told me about the affair. Don't make it worse. You have to let her go."

Tears welled up in Tim's eyes. "I promise you, Ally, there was no affair, and we didn't find anyone in the basement. I found your food down there, though. Mother said you got something to eat late last night. Did something happen afterward?"

Ally couldn't keep her eyelids open. They were so heavy. "She came here to break it off."

Something jabbed Ally's arm.

Dr. Bradley stood on the other side of her bed, a syringe in his hands. "That should calm her down and help her sleep. I'm a doctor, not a psychiatrist, which is what she needs."

"You forgot to say, 'Damn it, Jim,'" Ally chuckled. None of this was funny, but she couldn't help but laugh. It must make her appear even crazier.

"Ally," Tim stroked her face. "I didn't do anything. I promise you. We'll get through this, okay?"

"Did you kill Jane? Where is she, Tim? Where did you hide her body?"

Tim hung his head.

Dr. Bradley placed a hand on Tim's shoulder. "She's delusional. I wouldn't listen to what she's saying. You should go."

Tim shook his head. "I need to stay with my wife."

"She needs to rest. That's the best thing for her now." Dr. Bradley nudged his shoulder, and Tim rose. Dr. Bradley leaned over her and spoke in a condescending tone to Ally, his face only inches from hers. "I've given you a powerful sedative. It will help you sleep but will make you dizzy. Don't get out of bed."

Ally's eyes rolled up, and the lids slammed shut. He didn't have to worry about her getting out of bed. Her body felt like it was melting into the mattress. A warm glow spread through her, and her breathing slowed down.

Tim hovered back over her. "I'm going to be right here. We'll get through this. I love you."

―――――

Ally opened her eyes and took a deep breath. Sunlight filtered through the shade and slipped past the gap in the curtains. The beam spread across the bed and gleamed off the mahogany posts.

She sat up, feeling groggy and disoriented. Her head throbbed, and her stomach felt queasy. She rubbed her eyes, trying to clear the cobwebs from her mind. A faint memory of the previous night flickered, but she couldn't quite grasp it.

She swung her legs over the bed and stood up. Her feet sank into the plush carpet and she wavered a little, feeling unsteady. She stumbled toward the bathroom, holding onto the wall for support. As she splashed water on her face, the events of last night came back to her in a rush. The woman beneath the stairs, the affair, the broken saw, the sedative. Panic seized her. Her head spun. Ally sank to her knees on the tile floor.

Was it happening again, or was it real this time? It all started with her hearing Kim when she was in the shower. But this was different. Kim was not just a voice in her head; she'd seen her and spoken with her. It was all so vivid.

Ally covered her face with her hands and leaned against the wall. She swore it was real when she heard the children, too. Tears ran down her cheeks, and her hands trembled. Her right hand throbbed. She held it out and stared at the calluses on her palm. She arched her shoulders. The muscles in her back felt like a horse had kicked her.

Her eyes widened. She did use a saw last night. There was no way her imagining doing it would produce this soreness or the blisters on her hands.

Pulling herself to her feet, she grabbed hold of the sides of the sink with trembling hands. She stared at her reflection in the mirror. Her eyes were red-rimmed, and her hair was a mess.

Ally took a deep breath and tried to steady herself. Her heart raced so fast that she felt the vein in her neck throbbing. Kim was real and not a figment of her imagination. Who took her, and where did they go? Was she still alive?

A brief glimmer of hope ignited inside her. Maybe Kim escaped! Ally had left behind the broken piece of the saw. Had Kim used it to cut through the rest of the chain link while Ally ran to the boathouse? It was possible. And if that happened, she was still on the island somewhere.

Ally stared down at her trembling arms, her knuckles as white as the marble sink. If her dad were here, she knew what he'd say, "Keep your mouth shut, your eyes open, and figure out what's going on. And the only way to do that is with good intel."

Ally glared into the mirror. She needed to prove to herself she wasn't insane. She had to confirm that Kim was real. She needed to go back to the cellar.

Chapter Nineteen

Ally had finished dressing when there was a knock on the bedroom door. "Who is it?"

The door opened slightly, and Dr. Bradley stuck his head in. "I didn't expect you to be awake." He smiled, entered the room, and shut the door. "I was stopping by to check how you are doing." The slender man, dressed in dark suit pants, black shoes, and a gray shirt, stood holding his leather bag. "How did you sleep?"

"Very well, under the circumstances."

"I see that you may be preparing to be up and about. Might I suggest you think about resting today? I can provide some medication to help you relax."

Ally's lips pressed together. She needed to prove that Kim was real, and the last thing she was going to do was let someone give her drugs to knock her out. "I'm quite hungry. Maybe later?"

Dr. Bradley gave a slight disapproving frown.

She doubted he was used to his advice being rejected.

"While I'm not a therapist, I do have personal experience with mental illness. My wife suffers from autophobia." Dr. Bradley walked in and set his bag down next to the bed. "I'm concerned about your color. Your skin is rather pale, and the capillaries beneath your eyes are gray. I need to check your pulse."

Taken aback by the mention of his wife, Ally stared at Dr. Bradley's hand as he held her wrist. He didn't wear a wedding ring. "Autophobia is fear of being alone," she said. "Is anyone with your wife now?"

"No. I believe radical exposure therapy is the best way to treat irrational fears. In light of Victoria's need for me, I decided my wife should deal with her condition head-on."

Ally cleared her throat. She wondered if the doctor feared heights and how he'd feel about her pitching him out the window.

"Your pulse is very rapid. I need to check your vitals. Please, sit."

Ally stiffened. "I'm fine, thanks."

Dr. Bradley placed his hand on the small of her back. "I think—"

Someone knocked on the door, and it whipped open. "Lunch time!" Tom called out.

Dr. Bradley almost fell off the bed and staggered to his feet. "You should knock."

"I did." Tom shrugged. "What were you doing?"

"I'm conducting a physical." Dr. Bradley pointed at the door. "You need to leave."

Tom nodded. "Okay. I'll go tell Momma you're in Ally's bedroom."

"No!" Dr. Bradley's face flushed crimson. "You...." He muttered something Ally couldn't understand before yanking off his stethoscope and jamming it back into the bag. He turned to Ally and said, "We'll discuss treatment later," then stormed out of the room.

Tom made a face. "He's always grumpy," he whispered a little too loudly.

Ally smiled. "Good morning, Superhero. Thanks for the save."

Tom puffed out his chest and pointed at his blue T-shirt with the red, white, and blue round shield. "Like Captain America. I just saw the one where he fights his friend. But his friend doesn't remember him because he got his mind erased by the bad guys."

"Oh, my goodness. That's so sad." Ally followed Tom into the hallway.

"Don't be scared. It's okay. See..." Tom explained the movie to her as they headed to the dining room. Ally walked into the room with her head high. The chatter at the table stopped. Victoria sat at the head, Dr. Bradley beside her, with Mia opposite him.

Ally took the chair next to Mia, and Tom sat opposite her. It created a very lopsided seating arrangement, but there was no way she would sit next to Martin Bradley.

Victoria smiled. "I'm so glad you decided to join us, but if you prefer, I can have Nashwa bring something up to you."

Ally shook her head. "No, thank you. Where's Tim?"

"He, Philip, and the policemen are trying to repair the boat."

"Carter and Ziad went, too," Mia said.

"Would you like me to send Nashwa to fetch him?" Victoria asked.

Ally shook her head. She didn't want to speak with Tim, not just yet. "I'd like to discuss last night."

Dr. Bradley set down his water glass. "You had a significant psychotic episode. It's not surprising under the circumstances and your history." He turned to

Victoria. "I haven't had a chance to let you know that I checked on Ally this morning. I wanted to make sure she didn't have any adverse reaction to the sedative."

Victoria's brows knit together as she met his gaze. "How thoughtful." She smiled but not with her eyes, which were cold and narrow.

Tom leaned over and whispered, "I hope we have hamburgers and not salad or something."

"Me, too," Ally whispered back.

Victoria folded her hands in her lap. "After the incident last night, we all checked the cellar. My son went over every inch twice. His concern for you is unparalleled, and he blames himself for pushing you too fast, too soon. That's why he's trying to fix the boat — so he can sail to the mainland and get you help."

Ally wanted to deny she was imagining things but kept her mouth shut. She would find out the truth but do so without raising suspicion.

"I wouldn't worry about it." Mia leaned forward. "I had a meltdown in the middle of a party in the Hamptons two years ago. Carter told me the silliest joke about an actress who was going to be attending, but she had just been stabbed! He said her name was Reese something."

"Witherspoon?" Dr. Bradley asked.

"That's what I said!" Mia set her elbow on the table, her palm up and her fingers spread. "Then Carter says, no, with a knife!"

Dr. Bradley laughed hard, but one glance at Victoria's disapproving expression cut him off.

"And guess who walks into the party?" Mia rolled her eyes. "Reese Witherspoon! I don't know if it was because of the booze or the coke... Ah, Coca-Cola, but I lost it. I couldn't stop laughing. Here, this A-list actress says hi to me, and I crack up. I laughed so hard I wet my pants."

"That is entirely too much information," Victoria said.

Tom laughed, then covered his mouth. "Sorry. That's funny but not funny."

Mia kept her head turned away from Victoria and winked at Ally. "Just saying, these things happen. Don't worry about it."

Nashwa came in pushing a cart with plates of tomato tea sandwiches and creamy grape salads with pecans. She set out the plates in front of everyone except Tom. Reaching to a shelf underneath the cart, she picked up a plate with a hamburger and french fries.

Tom clapped. "Yeah, no gross salad!"

Nashwa smiled.

Victoria raised her glass. "I suggest we set this whole sordid affair behind us. "The boat will be repaired shortly. Philip and Tim will head to the mainland, and all will be well."

Everyone lifted their glasses and drank.

Tom leaned over and asked Ally, "Do you want to watch a movie with me? I'm on *Iron Man* 3."

Ally would love to spend time with her brother-in-law, but she was a woman on a mission. She opened her mouth to politely decline when she remembered the staircase in Tom's bedroom leading to the cellar. "That sounds wonderful. How about after lunch?"

"Great!" Tom stood up. "I'll go get it ready."

"Thomas!" Victoria called out. "Do sit back down."

"But Ally wants to watch a movie with me."

Ally placed a gentle hand on his arm. "I will, but after we eat. Okay?"

Tom sighed and made a face before flopping into his chair. He noticed the hamburger and smiled.

The front door bashed open. Heavy boot steps sounded in the foyer, and Philip appeared. He glared at Ally.

"Do you need something, Philip?"

"While you're all stuffing your faces, we're down at the boathouse in the rain trying to fix the mess Lizzie Borden made during her freakout."

"That's enough!" Victoria's chair slid back as she stood. "Why are you here?"

"We need some food and something to drink."

"Why didn't you send Ziad?"

"Because he's working on the engine with Scott." Philip's cold brown eyes bored into Ally. "What did you put in the gas tank?"

"I didn't do anything to the motor or the boat," Ally said.

"Yeah, right. You went down there, and don't deny it. They found my screwdriver and hacksaws. You took a sledgehammer to the side of my boat, you fruitcake."

"Stop calling her names!" Mia said.

"Shut your face, leech," Philip snapped.

"You're one to talk," Mia shot back.

Philip took a menacing step closer.

Tom started to stand, and Ally pulled him down into his chair.

"Do not make me raise my voice, Philip," Victoria said. "Go in the kitchen, have Nashwa prepare whatever you want, then leave and fix the boat."

"I don't know if it can be fixed." Philip ran a hand over the stubble on his chin. "She put something in the gas tank. We've cleaned it and tried to flush the lines, but it still won't start. Without a motor, even if we patch the giant hole, we're still stuck."

"Then I suggest you get it working," Victoria replied.

Philip glared at Victoria but leveled a finger at Ally. "I'll get it going. You keep Norma Bates in the house. I'm serious. I'm throwing her out to sea if she goes near the boathouse! And I'm blaming Tim for this. He's always gotta pick out the looney tunes who freak out."

Victoria slammed her hand on the table so hard the doctor's water glass fell over. "Outside. NOW!" She marched out of the dining with Philip stomping after her.

"What I wouldn't give to be a fly on the wall." Mia grinned and plopped a grape into her mouth.

"Uncle Philip can be a big jerk," Tom said.

"I didn't say a thing about her!" Philip shouted from the other room. "You know it's true, and I swear I'm not gonna clean up his mess again!"

"Don't pay any attention to that blowhard," Mia said. "Auntie keeps him on a short leash. Once he gets the motor going, he'll calm down."

"I don't know why she lets him talk to her like that." Dr. Bradley scowled. "If she'd permit, I'd give him a stern talking-to."

Mia rolled her eyes.

Ally wished they'd all shut up so she could hear what Victoria and Philip were discussing. But Philip had stopped shouting, and now she couldn't make out anything they said.

Tom's mouth fell open. A mischievous smile spread across his face. He picked up his plate. "Let's go watch the movie before they get back."

Ally grabbed her plate. She wasn't eager to face Philip's wrath again, and this gave her the excuse she was looking for to go to Tom's room.

Mia hurried after them, carrying her salad bowl with the sandwich stacked on top.

"Are you coming too?" Tom asked her hopefully.

Ally held her breath. If Mia came, it would throw a wrench into her plans.

"Maybe another time. I'm going to eat in the game room."

"Okie dokie!" Tom hurried down the hallway, and Ally followed him.

But she still had a problem. How could she distract Tom so she could get into the cellar?

Chapter Twenty

Ally walked next to Tom as he proudly showed off his room. The former summer kitchen had been renovated into an enormous open space. Tom's bed lay in the right corner. The door to the left led to a large private bathroom. Tom had his own kitchen with a microwave, sink, refrigerator, and freezer, but no stove.

"I can't keep any ice cream in this freezer," Tom said, his lips mashing together into a pout. "Mother says it's the wrong kind of freezer, and it would melt."

Ally frowned. Tom loved ice cream and tended to overindulge, but Victoria shouldn't lie to him.

"And these are my Avengers magnets." He pointed to the front of the refrigerator and a collection of magnets Tim had given him for his birthday. "Try to lift Thor's hammer." He smiled.

Ally approached the 3D silver hammer stuck to the fridge and grabbed the handle. It must have been a rare earth magnet because it was so difficult to pull off.

"You did it! You're worthy!" Tom grinned. "Only someone worthy can lift Thor's hammer," he explained, taking it back and setting it in place with a loud click. "And over there are my pinball and asteroid and Pac-Man games. Do you want some popcorn? Or a soda?" Tom pointed to a replica of a candy counter from an actual movie theater. The popcorn machine was fake, but the soda dispenser worked.

"Maybe later." She followed him over to the two rows of seats, glancing toward the far left of the room and the door which led to the basement. She cleared her throat. "You like Chinese food, right, Tom?"

"It's my favorite! Tim said all three of us were gonna get some after he fixed the boat. I can't wait. I like fried rice and egg rolls."

"Me, too. Did Tim take you out for Chinese food when he was here last time?"

"Yes. And a movie. I forgot what movie, but we got ice cream after. Strawberry with sprinkles."

Ally took a deep breath. "Did anyone go with you to the restaurant? Besides Tim?"

Tom shook his head.

"Nobody ate with you? No girl?"

He wrinkled his nose and shook his head again.

Ally relaxed into the seat.

"She wasn't hungry."

Ally's hands tightened on the armrests. "You did see a girl?"

Tom nodded. "When I came back from the restroom. She and Tim are friends, but she wasn't hungry, so she left."

"Did you talk to her?"

"Nope."

"How do you know they are friends?"

"Friends hold hands." Tom picked up a remote, and the lights dimmed.

"So you came out of the bathroom, and this girl and Tim were holding hands?"

"Because they're friends. Then she left. I got an

egg roll with the red sauce. That's super yummy." Tom pressed another button, and the enormous screen in front of them flickered to life. After a second, the movie began to play.

Ally sat in the dark room, her heart feeling like a dead weight in the center of her chest while her mind swirled with emotions. She felt anger and betrayal, but at the same time, there was sadness for what she had lost. Tears streamed down her face as she tried to come to terms with the fact that Tim had had an affair, yet all she could do was sit and cry in despair.

"That's Iron Man." Tom pointed at the screen.

"He's the guy with the glowing thing in his chest, right?" Ally asked, drying her eyes.

Tom's expression turned serious. He leaned so close to Ally his breath tickled her cheek. "A missile exploded, and metal got stuck in his chest. The glowy thing is a magnet that keeps the metal from going into his heart. That's what magnets do. They attract little pieces of metal."

Ally settled into the seat and pretended to pay attention to the movie. Inside her mind, she was busy watching a lifetime of memories starring Tim and her. The day they met slowly came into focus. She'd never been to an art show, let alone fallen for an artist. She fell deep, hard, and fast. So had he. From the first date, they'd become inseparable.

The lights on the screen flickered as an explosion played out in the movie, but Ally only saw Tim on one knee, a simple ring in his hand, and that irresistible smile on his face. She clamped her eyes closed as he repeated their wedding vows in her mind. All of that was gone now. He'd broken his vows to her and God.

She almost couldn't believe he'd cheat, but kidnapping? No. Not Tim. She knew it wasn't logical to think someone else hit Kim over the head and locked her in the cellar, but it couldn't be her husband. Infidelity was one thing. Chaining someone to a wall was something only a monster would do.

Had she been that blind?

Tom clapped and turned the lights in the room on. "That was so awesome! Did you like it?"

Ally sniffed and nodded. "Very much." Had she dozed off? It couldn't have been two hours she'd spent lost in thought!

"Can you watch the next one with me? Please? It will be even awesomer."

Ally eyed the cellar door. She needed to get downstairs but couldn't with Tom here. "Do you want to get us a snack from the kitchen?"

"I'm full. What about after the movie? Please?"

Ally rubbed her hands together. Getting Tom out of the room for any length of time might be more complicated than she expected. "Sure."

Tom cheered and started the next movie. An hour later, Tom yawned. His eyes drooped, and he reclined the chair back. He rolled toward her and gave her a sleepy smile.

Ally crossed to his bed, and he was already fast asleep when she returned with a blanket. She laid the blanket over him and was about to sit down when her eyes lit up. This was perfect. With Tom sleeping, she could slip into the cellar.

Doubt and depression slammed down on top of her. First, the miscarriage. Now, an affair. If those weren't traumatic enough, Tim questioning her sanity was rock bottom. Fresh tears came. "God, please help me." She whispered, but inside, she felt defeated and crushed.

Metal screeching boomed over the speakers. On the screen, the car that had landed on the hero shook and then rose into the air as Iron Man flung the vehicle aside. His chest glowed a bright blue as the magnet that powered his suit and kept the metal from reaching his heart surged with power.

Ally gasped.

That's it! That's how she could get the proof she needed. She hurried over to the fridge, grasped Thor's hammer, and tried to pull it off. The grip was so strong the refrigerator door opened a crack, sending light streaming across the floor before she managed to remove it again. The fridge shut with a click.

Glancing back at Tom, she waited until she saw his chest rising and falling. The light cast from the refrigerator had given her another idea. She crept to the shelves lining the wall beside Tom's bed. She scanned them until she located an Iron Man flashlight. Flicking it on and off to ensure it worked, she headed to the cellar door.

Tom softly snored in his chair, and the movie continued to play.

The door opened freely. Ally slipped through, turned on the flashlight, and shut the door behind her. Reaching the bottom steps, she expected to have to push the windows screens out of the way on the other side, but someone had already moved them. All of the screens were now stacked along the wall. Shining the light to her right, she saw the open wine cellar door. She hurried over and darted inside, her grip tightening on the handle of Thor's hammer.

The room was exactly as she remembered it, except Kim wasn't there. She moved toward the alcove, her light shining off the bricks on the back wall and wooden bench. The chains were gone. The rings in the wall they had been fastened to were still there, but there was no evidence that anything she'd seen had been real.

Stooping down, she carefully examined the floor for any trace of a broken saw blade or even a piece of it, but there was none. She held Thor's hammer by the handle and ran the magnet along the bricks. Her eyebrows knit together.

The bricks in the alcove floor differed from the rest of the room. The appraiser in Ally noted that the contractor had used refractory bricks. They were larger, thicker, and wider than regular bricks, so they were able to withstand high temperatures. Pushing aside the memory of the job she loved, she swept the hammer along the entire alcove, paying particular attention underneath the bench. When she finished, she held the hammer up and shined the flashlight on it — nothing. Not a piece of chain link or a bit of broken saw blade clung to the magnet.

Ally flopped down on the bench. Laying the flashlight and hammer beside her, she put her head in her hands and covered her face. Maybe she had imagined the whole thing. It all began with hearing voices again. Was it that much of a stretch to go from speaking to imaginary voices to having a conversation with a fictional person? Crazy is crazy.

Ally slowly rose and picked up the flashlight and hammer. The good news was, if she imagined everything, Tim didn't have an affair. If Ally made Kim up, she must have created the romance too.

But what about what Tom told her? He saw Tim holding hands with another woman. Ally might have imagined Kimberly Hall in the cellar, but Kim was a real person, and Tim knew her. Between the photograph Frank had and Tom's eyewitness account, part of the story had to be true.

Defeated, Ally trudged out of the wine cellar. She quietly climbed the stairs and slipped back into Tom's room. The movie was still playing, and Tom lay where he'd been sleeping.

Ally shut the flashlight off and walked over to the refrigerator. She stuck the hammer against its face, but it didn't sit flush. Puzzled, she stared down the handle, which stuck to the surface of the refrigerator at an odd angle.

Holding onto the grip, she pulled the hammer free and looked at the face of the magnet. A pile of dirt or dust clung to the top. How was that possible?

Ally turned the flashlight back on.

Thin silver metal shavings sparkled in the light.

Ally's eyes widened. The little mound stuck to the magnet wasn't dirt. While Ally had sawed the chain, tiny bits of ground metal from the link fell onto the bench. When she set the hammer next to her, the magnet attracted the shavings.

She wasn't crazy, and she didn't imagine it. It happened. She had spoken with Kim. She'd almost succeeded in setting her free.

Ally gasped.

Where was Kim now? Had the kidnapper come back and moved her somewhere else? Maybe Kim managed to free herself! Ally had sawed most of the way through the last link. She could have used that little piece of broken saw blade and the screwdriver to break free.

Either way, Kim was out there, and Ally had to find her.

Chapter Twenty-One

Ally stood at the counter beside the refrigerator, scraping the metal shavings off the magnet and into a napkin. After collecting all she could, she folded the napkin and placed it in her pocket.

She'd been vindicated. She hadn't imagined everything. But the truth came at a great price. Kim was missing. Tim had an affair. And Ally didn't trust anyone.

Silence descended on the room as the second movie ended.

Tom yawned and sat up. He glanced around, noticed Ally, and smiled. "Did you like the movie?"

She nodded. "I'm sorry you fell asleep."

Tom shrugged. "I'll watch it again." He grabbed the remote. "If I choose play from the beginning, it starts all over! We can watch it now!"

Ally opened her mouth, but a knock on the door cut her off. "Hold on." She opened the door.

Nashwa stood in the hallway. "Sorry to bother you. Mrs. Hawthorne wanted me to ask you both to join everyone in the sitting room for hors d'oeuvres and cocktails at six."

Tom bounded out of his chair. "Do you have the little hot dog things?"

Nashwa gave a sympathetic frown. "Your mother picked out everything."

Tom stuck his tongue out. "That means you made weird stuff. What about dinner? Did she pick that out, too?"

Nashwa nodded. "But I made you chicken with broccoli."

Tom grinned. "I like broccoli. It looks like little trees, and she puts butter on it."

"Do you want to join the others at dinner?"

"If momma said it's okay, I'll eat in my room."

"Mrs. Hawthorne said it was all right for you to do that."

"Yes!" Tom pumped his arm like he scored a touchdown. "I'm gonna take a shower." He marched to the bathroom and closed the door.

Ally followed Nashwa into the hallway. "Do you need help with anything?"

Nashwa stood there blinking for a moment, then smiled. "You and your husband are so nice. He's always offering to help Ziad and me, too. Thank you, but I'm all set."

The mention of Tim made Ally's chest tighten and her breath hitch. Fighting back her growing anxiety, she said, "He's that way at home, too. I hope he isn't a bother when he's here."

"Oh, no. You should see him around Tom. It's so sweet. They do everything together."

"Do they go to the mainland often?"

"Not really. Although on his last trip, they did go several times."

"Did you know the missing girl?"

Nashwa sped up down the hallway. "No. I didn't

recognize her until the police mentioned she worked in the cleaning crew. She wore a head scarf when she cleaned. A blue and red scarf."

"You were here when she was cleaning?"

"Only a few times. Everyone usually cleared out when they came. Mrs. Hawthorne doesn't like being around working people, so she asks them to be in and out quickly. While they are here, she makes a trip to the mainland."

"Working people? Does she think she's a queen?"

Nashwa's breath hitched, and her eyes darted across the foyer to the open door of the sitting room. "I have to go get dinner ready." She put her head down and rushed to the kitchen.

Ally watched her go. She'd certainly gotten spooked when Ally mentioned Victoria, but she wasn't comfortable talking about Kim, either. Did Nashwa know something, or was she simply freaked out because everyone told her Ally was crazy and seeing things?

Ally checked the grandfather clock. She had two hours before dinner. More than enough time to make a quick trip around the island and see if she could find Kim. She set the timer on her watch for an hour and forty-five minutes, grabbed her jacket, and headed out the front door.

The cold wind blew from the east, the salt stinging her cheeks. Stuffing her hands into her pockets, she hurried down the steps. The gray of the day was already beginning to darken.

If Kim had somehow managed to free herself, she would have ended up in a similar situation to a prisoner escaping Alcatraz. She would be out of the prison and trapped on the island by the sea. Last night was freezing, and Kim had only been barefoot wearing a dress. She would need to find shelter, and Ally could think of only one place she could go.

Jogging down the path, Ally scanned the area and listened for anyone watching her. No ships were visible on the ocean. Had whoever kidnapped Kim killed both Dennis and Gary? With all of the little beaches dotting the island, the killer might have moored Dennis's boat and come ashore.

Maybe they hid Kim on the boat? Or did they move her somewhere else, or had she escaped? Either way, her kidnapper knew she was gone.

Ally hurried past Philip's house. The single-story building looked like the coastal cottages on postcards from Maine. Faded wood and stone steps led up to an old, dull gray door with a small, rectangular glass window. A large oak tree would shade the front yard in the spring and summer, but now the bare branches looked like skeletal fingers clutching at the dark clouds.

Philip was busy repairing the boat with Tim, Ziad, and the police. She prayed they'd get it going soon. But a haunting question niggled at the back of her mind. What then? The kidnapper had to realize they'd be discovered once that boat was operational. Or did they not care?

Pushing those thoughts aside, Ally hurried on. The path wound down in front of the guest cottage, a duplicate of Philip's. She had asked to stay there on her visit, but Tim wanted to sleep in the house, so the adorable cottage lay empty and dark.

She hurried up the three stone steps and tried the knob. To her surprise, the door wasn't locked. She slipped inside, shutting the door behind her.

The cottage was furnished in the pine and stone décor that typifies the Maine style. A mix of woodland and sea motifs, the interior matched the outdoor scent of the forest and the smell of the salt breeze from the ocean just beyond the house.

In the living room to the right were a few chairs, a couch, and a large TV. A table, which looked like it had been put together from driftwood, held a driftwood lamp with a red shade. A small bedroom stood empty on the left. The kitchen sat in the rear of the cottage, and there was another bedroom behind the living room, but that door was shut.

"Hello?" Ally softly called out.

The house was quiet. She crossed the living room. Her sneakers against the wood floor sounded loud in the stillness. The brass knob turned in her hand, and the door swung open.

An old-fashioned wooden bed with a patchwork quilt took up one corner of the room. Another corner housed a simple nightstand and reading lamp. The whole place sported bright white ceilings and trim. A door led to a small bathroom. The closed sliding doors of a closet stood adjacent to it.

Ally stood in the doorway listening. Her heart felt like a jackhammer was tapping against her ribs. She crossed the carpeted floor and opened the closet. Two white bathrobes hung inside, and blankets and bedding were stacked in the back, but otherwise, it was empty.

Ally crouched down and peered underneath the bed — nothing. Running her hand through her hair, she marched over to the bathroom. The shower curtain was drawn. "Kim?" She whispered. "It's me, Ally."

Something banged behind her in the closet.

Ally spun around, but it was too late to avoid the

person rushing out of the closet and directly at her. She opened her mouth to scream.

Kim slammed against Ally. The terrified woman wrapped her arms around Ally's waist and sobbed uncontrollably.

"Shh. Quiet." Ally kept Kim from falling as she sank to her knees. "What happened?"

Kim sniffed and brushed the hair from her face, the shackles still attached to her wrists rattling. Her eyes lit up. "Mr. Waters. I always hated him, but I will kiss him if I ever see him again."

"You're not making sense. How did you get free?"

"Mr. Waters was my science teacher in high school. He taught us about levers and fulcrums and junk. I put the screwdriver through the chain link and used the metal ring on the wall as a base. The link broke!" She sobbed and hugged Ally again. "Then I just ran. I'm so sorry I couldn't wait. I had to get out of there."

"I understand. Believe me, I would have run like a bat out of hell, too." Ally's breath hitched. "Did you leave everything behind? The saw, the tools, everything?"

"I didn't even think about taking any of that. I ran."

Ally inhaled. "When I came back, they were all gone — even the chains. Everyone in the house thinks I'm crazy."

"Everyone except the person who put me there." Kim held Ally's hand. "You can't trust any of them. They're all evil."

Ally shook her head.

Kim tightened her grip so hard it hurt. "You don't know them! There's always been rumors in town. I didn't believe them before I met Tim. I thought it was gossip and conspiracy theories."

"You mean Jane Nelson?"

"There's more. Did you know Dr. Bradley moved to town right before Tim's father was killed?"

"Tim's father wasn't killed. He drowned."

"Right after Victoria and Dr. Bradley start having an affair? The police never looked into it, yet the morning the family was supposed to go on a trip to Disney, Tim's father decided to go out on the boat? They found him tangled in a fishing line. All of his friends and family said he hated fishing."

Ally sat back on her haunches. Tim never mentioned any of this.

"What about Philip's first wife?" Kim continued. "She drowned, too. She took a swim in October. Who does that? No one! And again, the police wrapped it up in a week and put a bow on it. Tim is just like them. I didn't want to believe it."

"I don't!" Ally said. "Anyone could have hit you from behind. Maybe it wasn't even one of them. What about Gary? I didn't tell you, but Dennis is dead. His boat and Gary are missing. Is it possible Gary killed Dennis and stole his boat? Could Gary have gotten jealous and tried to stop you?"

"Gary's an idiot, but why wouldn't he have killed me when I was in his apartment? Why would he wait and chain me up inside the Hawthorne's mansion?"

"To frame Tim," Ally said.

Kim's shoulders shook. "Oh, my gosh. Oh, my gosh. I'm such an idiot."

"What are you talking about?"

"Maybe it was Gary." Kim's fingers dug into the carpeting so hard her knuckles turned white. "I told him all about the house. I've cleaned every inch of it, including that wine cellar. Gary also has access to my phone. That had Tim's number. He'd even know the alarm code to the house."

"But would Gary go through all that because of jealousy?" Ally asked.

"No." Kim covered her mouth with her hand and slowly shook her head. Her eyes bulged out like she was choking. "It is him. But it's not about me. This whole thing is about Jane," Kim whispered.

"Try to calm down and explain why you think that," Ally said.

"It all makes sense. I met Gary on the docks when we returned from cleaning the house. He gave me the full-court press. Flowers, candies, jewelry, but all he wanted to talk about was the Hawthorne's and Jane. He was obsessed with her. He said he had seen some TV show about her disappearance and was writing a book about it. He grilled me for details on the island. And then I met Tim."

"And Gary became jealous?"

Kim shook her head. "No. I'm not a cheater, so I told Gary about Tim. But Gary didn't flip out. He said he wanted to stay friends and asked if I would do him a favor. I thought he hoped to be some backup plan, but he begged me to ask Tim about Jane. He even offered me money. I said that was too weird, but Gary said he needed it for his book."

"Why does he care so much about Jane?"

"I don't know, but he's obsessed. Jane might be the reason why Gary is doing this."

"But no one knows what happened to her."

"Someone on this island does. And I'm certain that Tim knows something. I could tell when I asked him. I could see it in his eyes."

They both jumped when the alarm on Ally's watch went off.

"They're having dinner at the house," Ally said, shutting off the alarm. "I'd better go so people don't come looking for me. "Do you have food? Water?"

"I found some in the kitchen."

"Go back and hide in the closet. It's a good spot. They're almost done fixing the boat. Help will be here soon. Stay hidden."

Kim grabbed Ally's hands. "Gary won't stop. He's fixated on finding out what happened to Jane. She's the key. If Gary is after the truth, maybe that's what can stop him. If I could only talk to Tim."

The sound of her husband's name and the thought that another woman felt so close to Tim that he'd confide in her instead of his wife hit Ally like a spear in the chest.

"You can't talk to Tim, but I can. You stay out of sight. Agreed?"

Kim squeezed Ally's hand and nodded.

Ally hugged her and rose. She watched Kim, dirty and scared, return to the closet and close the door. Hurrying down the hallway, Ally locked the front door before closing it.

Dashing back along the path, Ally sprinted up the hill and down the other side. She rounded the corner where the trail branched off toward the boat dock.

A large evergreen bush shook, and Philip charged out, zipping up his fly. "I thought I told you to stay away!" He stomped toward her.

Ally held her hands up. "I was just letting you know that dinner is almost ready."

"Carter already came and told us." He eyed her suspiciously. "So unless you want me to tie you to the bed, you'll take your crazy butt back to the house and stay there. Got it?"

Ally nodded, circling him as he spoke. As soon as she had an opening, she ran toward the house.

Philip stood on the path with his arms crossed, watching her.

Ally's mind raced faster than her feet on the gravel. Kim was real, and she was safe — for now. While the fact that her husband was an adulterous scumbag hurt, the possibility he wasn't a kidnapper gave her some hope. While she waited for them to fix the boat, she wasn't about to sit around on her hands. Kim was right. This whole thing revolved around Jane.

Ally needed to find out what happened to her.

Chapter Twenty-Two

Ally hurried through the front door and hung up her jacket. She shivered as she walked into the foyer.

"I thought I heard you come in," Carter called from the sitting room doorway. "We're all in here."

Ally crossed over to him. Victoria and Dr. Bradley sat at a table with Frank and Scott. Mia stood beside the fireplace, a plate of food and a tall glass filled with greenish liquid on the mantle beside her.

Victoria lifted her chin. "Tim, Philip, and Ziad are still down at the boathouse. They've opted to forgo dinner until they get the motor running."

"If they get the motor running," Carter said, munching on cheese and crackers. "We," he circled his hand, "were responsible for patching the hole in the boat. That's done."

"That was the easy job," Scott said. "I'm glad I don't know anything about engines. They've stripped the motor down to the base, but it refuses to stay running. It will turn over but dies almost immediately."

Ally stared at Scott. He was the one person she thought she might be able to trust. Being new to the police force, he might not yet be tainted even by Victoria's proposed bribe.

Scott met her gaze and raised an eyebrow.

Suddenly unsure, Ally looked away and headed to the hors d'oeuvres table. She reached for a cracker and felt someone's presence beside her.

Dr. Bradley approached closer, his piercing blue eyes studying her intently. "How are you holding up, Ally?" he asked, his voice low.

Ally hesitated, unsure of how to answer. "I'm okay," she finally said, forcing a smile.

Dr. Bradley didn't look convinced as he loaded a small plate with crackers and cheese. "Have you taken your medication?"

A lump formed in her throat. "Yes. I'm feeling much better."

"Great. Good to hear. Still, I will need to check your vitals and conduct a complete physical examination. Perhaps after dinner?"

Before she could tell him where to stick his stethoscope, he hurried back to Victoria and handed her the plate he'd gathered, accompanied by a slight bow.

As Ally reached for a mini quiche, Mia took the doctor's place beside her. "Ally, can I talk to you for a moment?"

Ally's heart skipped a beat. The way Mia said her name made her feel uneasy. "Sure."

Mia led her to a corner of the room, away from the others. "I know this must be difficult for you with everything happening. My nerves are completely shot, too. Do you need something to take the edge off? Something a little stronger than the medicine?"

"What do you mean?" Ally asked, trying to keep her voice steady. "A cocktail?"

Mia leaned in closer. "No. I've got a stash of just about anything you need. It's technically not legal in the United States, but they are in Amsterdam. Some of them are, anyway. Others, the ones with a real kick aren't, but we won't tell anybody."

Ally pressed her lips together. "I'm feeling a little better." She tapped the side of her head for emphasis. "Up here. But thank you."

Mia placed a hand on Ally's arm. "I'm here to help you. So is Carter." Mia glanced around the room until she spotted Carter. He stood next to the door leading into the sunroom. He was busy examining a large round shield with a crossbow and axe mounted to the front. He lifted up a corner of the shield, peering behind it.

"Carter!" Mia called out.

Carter jumped. The shield and the weapons attached to it slid off the wall and landed on the floor with a loud clatter.

Dr. Bradley spilled his cocktail across the table.

Victoria leaped up, moving away from the pool of liquid. She glared at Mia. "You married an imbecile!"

"I'm well aware." Mia crossed her arms.

Carter lifted the shield. The attached weapons dangled off, clinking together. The axe slipped out of the strap and banged off the floor, the blade just missing his leg.

"Careful!" Scott rushed over and removed everything from Carter's hands. "That crossbow is loaded."

"No, it isn't." Carter made a face.

Victoria, wiping her hand on a napkin, leveled an icy stare his way. "Why don't you point it at your foot and pull the trigger so we can all find out?"

Carter laughed, then swallowed it down when he realized she was serious. "I apologize, Auntie." He inclined his head so far it turned into a bow. "I was only admiring your fabulous collection. You have the finest taste. Haven't I always said that, Mia?"

"Do stop groveling. But you can continue to bow. I rather enjoy that." Victoria said.

The cheery twinkling of a bell sounded from the kitchen.

"Dinner is ready," Victoria said. "I have been informed that tonight, we have a special treat to look forward to."

Everyone followed Victoria to the dining room. Carter whispered something to Mia, who covered her mouth and giggled.

The large mahogany table sat in the center of the dining room. It could easily be adjusted to seat sixteen with inserts but had been set for eight. Lit candles formed a column down the middle of the table, casting a warm glow through the room. The table was spread with a crisp, white cloth, silver beach roses, and starfish adorning it. The fine china was patterned with an undersea motif. The stemware was crystal clear, and a silver cloth napkin folded into the shape of a sea shell sat at each place setting.

"And what is this?" Carter asked as he circled to his chair.

Sitting on each plate was a white box five inches square. A silver knob was fastened in the center of the lid. Each box had a name written on the top, along with a number. Ally had number 3.

"I'll open mine first!" Carter said.

"Why you?" Mia asked.

Carter pointed to a note lying in the middle of the table. "I have number one, and the instructions say to open your treats in numerical order."

"This is so kind of you, Auntie." Mia squeezed her shoulders together and grinned.

Victoria gave a thin-lipped smile and sat.

Carter picked up his box and gave it a shake.

Something slid around inside of it. Setting it back down, he grabbed the silver knob and lifted it high.

The sides of the box folded out, landing on the plate. Blue paper butterflies rose into the air and fluttered around the room.

Carter laughed while Mia clapped. "I've seen these before," he exclaimed before peering into the box. He removed a tiny silver charm.

"What is it?" Frank asked, leaning forward.

"I think it's a cartoon character." Carter stared at the object twirling around on the end of a silver ring.

"It's Dopey!" Mia laughed. "From Snow White!"

Victoria nodded approvingly. "How appropriate."

"My turn." Mia lifted her lid, and pink paper butterflies sprang out, fluttering around her head before landing on the table. She eagerly reached inside and frowned. "Sleepy?" She made a face as she showed her charm around the room.

Ally took a deep breath. Green butterflies soared into the air, but she didn't receive a character. Inside was a small silver charm mirror.

"I don't get it," Carter said.

Mia's hand slapped down on the table. "You know, mirror, mirror on the wall! It's the mirror from Snow White."

"You know what's funny?" Frank said. "That's not the real quote. The wicked Queen says, magic mirror on the wall, who's the fairest one of all? But everyone remembers it wrong."

"I've heard of that phenomenon." Dr. Bradley said. "It's referred to as a collective false memory. It occurs when a group of people remembers an event a certain way when, in reality, they are all calling to mind the same thing incorrectly."

"Like people think the guy with the top hat in Monopoly has a monocle?" Mia asked.

"He doesn't?" Carter wrinkled his nose.

"See!" Mia and the others laughed.

Scott went next and got purple butterflies with Sneezy.

Frank's color was yellow, and his character was Grumpy. When he scowled, everyone cracked up.

Victoria reached for her handle.

Carter leaned over and whispered to Mia, "If she gets the witch, I'm running."

Ally coughed to cover her laugh.

Victoria dramatically raised her lid. The red butterflies seemed to fly higher than all the others. Victoria's eyebrows arched. She reached into her box and lifted out a silver apple.

Dr. Bradley said, "That makes you Snow White."

Victoria cocked an eyebrow. "I think not. The queen possessed the apple." Her arm shifted over underneath the table.

Dr. Bradley jumped in his chair, and his cheeks flushed. "I bet I know who I got." He cleared his throat. "DOC!" He leaned slightly forward, laid hold of the handle, and yanked.

Black butterflies filled the air. A thin jet of white powder sprayed Dr. Bradley directly in the mouth. He gasped, inhaling most of the cloud.

Frank fell out of his chair as he moved away.

Victoria hurried back, her chair tipping over and clattering to the floor.

Dr. Bradley coughed twice, and then a huge smile broadened on his face. He shook his head. His eyes were so bright that they practically glowed blue.

Carter chuckled. "Oh, I did not like that one. But

Martin, you seem to enjoy whatever it was. What is that white stuff?"

Dr. Bradley coughed again and chuckled. "I don't know, but it's... Whoo!" He held his hand in front of his face, gazing at it like he'd never seen it before. "Wow. Now that is something." He gasped and clutched his throat. His eyes rolled up in his head. He staggered back and collapsed.

Victoria started forward. "Martin, are you—"

"DON'T TOUCH HIM!" Frank shouted. The detective shoved the table back, kicked a chair out of the way, and cleared a space around the doctor. His hands shook as he pulled blue gloves out of his coat pocket.

"What was that stuff?" Carter asked again.

"We don't know, so treat it like it's toxic!" Frank handed Scott a pair of gloves before putting his on. He grabbed Dr. Bradley by the jacket collar and dragged him away from the circle of dust on the floor. "Everyone get back."

Dr. Bradley gasped for breath.

Ally crossed to stand beside Victoria.

Frank turned to Scott. "Do you have test strips?"

"Yes, sir." Flustered, Scott reached into the sleeve pocket of his police uniform and pulled out something that looked like a chemical strip Ally used to check the water in her fish tank.

"Don't just stand there. Help him." Victoria said, her voice surprisingly calm.

"I'm trying." Frank placed the test strip into the powder on Dr. Bradley's chin. "After a moment, it turned blue. He looked up at Scott. "It's fentanyl. My pen is still in my cruiser."

Frank pointed at Carter and Mia, cowering in the corner. "Do you have Naloxone?"

They shook their heads.

Dr. Bradley gasped and stopped breathing.

Frank grabbed the water pitcher off the table and poured it on Dr. Bradley's face.

"He can't breathe!" Victoria shouted. "Drowning him won't help you fool!"

Scott moved between Victoria and Frank. "He's trying not to get himself killed."

Frank pinched Dr. Bradley's nose closed, then covered Martin's mouth with a gloved hand, leaving an open spot to breathe into. "Scott! Chest compressions." He said before breathing into Dr. Bradley's mouth.

Ally remembered the black bag Dr. Bradley had with him when he came into her room. "I'll get the doctor's bag." She raced out of the room and down the hallway. Dr. Bradley's room was unlocked, and his bag sat beside the bed. She snatched it up and dashed back to the dining room.

Frank and Scott were still administering CPR.

Ally swept a place on the table clean and dumped the bag's contents out. Ally, Carter, and Mia rummaged through the dozen or so prescription bottles, calling out the names of random medicines, but none of them would counter the effects of an overdose.

Frank and Scott tried for what seemed like ages, but Dr. Bradley didn't respond. His lips had turned blue, and his skin a light gray. Sweat matted both of their shirts, and Frank's skin was pale, but he kept at it.

Ally stood there, shocked. She'd never witnessed a person die in front of her. Helplessness washed over her. Her legs shook, and she held onto the chair for support.

Mia stared down at the doctor. "We're all only one breath away from death."

Victoria placed her hand on Frank's shoulder. "Stop. It's useless. He's gone."

Frank shook his head.

Victoria grabbed his arm. "You need to look to the living. I need you alive to find Gary. If we don't stop him, we'll all be dead."

Chapter Twenty-Three

Ally stared down at Dr. Bradley's body. His lips were blue, and pulled back so far, all of his teeth were visible. The last moments of agony he'd endured were frozen on his face.

Scott helped Frank up and over to a chair. The detective was shaking and pale.

Ally didn't know if Frank's condition was due to the CPR or if he'd been exposed to the fentanyl trying to save Dr. Bradley. She brought the detective a glass of water. It was all she could think to do.

"Stop, ma'am. Set it down on the table." Frank peeled his rubber gloves off, putting one within the other, then dropped them into a cloth napkin he bundled up and tossed into the corner of the room. "No one touch anything."

Victoria lifted her chin. She spoke in a calm, clear voice, "Detective Burgess and Officer Davis, I lay the blame for this man's death squarely on your shoulders. You let that deranged drug addict wander away, and now Gary has killed two men. There's a murderer loose on my island. Seeing how it is your responsibility and that you are the only people armed, get off your asses and go find him!"

Ally stared at her mother-in-law in horror. Here, both of those men risked their lives to save Dr. Bradley, and still, she felt entitled to send them outside to hunt a killer when one looked barely able to stand.

Nashwa raced into the room and skidded to a halt. She removed an earbud from her left ear and glanced around the room. She stared at Dr. Bradley lying on the floor, his face twisted in death. Her mouth opened, but no sound came out. She crumpled to the floor like a ragdoll cut from its string.

Ally rushed over to Nashwa and knelt beside her. "She's fainted."

Victoria pointed at the door. "Mia, help Ally remove Nashwa from the room."

"Everyone needs to get out," Frank said. "It isn't safe in here." He pointed at the door. He was sweating, and his arm shook.

"I think you need to follow your own advice," Scott said.

"I'm okay." Frank rose, grabbed a glass of water, dumped it onto a cloth napkin, and began rubbing down his face. "Everyone out!" he repeated. "This is a crime scene."

Victoria snatched off a blue butterfly clinging to the back of Carter's shirt. "Stop!" she seized Carter by the shoulder and spun him around so he was facing her.

Carter's brows arched. "What?"

Victoria slapped him hard across the face. "What did you put inside that box?"

"Auntie!" Mia shouted.

Carter stepped back, his hand moving to his red cheek. "Nothing. I've never... Oh, my word. Oh, no."

Victoria held up the butterfly and crushed it in

her hand. "Two years ago, you brought another one of your get-rich schemes to me for backing. Only that time, it wasn't doggie snacks. It was these clever little boxes. You said you'd make millions. I thought you abandoned the idea like all the others, but this is the product."

Carter shook his head. "They are, but I never sold them. The supplier had a problem, and the deal fell through."

Frank marched over to Carter. "These boxes belong to you?"

"Mine? No. Maybe. I don't know." Carter stared desperately at Mia. "Are they?"

Nashwa groaned and rolled onto her side. She made a gagging noise like she was about to vomit.

Ally placed her hands underneath Nashwa's shoulders. "Mia, help me bring her into the foyer."

Mia grabbed one leg, and Carter took hold of the other. The three of them lifted Nashwa and carried her out of the room, laying her down on the small rug near the grandfather clock.

With her fists clenched at her sides, Victoria silently marched through the foyer and headed upstairs. Her shoes rang off the marble as she climbed to the second floor and disappeared.

Nashwa groaned, and Ally knelt beside her. "It's okay, Nashwa. Everything is going to be all right."

"Where's Ziad?"

"He's at the boathouse. We'll get him. Try to stay calm. You should stay lying down."

Frank appeared in the doorway and pointed at Carter. "Don't go anywhere." As soon as he said the words, he made a face. "I know you can't leave the island, but don't leave this house."

Carter opened his mouth, but Mia grabbed his

wrist and squeezed. She whispered something to him, and his eyes went wide. "Yes, Detective."

"Everyone needs to keep out of this room. It's off-limits from here out." Frank closed the door.

Mia and Carter exchanged glances and sprinted down the hallway toward their room. As they passed Tom's door, it opened, and he appeared.

"Did I miss dinner?" Tom called out as he walked down the hall. "Where's everyone going?"

"Tom! I need you to do me a huge favor." Ally said. With a killer on the loose, there was no way she could ask Tom to get Ziad. She'd have to go herself. "I need you to stay with Nashwa. She isn't feeling well. Stay with her, okay?"

Tom hurried over. "Does she need water?"

"No. She's okay. Just stay with her."

"You can count on me."

Nashwa blinked and opened her eyes. She tried to sit up but slumped back onto the rug.

"I'm going to get Ziad," Ally said. "Please don't leave Tom alone. Stay right here, okay?"

Nashwa covered her face with her hands. Whatever she said was drowned out by her sobs.

With Tom patting Nashwa's shoulder, Ally rushed to the front door, grabbed her jacket, and raced into the night. A light rain continued to fall, but there was very little wind. Ally made her way down the steps and then broke into a sprint. She dashed down the curving path until the light from the boathouse shined through the trees.

The sound of a hammer on metal rose out of the building.

Ally yanked the door open and froze.

Philip stood at the bench, a hammer tightly

gripped in his hand and a half-empty bottle of whiskey in front of him. Pointing at her with the hammer, he stomped forward. "What did I say I'd do if I caught you down here? You looking to break everything again?"

"Dr. Bradley is dead," Ally panted. "Where's Tim and Ziad?"

"Back up, Fruitloop. Did you say Martin is dead?"

Ally nodded. "Frank thinks it was fentanyl."

Philip screamed and threw the hammer at the wall. It shattered a bottle on the shelf and punched through the aluminum siding. "Gary! I warned everyone that druggie wasn't done." Philip ran for the door, and Ally hurried out of his way as he charged by.

"Where's Tim?" she called after him.

"My place," Philip snarled and kept running.

Ally glanced around the shop and picked up a silver wrench. It wasn't much, but it would do if she ran into Gary.

Ally ran toward Philip's cottage. The path curved and turned, rising and falling, making the way treacherous in the dark. Ally slid on a rock, catching herself just in time to avoid a twisted ankle. She rounded the corner and stopped.

Footsteps sounded ahead of her on the path. They were coming closer.

Ally crept off the trail and into the shadows. Crouching down, she waited. Her palms became slick as she clutched the metal wrench.

Huffing and puffing, Ziad ran up the hill. In his arms, he carried a large metal piece of an engine that appeared extremely heavy.

"Ziad!" Ally jumped from her hiding spot.

Ziad shrieked, dropping the part that landed with a splat in the mud. He clutched his chest and doubled over. "You scared the life out of me, Mrs. Hawthorne. Are you all right?"

"Where's Tim?"

"He said he needed to go to the house. Is he not there?"

"No. And Dr. Bradley is dead. Nashwa fainted —"

"My Nashwsa!" Ziad sprinted toward the house.

Ally tried to catch him or at least keep up, but he ran like his feet were on fire. She soon lost sight of him. She continued to run, her eyes darting around, expecting any moment for Gary to charge her from the shadows.

Reaching the base of the cement staircase leading up to the house, she stopped at the railing and took a second to catch her breath. Above her, the mansion glowed. It appeared someone had turned every light on both inside and out.

Ally jogged up the stairs. As she entered the front door, Mia exited the kitchen carrying a bucket. "Oh, Ally." Mia pouted. "It's like a bomb has gone off."

"Have you seen Tim?"

"He's with Auntie. So are Philip and Tom. Ziad is with Nashwa."

"Where are Frank and Scott?"

"Processing the crime scene. This is terrible. Just terrible. Why would Gary kill Dr. Bradley?" Mia started up the stairs. "I have to go to poor Carter. He won't stop throwing up."

Ally debated about returning to her bedroom, but the thought of being alone in that dark place sent a cold shiver racing through her. She didn't dare go warn Kim. Kim had a good hiding place, and it would be more dangerous for her if Ally were spotted coming or going from the little cottage.

Ally headed to the sitting room. The hors d'oeuvres were still out, but the room was empty. Ally crossed over to the window. She stared at the darkness beyond the faint glow of the house. Somewhere out there, a monster lurked.

Ally gasped. Who was to say that Gary was outside? He'd managed to get in to put the boxes on the plates. Was he hiding in the house now? Kim had said that she told him all about the home's layout. Ally shivered even though she was still wearing her coat.

Scott crossed the foyer. He spotted Ally and headed over. "Have you seen Tim or Ziad?"

"Tim is with his mother, and Ziad is with Nashwa."

Scott nodded. "It can wait."

"Can I help?"

Scott shook his head. "We need to move Dr. Bradley."

The memory of Dr. Bradley's death mask made her stomach flip. "I'll try to help," Ally offered.

"I don't want to put you through that. We'll deal with it."

Ally took a deep breath. Gary was loose on the island. She needed to trust someone. "Can I talk with you about something?"

Scott glanced back at the dining room door. "I only have a minute, Mrs. Hawthorne."

"I understand, but you need to know this. I'm trusting you, Officer."

Scott stood with his hands folded in front of himself. "Thank you. Go ahead."

"I was watching *Iron Man* with Tom, and it gave me an idea. I went back to the wine cellar."

A wince of dread flickered across his face. "You shouldn't have done that, Mrs. Hawthorne. I'm not a psychologist or anything, but —"

"I'm not crazy. You need to listen. I took a magnet with me." Ally reached into her pocket and pulled out the napkin. "I found this on the bench of the alcove." She opened it up. She didn't know what she expected from him, but it wasn't the one-shouldered shrug he had given her.

Scott peered at the silver fillings. "Is that metal?"

"They're pieces of the chain that fell off as I sawed. I don't care if you think I'm nuts, but this proves Kim was there."

"Mrs. Hawthorne, I need to be honest with you. I know you believe you spoke with this Kim, but we haven't found any evidence she's been here."

"This does!" She held out the napkin.

"These metal shavings don't mean anything. Philip said you took a number of tools from the boathouse. Maybe the metal is from that, or it's from twenty years ago. The point is, you are currently under psychiatric care and —"

"I'm not crazy!"

"I'm going to ask you to lower your voice. My point is that with everything going on, let us handle things. Right now, we need to deal with the situation regarding Dr. Bradley. In the morning, I'll check with Frank and Victoria about conducting another search for Kim. Under the circumstances, that's the best I can do."

Ally's wounded pride wanted to grab Scott by the arm, march him to the guest cottage, and show him Kim. But Ally clamped her mouth shut. Scott said he wanted to check with Frank and Victoria. Had her bribe already hooked him in? It may have, but the trust she'd hoped for was no longer there.

"Thank you," Ally mumbled before beating a hasty retreat out of the room.

She couldn't tell anyone about Kim. She had to wait and pray they got the boat working.

Chapter Twenty-Four

Ally woke with a start. She rubbed her eyes, amazed she'd slept at all. She glanced at the empty place on the bed beside her and remembered that Ziad told her Tim, Carter, and Philip would sleep at the boathouse. Even though the motor was still not working, Philip said that he'd worked too hard to fix the boat to let it get destroyed again. Victoria insisted the other men stand guard with him.

Ally stumbled to the bathroom and splashed water on her face. Frank announced that no one besides the three men could leave the house that night. Ally was trapped inside, unable to check on Kim hiding in the guest cottage.

Drying her face with a towel, Ally glanced out the window at the rising sun. The day was overcast and gray, but that beat dark, windy, and raining. Pushing the cabinet she had slid in front of the door out of the way, Ally unlocked the door and peered into the empty hallway. The house was quiet.

Walking to the railing above the foyer, Ally listened. The quiet ticking of the grandfather clock was the only sound. She descended the steps, her heels making a faint noise against the marble. Halfway to the kitchen, she spotted Frank slumped in a leather chair in the sitting room. Underneath his eyes were dark, almost purple circles.

"Have you been there all night?" Ally asked.

"I tried to sleep. Couldn't. You?"

"A little. Can I get you anything? A cup of coffee or something to eat?" Ally was slightly perplexed by how much the murder disturbed him. After all, he was a detective, and violent crime was part of the job.

"I'm good. I will let it get a little brighter, and then Scott and I will head down to the boathouse to give the others a hand." He stared at her for a minute, a mixture of emotions playing across his face. "You want to know something funny, Mrs. Hawthorne?" He planted his hands on the arms of the chair and groaned as he stood up. "Sometimes, when you're sitting in the dark, other things become clear."

"What do you mean?"

"Pieces are coming together. This whole thing is starting to make sense to me."

Ally jerked her head back. "Please enlighten me because none of this makes any sense."

Frank rubbed the back of his neck. "Not yet, it doesn't. But it will. Once I put the whole thing together, you'll be the first to know." He nodded and walked out of the room and down the hallway.

Ally hurried to the front door and grabbed her jacket. Maybe it was lack of sleep, or Frank was trying some detective trick on her, but either way, she didn't have time to worry about what he was talking about.

Circling the house to the rear path, Ally broke into a jog. The sun lit a small spot on the horizon in muddled purples and reds. The day was cold, but the gulls were already soaring on the wind, filling the air with their caws.

As she neared the guest cottage, wood knocking against wood made Ally's head turn toward the noise. The sound was coming from the direction of the cottage. She sped up, flying down the path, craning her neck until the house appeared.

The cottage shone in the rising sun. It looked the same as it had yesterday. She slowed down and started to breathe easier until the wind brushed her cheek. The breeze pushed the front door open, and it closed with a bang.

"Oh, no. No."

Ally sprinted the rest of the way and leaped up the steps. She shoved the door open. Pieces of broken wood lay on the floor. The lock had been smashed.

"KIM!" Ally dashed down the hallway to the back bedroom. The closet doors were open, and the carpet was bunched against the bed.

Ally hurried over to the closet. The right sliding door had been knocked off its track and was stuck open. Inside, the pile Kim had hidden underneath was strewn about.

Ally grabbed onto the door frame to keep from falling over. "KIM!" she shouted as she dashed back to the front of the house.

The front door opened in the breeze and banged shut again. Gary must have found Kim. He kicked in the door, but where could he have taken her?

She couldn't do this on her own. She needed help. Running outside, Ally sprinted back toward the house. As she crested the hill, muffled cries echoed from out front.

Ally headed toward the shouts.

Nashwa stood on the front steps, jumping up and down, waving her arms, and pointing at the sea. "A boat! A boat! In the harbor!"

Frank dashed out the front door and down the steps toward the dock. Ally raced after him. Behind her, more people shouted as they came outside and saw the ship. Ally darted past Frank as she flew down the stairs.

An old fishing boat with a red hull lay at anchor in the little bay.

Ally screamed and shouted, waving her arms as she raced toward the dock.

Tim, Philip, and Ziad were already there. But they weren't excitedly pointing or jumping. They were standing with their arms crossed and staring.

Ally's feet drummed off the wooden planks as she sped down the dock. She slowed to a halt as she saw the name of the boat. *THE SEA SPIT* was painted in black letters on the red hull.

"That's Dennis' boat. It came back?" Ally asked.

Philip spit. "That psycho Gary is goading us."

Scott and Frank reached the dock, followed by Carter, Mia, and Nashwa.

Nashwa gulped in air as she hurried over to her husband. "This is wonderful, right, Ziad?"

"We're not sure," Ziad said.

"No, it isn't." Ally's stomach clenched. "I found Kim last night, but Gary took her."

Philip rolled his eyes. "Here we go again. The cuckoo is off her meds."

Tim got right in his uncle's face. "Don't say another word about my wife."

"You think you're man enough to go head to head with me, boy?" Philip shouted.

Frank separated the two by moving between them. "We've got bigger problems. Back off. Both of you!"

Scott held his hand against his forehead, shielding

his eyes from the sun. "There's someone in the deck-house. Look at the window."

Philip squinted. "You've got a gun. Don't just stand there. Shoot the murdering bastard!"

"I can't tell who it is," Frank said. "For all we know, someone found Dennis' boat adrift. It could be anyone on there."

A woman's shrill scream carried over the water. "Help! Please, someone, help!"

Ally's hand covered her mouth. "It's Kim! That's Kim's voice! I told you, Gary got her. She was hiding in the guest cottage, but he found her. The front door was kicked in, and she was gone."

Tim started forward, and Frank grabbed his arm.

"It's a trap," Frank said. "He's trying to lure us out there."

"She needs our help." Tim kicked off his sneakers. "We can't just leave her."

"Can you even swim?" Ally asked.

"FIRE!" Mia thrust her arm out, pointing at the boat.

In the stern, near the engine, bright red flames appeared. They flickered and danced. The column of white smoke quickly turned gray and then black.

"HELP ME!" Kim shrieked.

Tim took three steps forward and dove off the dock.

"TIM!" Ally cried as Scott grabbed her around the waist.

Tim never went into the water in all the years she'd known him, not at the beach or even a pool. Yet here he was, trying frantically to swim in the open sea. The waves pushed him back, slowing his progress. He circled his arms and kicked frantically, rising up a wave and shooting down the other side.

The fire grew in intensity but stayed contained to the back of the boat. Something hissed, and bright blue flames arched high over the engine.

"It's reached the motor," Philip said. "That idiot is going to get himself killed."

"Hurry, Tim!" Ally begged.

A thunderous explosion echoed across the sea. The boat lifted partway out of the ocean as shrapnel sailed into the air and peppered the water like a handful of gravel tossed into the sea.

The hull crashed down, sending out waves that pushed Tim backward. Smoke poured across the deckhouse, but somehow, the boat was still afloat.

Tim continued to swim toward it.

A second explosion, louder and more powerful than the first, blasted the remainder of the boat to pieces.

Everyone on the dock ducked as burning debris rained down all around them. Most of the pieces landed hissing in the water, but a few struck the dock and quickly burned themselves out.

Ally frantically searched the water for any sign of Tim. With all the debris floating on the surface, it was hard to pick him out, but she finally did. He was treading water, staring at the spot where the boat had been.

"He murdered that poor girl." Mia sank to her knees. "Why? Why is he doing this?"

"Tim!" Ally shouted. "Come back! Please!"

Tim began to swim toward the dock.

"Why?" Mia asked again.

"Does a drug addict need a reason?" Philip shouted. "Maybe he wet the bed as a kid, or his mommy was mean. The guy is crazy. Crazy people don't need a reason to kill."

Carter knelt beside his wife and held her. "It's a good thing Tim isn't a good swimmer. If he were faster, he would have been on the boat."

Ally ran to the end of the dock and helped Tim out of the water. He was freezing, but the expression on his face stabbed her heart. His eyes were so dark and filled with such pain it looked like a piece of his soul had died.

"Are you hurt?" Ally asked. "Did any of those pieces hit you?" Tim stared at her like he didn't know her. He blinked and wiped the water from his face. "Tim?" Ally started checking his head and torso for injuries.

Tim shuffled forward and down the dock.

Frank lightly held Ally's arm. "Let him go. He needs time."

Ally ground her teeth. How dare anyone tell her what her husband needed? She looked at the detective, her eyes shifting over his shoulder and up to the sky. A column of black smoke rose above the trees.

Frank followed the direction she was looking.

"NO! That's the boathouse!" Philip shoved Frank out of the way, almost knocking him off the dock and into the water.

Frank, Scott, Philip, and Ally ran down the path. Branches whipped back at her as everyone sprinted along the muddy trail.

Ally heard the crackle of the fire before she saw it. Both the building and the boat were completely engulfed in flames. The fire was so intense it appeared to be one blaze.

Philip swore and shouted. He picked up a rock and flung it at the building. It crashed off metal and sent sparks kicking upward.

"Gary used the boat as a distraction," Frank said.

"He lured everyone away from the boathouse. Now he has us all trapped."

"We'll see," Philip snarled. "But I'm sick of hanging back and letting that creep throw all the punches. It's time for me to start hitting back." He stomped down the path in the direction of his cottage.

"What are you going to do?" Frank asked.

"Now, I'm the one doing the hunting."

Chapter Twenty-Five

Ally followed the drops of water through the foyer and up the stairs. The trail stopped at the bedroom door, and so did she. She knocked, waited, and then opened the door.

Tim stood dressed in new clothes, staring out the window at the sea.

Ally crossed over and sat on the edge of the bed. A profound silence descended upon the room. She didn't know what to say. Sadness, hurt, and anger swirled like the gathering rain clouds outside.

"Did you love her?" Ally whispered. The question had come from somewhere deep within her soul. Why it was the first thing she said, she didn't know, but now she needed the answer.

Tim closed his eyes and hung his head. "I didn't even know her. You'll never believe me now."

Ally twisted her wedding ring. "Kim told me about the affair."

"It's a lie. There never was one."

Ally's smoldering pain ignited into a flash of anger. She stood. "And the text message? What about the photograph? Those were all lies?"

Tim pressed his index finger and thumb against his eyes. "What does it matter? To you, they're proof."

"To anyone, they'd be proof. I could walk into any court and lay out the evidence, and they'd all find you guilty. I didn't want to believe it. I gave you every benefit of the doubt until this morning."

"What did I do this morning to change your mind?"

Ally covered her mouth with her hand. She never dreamed she'd be having this conversation with Tim. She thought he was the love of her life. A rock she'd clung to.

"What did I do?" Tim's voice had a hard edge to it.

"You confessed."

He shook his head like he still had water in his ears. "What are you talking about? I didn't have an affair. How could I confess to something I didn't even do!"

"Why did you jump into the sea? I didn't even know you could swim. But when you heard Kim cry out, you didn't hesitate to risk your life for her."

"You think I tried to save her because I loved her?" Tim's mouth curled in disgust. "Is that how little you think of ME?"

Ally stepped back. "Why else would you risk your life for someone you don't know?"

"Because it was the right thing to do. What if you or Tom or Mia were on the boat? What about Nashwa or Ziad? Do you think I'd sit by and let them burn to death? Is that the kind of person you think I am?" Tim's voice dropped to just above a whisper. "You don't know me at all." He marched over and ripped open the door. "I'm going with Uncle Philip to find Gary. Please don't leave the house." He slammed the door so hard the wall shook.

The painting of guillemots on the beach slid on its mount, coming to rest hanging at an angle.

Ally covered her mouth and sobbed. What had she done? Her mind felt like it was splitting. She lay on the bed and cried until there were no more tears to shed.

Her legs shook as she stood. Tim was right about one thing. The man she loved wouldn't have hesitated to risk his life for someone else. She knew that, but still, she doubted him now. It was obvious he had an affair. Love must have enabled him to overcome his fears of the ocean and risk his life for Kim, wasn't it?

Kim couldn't have been mistaken, but why would she lie? None of this made sense — first Dennis, and then Dr. Bradley. Now Gary had murdered Kim and trapped them on the island.

Frank said that he was starting to figure it out. She needed to find him.

Ally raced out of the room and went to the first floor. The grandfather clock echoed across the foyer. Each tick rang with an ominous tone, like the timer of a bomb slowly counting down. In between those moments, the house was oddly silent. Ally hesitated on the bottom steps. Something was wrong. She didn't know what, but the hairs rose on her neck, and a chill swept over her skin.

Someone was in the sitting room. She couldn't see or hear them but knew they were there. Creeping forward, she exhaled when, once again, she saw Frank sitting in the leather chair with its back to the open door leading to the sunroom.

"You really should get some rest, Detective," Ally said as she walked closer.

"I'm going to." Frank nodded to a chair near him. His voice was soft and quiet, like he was speaking in a library. "I was hoping you'd come down."

"I need to talk to you." Ally moved the chair so she was facing him. "You said you might know why Gary is doing this. Do you?"

"Is Tim around?"

"He went with Philip."

"Fair enough. I think you should be the one to tell him anyway." Frank took a deep breath and winced.

"Are you okay?"

"There's something I need to get off my chest. Let me start by saying I'm not a bad guy."

"I apologize for accusing you of kidnapping Kim that night. I was wrong."

"It's all right. I'm glad Scott didn't believe you. He trusted me. He's a smart kid. He'll go far as a cop. He knew I have an ankle holster. That's why he told me to give up my sidearm."

Ally stuck her tongue in her cheek. "So he didn't trust me?"

"Can you blame him? The whole thing sounded crazy, and so did you. But it all makes sense now."

"Not to me." Ally leaned forward to hear him, putting her elbows on her knees. "Can you please explain your theory?"

"It's all connected to the disappearance of Jane Nelson, Tim's former girlfriend. How much has Tim told you about Jane?"

"He said they dated in high school. She didn't live here. It was a divorce situation. They broke up the summer of his freshman year. He never saw her again, but a year after that, you showed up at the house looking for her."

"Jane lived with her grandmother. Jane's mother

died of an overdose when she was little. Her father, who lived on the mainland, was on and off the wagon. Off mostly, but Jane's grandmother still sent her here every summer. I didn't know any of this until Jane went missing and the grandmother called. She said Jane flew up here to talk to Tim Hawthorne and never came home." Frank swallowed and closed his eyes.

Ally held her breath. The more she learned about Jane, the more she cared for the poor girl.

"It's a small town, and people talk, but the only person I found at the docks who said they saw Jane was Dennis. He even described what she was wearing. He said she seemed like a nice kid. And he didn't bat an eye when he told me he ferried her to the island. But everyone out here swore no girl ever came out. Victoria, Tim, Philip, Carter, Mia, and Martin were all here, but none saw anything."

"You think they were lying?"

"I knew they were lying. One of them was, anyway. But you see, Dennis changed his story. He said he was drunk and got confused. I had no leads and nothing to go on."

Frank stared down at his hands resting in his lap. He wet his lips and sighed. "And then I got promoted to detective second grade. I got a big raise and a new official car. New computer, too. But the thing is, I had only been a detective for three months. I couldn't figure out how I got the promotion until the Chief asked me when I would close Jane's case. Then it all clicked."

"So you stopped looking?"

Frank nodded. "I called the grandmother to tell her I was closing the case. She was heartbroken. Then she dropped a bombshell — Jane left the year before because she had gotten pregnant."

Ally's hands tightened on the arms of the chair. The room seemed to shift.

"Jane never wanted her father to know, so the grandmother didn't tell me at first. She'd given the baby up for adoption."

Ally swayed in her seat. She held onto the chair to keep from tumbling out. "Are you saying Tim was the father?"

"I can't be sure. I talked to Victoria about it, and she threatened me with everything from having the Chief fire me to suing me for defamation. So, not only did I stop looking, but I looked the other way. Until three days ago."

"When Gary came to the police station."

"Yeah. I think I saw it as a chance for redemption. When you sell your soul, you tend not to sleep well at night afterward. It never occurred to me it was a setup."

Ally's eyes widened. "Gary lured you out here?"

Frank nodded. "Tim's thirty-eight. Gary's twenty-two."

"You think Gary is Tim's son?"

"I can't say for sure, but I figure Gary thinks that. And he's looking to avenge his mother. Look at who has been targeted so far. They're all connected to Jane. Dennis changed his story. Martin Bradley, he was here the night Jane came out but swore he never saw her."

"You're right. That's what Kim thought. When she was hiding in the cottage, she said that Gary was obsessed with Jane. When Gary found out Kim worked here, he started dating her. He got the alarm code and knew the layout of the house."

"The missing piece." Frank sighed. "And Gary killed her because Tim was having an affair—"

"Tim swears he wasn't. He promised me."

"If I had a nickel for every time a guilty person swore to me they were innocent, I'd be on an island in the Bahamas right now." He chuckled and winced. "But even if Tim wasn't, Gary may have believed it. I think he's going scorched earth and killing everyone involved in his mother's disappearance and everyone that Tim cares about. That's why I wanted to talk to you. You need to be careful, and you need to tell Tim about his son."

"But Gary doesn't even know his mother is dead. Maybe Jane came here and left?"

Frank shook his head. "Dennis dropped her off. I questioned anyone with a boat, and nobody picked her up. Jane never left this island. That I'm sure of."

"You need to tell Tim."

Frank sighed and shook his head. "I can't."

"It's your job." Ally's hand smacked the arm of her chair.

Frank lifted his chin. "Not anymore. The chickens have come home to roost."

Ally hadn't realized how pale he'd become. "Are you sure you're all right?"

"Tell Scott I'm sorry I got him involved in this mess." Frank's head slumped forward, and his chin rested on his chest.

"Detective?" Ally stood up and touched his arm. He didn't move. "Frank?" She shook him hard, but he didn't respond. "HELP! HELP ME!"

Running footsteps sounded in the hallway, and Scott raced into the room. "What happened? What's wrong with him?"

"I don't know. He was talking and just stopped."

"Frank! Frank, can you hear me?" Scott grabbed Frank's shoulders and pulled him slightly forward. Leather tore. Scott peered at the back of the chair and gasped.

Ally walked forward. Like passing the scene of an accident, she didn't want to look, but she couldn't turn away. In the back of the chair, the end of a crossbow bolt protruded, its feathers and notch visible. Blood dripped down the shaft and onto the floor.

Ally couldn't breathe. Gary killed Frank. And if Frank was correct, Gary was coming after her, too.

Chapter Twenty-Six

Ally stood staring at Frank's body pinned to the chair by a crossbow bolt through his back. Her body had gone numb and felt so heavy it was weighing her down to the floor.

Ziad and Carter hovered in the doorway, a look of horror on their faces as well.

Scott lifted his hand, motioning for them to stay where they were. "I shouldn't move him now." His voice broke. He removed his phone from his pocket. "I need to process the crime scene. I'll call when I need you."

Ally motioned for the others to follow her out of the room.

"Was that an arrow?" Ziad whispered after closing the door.

"It was a crossbow bolt," Carter said. "I guess Victoria was right. It did still work."

Ally remembered the shield with the crossbow and axe that Carter had knocked off the wall. Someone had moved it to the sunroom, and Gary must have found it.

"He's picking us off, one by one," Ziad said.

"Why?" Carter's voice rose.

"Frank said it had something to do with the disappearance of Jane Nelson," Ally said.

"Tim's girlfriend? That was in high school." Carter said.

"We're not talking about getting over a crush," Ally said. "Jane's never been seen again. Most likely, she's dead. Gary is killing anyone connected to her disappearance."

Carter scratched the side of his head. "So this Gary is killing people who were here that night?"

Ziad's shoulders rose to the bottom of his ears as a grin dawned on his face. He lifted his hands over his head like he scored a touchdown. "Nashwa and I weren't here. We had nothing to do with any girl. We're safe!"

Carter crossed his arms. "There's a little problem with your theory, Ziad. That woman Kim wasn't here either. And Gary blew her up."

Ally couldn't believe how calmly Carter was taking everything in. She had expected him to run off screaming when he realized Gary was after him.

Ziad frowned. "But Gary said Kim was his girlfriend. Why did he kill her?"

Ally swallowed down her shame. People's lives were at stake. They deserved to know the truth. "Gary killed Kim to get at my husband. Tim was having an affair with Kim."

"But why does he hate Tim?" Ziad asked.

"Gary hates Tim and everyone here the night Jane disappeared, especially Tim. Jane was Gary's mother. He wants revenge."

Carter did a double-take. "Wait a minute! Do you think Gary is after Mia and me?"

"You were here that night," Ziad said.

"But we were down at the guest cottage! We'd

just gotten back from our honeymoon and tend to get a little vocal. Do you know what I mean? So we weren't *really* here. I never saw the girl. I'll swear to that on a stack of Bibles," Carter said.

"Does Gary know that?" Ally asked.

Carter took two steps back. "I need to tell him. Somehow. I have to let Mia know." Carter raced out of the room and down the hallway.

Ziad shook his head. "My poor Nashwa. She's falling apart." He shuffled off toward the kitchen. "This is going to push her over the edge."

Ally tried to calm her rapid breathing and scattered thoughts. She had to warn the others. She marched down the hallway. She stopped and knocked at Tom's door. "Tom, it's me. Ally."

The door opened a crack. "Ally?" Tim called out from inside.

"Tim! I didn't know you were here."

The door whipped open. Only Tom stood there laughing. He lowered his voice and said, "Ally?" He sounded just like Tim. Somehow, his sweet grin lightened the gloom clinging to her heart. "Do you want to watch a movie?"

"I can't right now." Ally walked into the room. "But I need you to do me a great big favor." She crossed to the door leading to the cellar and locked it.

"What's that?"

"I want you to stay in here and not open the door for any stranger." She tried to push the bookshelf in front of the cellar door, but it was too heavy.

Tom set his shoulder against it and slid it so it blocked the door. "I'm strong!"

"Yes, you are." Ally smiled. "When I go, can you put the bureau in front of the door to the hallway?"

"Why? Do you want to watch a movie? It's another Captain America!" He pointed at his T-shirt's red, white, and blue shield.

"I can't right now. But this is very important. Can you do that for me?"

"Is everything okay? Do you need help?"

Ally thought for a minute and shook her head. "You're my superhero. When I really, really need you, I'll call."

Tom puffed out his chest. "I'll be ready!"

Ally squeezed his hand and opened the door. "Remember, don't open it for a stranger. Lock it and then push the bureau in front."

Tom flexed again. "I got this!"

"You can do it! You're strong like Captain America."

"He's my favorite." Tom grinned.

Ally shut the door, waited until she heard the lock turn and wood scrape across the floor, then returned to the foyer.

Victoria stood staring at the closed sitting room door. She didn't look at Ally when she spoke. "The madman killed Frank."

Ally pictured the detective slumping forward, the arrow pinning him to the chair.

"Frank came and spoke with me this morning," Victoria said. "The stress and not sleeping had gotten to him. He cracked. Frank could have been a great detective, but he woman blineded by his conspiracy theories, wondering who shot Kennedy, who murdered Hoffa, and if Elvis was really dead. The answers were so simple he chose not to believe them." Victoria met Ally's gaze. "Oswald, the Mafia, and yes, Elvis has left the building. If he confided his preposterous idea to you regarding Gary's motive, I suggest you forget it."

"Frank wasn't wrong, and neither was Kim. She

said Gary was obsessed with discovering what happened to Jane; now I know why. Gary isn't going to stop killing people, Victoria. I need to know the truth. Did you pay Frank off so he'd drop Jane's case?"

"No, I did not." Victoria crossed her arms. "I paid the Chief of Police to bribe Frank to close his frivolous witch hunt. It cost me a great deal of money."

Ally closed her eyes. Her mother-in-law was splitting hairs, but at least she was being honest. "And Dennis? You paid him to change his story?"

"Dennis, I gave nothing to. My brother, on the other hand, has different methods of being persuasive than I have. Since you are a member of this family, I have decided it is time for you to know the truth."

Ally's back stiffened as she braced herself for whatever she was about to learn.

"Let me begin by stressing how greatly disappointed I am in you. Tim had nothing to do with Jane's disappearance or Kim's. I know my son. He never had an affair, but now that she is dead, the proof you seek may have perished with her. I am sorry she was murdered, but it wasn't my son's fault. The blame lies at her boyfriend's feet."

Ally could feel her cheeks burning. "Gary used Kim to gather information about the island and everyone on it. He wants revenge for his mother's death. You promised me the truth. Did Jane come here the night she disappeared?"

Victoria's eyes hardened into black diamonds. "I explained that I was taking you into my confidence, and I do not lie. Jane was never here that night. But there is something that I kept from my son and you. A year before she disappeared and shortly before she called off the relationship with Tim, she came here. She appeared on my doorstep with a fake sob story of being expectant. She had no proof it was Tim's, and I had no desire for my son to have a baby mama. If you're wondering if I paid her off, I did. I provided an airline ticket for her to return home and offered a more than significant amount of compensation. My only condition was that she stay away from my son, and she agreed. To my knowledge, she upheld her end of the bargain. End of story."

"What happened? Did Jane come back looking for more money?"

"No, she didn't. Did Frank mention I hired my own private investigators? From the look on your face, I'd say no. Let me tell you their conclusion. Jane did have a child and gave it up for adoption. A year later, she returned to Maine but not here. Her father had relocated to Portland, and she flew to Maine to visit him. Do you know where he currently resides? The penitentiary. He's incarcerated for the rape and murder of a fifteen-year-old girl — no, not Jane. But is it really that great of a leap to conclude an animal like that would be capable of anything in a drunken state, including the death of his own daughter?"

Ally glanced down at her hands. They shook. Her palms were sweaty, and her breathing was labored.

"I agree that Gary is likely Jane's child," Victoria continued. "But that does not make Tim the father or any of us responsible for Jane's disappearance. Gary is obviously deranged. Who knows what is going on in his mind? But we are the victims, not him. Where is Tim now?"

"He said he was going to help Philip look for Gary."

Victoria slowly inhaled and glared at the closed doors of the sitting room, then suddenly marched over and shoved them open.

Scott jumped and almost dropped his phone.

"If you don't stop processing this crime scene, I'm certain there will be another," Victoria said. "I will fetch Ziad and Carter to handle the body. You will help my son and brother as they track down the murderer, which, let me remind you, is your job, and it's your fault that he is loose."

Scott glanced at Frank's body, stuffing his phone into his pocket. "Tell them not to remove the arrow from the chair," he said before leaving the room and exiting the house.

Victoria turned to Ally. "I will get Ziad, go find Carter."

Ally nodded.

Victoria seized Ally's arm in a surprisingly firm grip. "If you still doubt me, let it go until this matter is resolved. If not, neither of us may make it off this island."

Chapter Twenty-Seven

Ally rushed up the stairs and down the hallway. Carter and Mia's room was on the house's far left side. She stopped in front of the door and knocked.

It swung freely open as soon as her knuckles hit the wood. Ally's heart raced as she stepped inside. Clothes were strewn across the floor, drawers were pulled out, and their contents scattered around the room. It was as if a tornado had swept through the bedroom, leaving nothing untouched.

"Carter? Mia?" Ally called out.

Above her, the wood creaked. She stared at the high ceiling. The chandelier swayed slightly. Dust shimmered in the light as it fell to the carpet.

"Carter?"

Muffled whispers echoed from above. The chandelier shook, raining more dust onto Ally's face. Coughing, blinking, and rubbing her eyes, Ally moved out of the way and toward the door.

Ally tried to picture the layout of the house. The only thing above them was an attic. Tim had shown her once, and it was nothing but crossbeams with some narrow boards above the plaster. You couldn't walk up there.

"Mia! Carter!" Ally shouted.

The plaster in the ceiling cracked and then split. A shoe appeared, followed by a leg.

Carter screamed.

Dust and chunks of plaster rained down.

Ally dashed next to the wall just as Carter plunged through the ceiling and landed on top of the end table next to the bed, breaking it. He rolled on the carpet, shrieking and holding his knee in pain.

"Baby!" Mia called out from the hole in the ceiling. She stepped forward. The plaster broke under her feet. She fell screaming into the room. She landed on Carter, and they both groaned.

Ally stared down at them in disbelief. They were covered in dust and plaster.

Carter held up a shaking hand. "Please don't kill us, Ally. We always liked you."

"Me?" Ally's voice rose high. "Why would I kill you?"

"There's no reason to!" Mia said. "We weren't even here that night."

Ally touched her hand to her chest. "I didn't kill anyone. Gary did."

"We're not a hundred percent sure of that," Carter grimaced as he pulled himself into a sitting position. "Anybody could be the killer — including you."

"Except Tom," Mia added. "It isn't him. I'm sure of that."

Carter shrugged. "Tom's still on my list."

"Shut up," Ally said. "Why were you in the attic?"

"We were hiding," Carter said.

"At least trying to," Mia said. "I told him everyone would know we were up there with him stomping around like an elephant."

"Ziad gave me the idea," Carter admitted. "We saw him and Nashwa run across the backyard. It would be safer getting out of Dodge, but why freeze to death when you can hide where it's warm?"

"They're not safe outside. Gary's out there!" Ally exclaimed.

"Isn't safe inside either," Carter said. "Frank was inside, and it didn't do him any good."

Something fell out of the attic. A loud pop and breaking glass made them all jump. Ally stared at the floor, puzzled, as a wet spot appeared on the carpet surrounded by broken glass, and another bottle rolled out of the ceiling and shattered on the floor beside it.

"Not the Scotch!" Carter groaned.

"We took supplies," Mia explained.

"We had to flush all our pick-me-ups after Dr. Bradley died," Carter said. "We had nothing to do with his murder, of course, but Frank thought we might have. And if he searched our room, we couldn't have him finding them."

"Stop talking and let me think." Ally bit her lip.

"There's nothing to think about," Carter said. "We have no phones. There is no way of communicating with the mainland. And no boat. The only thing we can do is hide."

Ally nodded. "You're right, but you picked a horrible spot."

"I told you so," Mia stood up and dusted herself off, sending a cloud of white particles onto Carter.

"It was a great place until it wasn't," Carter said. He tried to stand but grabbed his knee and sank back down, whimpering in pain.

Mia knelt beside him. "Are you all right?"

Carter flexed his leg and winced. "I don't think I can make it far."

"You don't have to," Ally said. "The laundry room is two doors down. You can hide in there. If Mia pushes the machines against the door, I doubt anyone could make it through."

"But what if they did? We'd be trapped," Carter said.

"No, you aren't. There's a dumbwaiter in the back of the room. I remember being so jealous of it when Tim first showed me. If someone comes to the door, you can get in the dumbwaiter and lower yourselves down to the first floor."

Mia helped Carter onto the edge of the bed. "Can you stand?"

"I think so." Carter looked at Ally. "Come with us."

Ally shook her head. "I have to warn Tim and try to stop Gary."

"Stop him? How? He's a giant compared to you," Carter said.

"Gary is trying to find out what happened to his mother, Jane. I'm going to try to talk to him. Do you two know anything about that night?"

Mia looked at the floor, and Carter clamped his mouth shut.

Ally clenched her fists. "You do know something! Tell me! It may save us all."

Carter held up his hand. "We don't know anything. I swear. We were both drunk and passed out. It was right after our honeymoon, and we had sex like seven times."

Mia shook her head.

Carter's mouth fell open. "I remember you telling me that specifically. I'm very proud of that feat."

"I lied. It was once, and you fell asleep."

"Enough about your sex life," Ally snapped. "Tell me whatever you know."

Carter took a deep breath. "The next day, everyone was acting so strange. It was obvious something untoward had occurred, but no one would tell us anything."

"And they never did," Mia added. "Their behavior was suspicious, but we had no proof of anything."

"Who was acting strangely?" Ally asked.

Mia and Carter stared at each other for a moment. It was weird like they were each searching for the memory in the other person's eyes.

"Uncle Philip," Mia said. "He and Carter got into a huge row over our firepit."

"We had a little patio out in the yard where Mia and I would sit at night and have a few cocktails by the fire," Carter explained. "That weekend, Philip tore the whole firepit down. He said he needed the bricks to renovate the wine cellar. And then he brought us back a pile of broken bricks."

Mia scowled. "When poor Carter complained, Philip hit him."

Their answer hit Ally like a punch in the face. She blinked rapidly, closed her eyes, and pinched the bridge of her nose.

"Are you okay?" Carter asked.

Ally nodded as he tried to process these facts. "Both of you go to the laundry room. Use the machines to block the door, and don't let anyone in."

Carter looked up to the hole in the ceiling. "What about our supplies? Do you think it's safe for Mia to go back up and get a bottle or two?"

"No." Ally grabbed the doorknob. "Now get moving."

"Where are you going?" Mia asked.
"To find answers."

Chapter Twenty-Eight

Ally rushed down the hallway. She needed to find Tim. He could be telling her the truth. He might know nothing about Jane's disappearance, and she owed it to him to give him the benefit of the doubt.

She stopped at her bedroom and shoved open the door. The room stood empty. Turning around, she noticed the painting of the guillemots on the beach hanging at an angle next to the door. Tim had knocked the frame askew when he slammed the door.

Ally froze. An electrical wire peeked out behind the painting. It protruded from a small hole in the wall and ran along the picture frame. In the corner of the wood, what Ally had thought was a polished stone inset was really a camera lens.

Her first instinct was to rip the wire out, but she blocked that impulse and instead stepped out of view of the lens.

What should she do? Someone had been watching the room. Could they hear what she said? Were the other rooms in the house bugged?

Stepping into the hallway, Ally pulled the door closed. It felt like iron bands tightened around her chest as she marched down the hallway. Gary, the murdering creep, was also a peeping Tom. He had been watching them, listening to them. Why?

Kim's words echoed in her mind.

Gary won't stop. He's fixated on finding out what happened to Jane. She's the key. If Gary is after the truth, maybe that's what can stop him.

She descended the staircase to the first floor. That was why Gary bugged the rooms. He was trying to figure out what happened to his mother. How long had he been planning this?

Ally pictured Gary listening to the conversations and watching the inhabitants of the house, hoping they'd reveal some information about what happened to his mother.

Kim was right. Jane was the key. If Ally was correct and she found Jane, would that convince Gary to stop his murderous rampage?

Ally hurried through the foyer and into the kitchen. Turning the cellar light on, she gazed down the stairs, feeling like she was about to head into a mine. She swallowed, took three deep breaths, and started down.

At the foot of the stairs, she glanced at the shelves filled with tools. Was it only two nights ago when she searched them for a saw?

Grabbing a crowbar, she crept toward the wine cellar. The door was open, and the lights were still on. She crossed to the alcove in the back and stared at the floor. When she first noticed the incorrect bricks that were used, as an appraiser, she'd blamed poor contractors who didn't know what they were doing.

Now, she wasn't so sure.

Scrapping the crowbar back and forth along the mortar line, she chipped pieces out. Once she had removed enough, she wedged the bar's tip into the gap she created and pried it back and forth. Slowly, it set-tled between two bricks.

She grabbed the crowbar with both hands and pushed. The mortar cracked. The bricks ground to-gether, and one lifted at the corner. She cleared a two-foot section of bricks by twisting, pulling, prying, and pushing. The ground beneath was fine sand but packed hard. Using the crowbar like a sledgehammer, she bashed through the hard crust and pulled that away in large sections. Switching between breaking with the crowbar and scooping with her hands, she quickly created a hole.

The sand scratched her fingers, but it became easier with every inch she dug. She flung sand up and out of the hole until her fingers touched plastic.

Ally gasped. She pulled her hands out like she'd touched a snake. She closed her eyes and balled her hands into fists. She didn't want to do this, but she had no choice. Reaching into the hole, she scooped until a clear corner of a plastic sheet appeared.

Her heart pounded, and her mouth was so dry it was difficult to breathe. Her hands trembled as she grabbed hold of the sheet and pulled. Sand slid down the sides of the hole as the sheeting lifted. Planting her feet, she seized the plastic with both hands and pulled.

The sheet jerked partially free. Inside the clear plastic were the skeletal remains of a human arm and hand. Pink fabric covered part of the wrist, and a silver charm bracelet.

Ally let go and stared in horror at the remains of Jane Nelson.

Frank was right. Jane had come here that night and never left the island. Someone had killed her. She didn't know who murdered Jane, but it was Philip who had buried her in the basement.

"You couldn't leave it alone, could you?"

Ally froze. She didn't scream. She couldn't even breathe.

Philip stood in the middle of the wine cellar, glaring at her. He ambled forward like an angry bear who found a fox in his cave. He held a shotgun in his right hand.

"You could have simply shut your mouth and stayed in your room. But no. That wasn't good enough for you." He reeked of whiskey.

Ally's fingers tightened on the crowbar. Philip was too far to strike him with it.

"I'm family, Philip. I won't tell anyone." Ally knelt in the sand, staring up at him.

"I know you won't. But you're not blood. Tim can always remarry." He stopped out of her reach.

Ally threw the crowbar as hard as she could. She aimed for his face, but it flew over his head and clattered on the cement floor.

Philip laughed. "I'm glad you tried something. I would have been disappointed if you'd just rolled over. Now turn around and face the wall." He strolled forward and stopped. The shotgun dangled in his right hand, the barrel pointing at the ground, and his finger resting on the trigger. All he needed to do was pivot the gun up, and she'd be dead.

She'd never fired a shotgun. The only thing she knew about them was that they kicked like a mule. She'd seen videos of people breaking their shoulders when they didn't hold the gun tightly when they fired it.

Ally pressed her hands together like she was praying and crawled forward, begging for her life.

"Please, Philip. I swear that I'll — " She lunged forward, grabbed the barrel of the shotgun with both hands, and yanked it toward the ground.

Philip's finger hit the trigger, and it fired.

The barrel of the gun shot out of her grip. The boom in the enclosed room was so loud that it felt like someone had stuffed her head inside a bell and rung it with a sledgehammer.

The shotgun kicked straight up. The butt struck Philip in the face. Sand, dust, and smoke filled the air. Philip flew backward and crashed onto the cement. He lay on his back, still clutching the weapon. Blood streamed out of his nose and mouth.

Ally sprinted for the door.

Philip screamed. His cry was filled with pain and rage. It rang off the walls and followed her out of the room.

Ally grabbed the door frame and spun out into the cellar. She crashed into the boxes, sending them tumbling to the floor. She raced for the stairs.

The shotgun fired again. The boxes outside the wine cellar blasted to pieces.

Ally grabbed the railing. Momentum swung her around. Her shoulder felt like it would pop out of the socket, but she hung on as she pivoted and saw the safety of the kitchen above. She flew up the stairs, taking them three at a time.

Another blast struck the stone wall behind her. Pellets and chunks of rock ricocheted against the cement and pinged off the metal shelves.

Ally reached the top step, spun, slammed the door, and slid the locking latch into place. She doubted it would stop Philip but hoped it would slow him down. Racing across the kitchen, she started to head outside and skidded to a stop. She remembered

Scott pointing his gun at Frank and demanding he turn over his sidearm.

Ally dashed across the foyer and into the sitting room. Frank's body still sat in the chair, pinned to the back with the crossbow bolt. She grabbed his pant leg, yanked it up, and silently cheered when she saw the pistol in his ankle holster.

The sound of breaking wood came from the kitchen as Philip attempted to break the door down.

Ripping the gun free, Ally ran into the sunroom and over to the window. She shoved it open, scrambled outside, and fell to the ground. Keeping low, she sprinted across the backyard. The path around the island came into view. She streaked past the little wooden bench next to the tree when pellets peppered the leaves above her head. The reverb from the shotgun rolled across the grass like thunder.

Ally's feet became a blur as she ran faster than she ever had. Clutching the gun tighter, she headed deeper into the island. Now, she had two madmen after her.

The path curved gently downhill, and she sped up. She needed to find Tim and warn him. As she raced down the trail, the day continued to darken. It had to be at least an hour before sunset.

Twisting and turning, the path followed the cliffs along the island. At one point, it seemed like she was headed back toward the house, but the route curved around, and she was again next to the sea.

The snub nose gun in her hand was heavy. As she passed a large, dead stump, she debated hiding behind it and ambushing Philip as he came by. The six-shot pistol was supposed to be used at close range but was no match for Philip's shotgun. The last thing she wanted to do was get in a close-quarters shootout.

The pistol was her last line of defense. Her feet and mind were the better weapons right now.

Pellets blasted the tree to her left. Pieces of bark flew off like shrapnel, striking the bushes and path.

Ally ducked low and raced off the trail.

How had he caught up to her so fast? He must have taken a shortcut. Philip grew up on the island. He knew it better than anyone and certainly better than she did.

Branches sliced her skin, and briars caught in her hair and tore at her clothes as Philip charged through the brush like a mad bear. His heavy footsteps thudded behind her, getting closer with every passing second.

Ally's heart raced as she stumbled over a fallen log, nearly losing her grip on the gun. Off the trail, Philip had the speed advantage. She couldn't outrun him forever. She needed a plan.

As she ducked and weaved through the thick brush, she reached the cliff's edge. Forty feet below, the waves crashed onto the narrow beach.

"Give it up, Ally. You're not getting off this island alive," he taunted. "You've got nowhere to run."

It was too far to jump. Ally scanned the cliffside. The ground had eroded to her left, dislodging a tall pine tree that had toppled over. Some tree roots clung to the soil, causing it to dangle like a Christmas ornament above the beach, its top almost reaching the sand below.

She sprinted for the tree and scanned the woods as she ran.

Branches snapped, and bushes swayed as Philip barreled toward her through the brush.

Her Marine father had drilled it into her head that you never shoot at something you can't see, but she figured he'd make an exception in this case. Ally aimed at the noise and pulled the trigger. She fired off two shots, then jammed the gun into her pocket.

She grabbed the rough bark at the base of the upside-down pine tree. The moment her sneakers landed on the mossy surface, she slid. The skin of her hands burned as she tried vainly to stop. Her feet hit a branch, and she pitched backward. Feeling like gravity had reversed, she fell through the branches of the inverted tree. Bouncing off one and then another, she grasped a limb only to have it snap in her hand.

She bashed off another branch and fell onto the beach, slamming against the wet sand. The impact knocked all the air from her lungs. She tried to draw a breath, but it felt like something vital to the breathing process inside her was broken. Her mouth hung open, but no air came in or out. Her diaphragm spasmed, and she gasped. Pain squeezed her stomach, and she vomited.

Ally lay with her face resting against the icy sand. Freezing water lapped at her ankles. She crawled forward, hiding beneath the branches in case Philip fired at her.

The waves rolled along the shore, and birds cawed above, but she didn't hear him. She pressed her bleeding hands against her shirt. She shook uncontrollably but forced herself to check for injuries. A nasty cut ran along the side of her left arm. Her right side was scraped raw and bleeding, but not severely. When she moved her left arm, she winced as pain raced down her wrist from her elbow. Much to her relief, her legs and feet felt fine.

Grabbing onto a tree limb, Ally's legs wobbled, but she managed to stand. She doubted Philip would try to climb down the tree because of his weight, but he'd find another way onto the beach. She couldn't stay here.

Crouching and sticking to the shadows of the cliff, Ally made her way along the shore. The sky continued to darken, and sprinkles of rain fell. Salt stung her eyes and made each cut burn. The sandy beach ended, changing to grayish-green rock underfoot. She stopped at the edge of a small lagoon spanning about forty yards. There was no circling it. She could either climb the cliff or cross the cold pool. It didn't look deep, but with night coming, the last thing she wanted was to get soaking wet.

Yanking off her shoes and socks, she rolled up her pants and started across. The rocks were slick, and the going was slow. Her feet were soon numb, and the chill raced up her legs. Her teeth clicked together as they chattered, but she couldn't clamp her mouth together hard enough to get them to stop. The heat drained entirely from her body. Even her head felt like it was freezing up. Pushing herself forward, she reached the other side.

Ally sat down on a rock and did her best to dry her wet feet with the sleeve of her shirt. Once she finished, she tugged her socks and shoes back on. The wind shifted, and a foul stench wafted across her face. She gagged. Pulling her shirt up over her nose, she peered over the rock. Lying on his back, partially submerged, Gary's corpse rotted on the rocks. His eyes were gone, and it was apparent he'd been dead awhile.

Ally gagged again and hurried several yards away. The truth slammed into her with the force of a speeding truck. All the strength evaporated from her legs, and she sank to her knees. Gary was dead and had been dead for days. He couldn't be responsible for killing the others!

Ally's breath came in short gasps. Between the freezing and the sudden mind trip, she felt ready to faint. She closed her eyes, stuck her hands underneath her arms, and forced herself to calm down.

Think. Assess the situation. Who killed Gary? Philip had shot at her and buried Jane, so it wasn't a stretch to think that he killed Gary, but Philip had no reason to kill the others. Or did he? If Philip killed Jane, he did have a motive to kill Dennis. Dennis witnessed both Jane and Kim come out to the island. Victoria admitted that Philip had paid Dennis off before and would do so again. Had Dennis refused the offer this time?

Philip also hated law enforcement, and Frank was searching for Kim. Maybe he thought Frank was close to solving the case.

But why would Philip kill Martin? Why kidnap and kill Kim?

Ally opened her eyes. Her head spun. She held her hands against her temples like somehow she could prevent her mind from flying away with the strength of her fingers.

Just because Ally didn't know the reason Philip killed everyone, it didn't mean that he wasn't responsible. Either way, Philip wanted Ally dead, and now he was the prime suspect in killing Gary, Dennis, Frank, Martin, and Kim.

She needed to warn the others.

Chapter Twenty-Nine

Ally needed to return to the house to warn the others about Philip. Where were Tim and Scott? Were they still out searching for Gary? What if they ran into Philip, not knowing he may be the real killer? Ally drove the thought from her head. They had been gone hours, and now that it was almost dark, surely they'd head back to the house where she could warn them — if she could make it there.

She raced along the bottom of the cliff until she saw the trail curving up from the beach. The last light of day gleamed in the distance, and she smiled at the cloud cover. Since she was being hunted, darkness would give her an advantage over Philip.

The trail was steep. Slipping in the sand, she pitched forward. She landed with her arms stretched out before her, cushioning the fall. Her palms sank into the sandy mud. Her cuts burned as the saltwater seeped into them. She shook off her hands, holding them out in the cold air, but it did little to dull the pain.

Getting back to her feet, she raced up the slope and jogged along the trail. The bare tree branches stood silhouetted against the sky. Several bats darted overhead. She reached the fork in the path. One way curved around to the boathouse, the other to the cottages. Both eventually led back to the house.

Ally picked the route that would bring her past Philip's cottage. She doubted the arrogant man would expect to find her on his doorstep.

As the sky faded to night, her pace slowed. Her eyes adjusted to the dark path. She could make out the different shades of night, from the gray sky to the black of the trees, and the path's lighter shadows. She used her outstretched right hand to feel along the trail, and she listened to the crunch of gravel beneath her feet to be sure she didn't wander off it.

She hurried by Philip's darkened cottage. The path wound down in front of the guest cottage. Inside, a flashlight flicked on and off. It was only a moment, but she saw Ziad and Nashwa in the kitchen.

Ally ducked low and listened. That light glowed like a lighthouse beam in the dark. Philip may have noticed it. Should she warn them? They had run away without letting anyone know they were going. They chose to go alone, so it wasn't her responsibility now.

Creeping past the cottage, her conscience pricked her heart. Nashwa had been falling apart ever since Dr. Bradley died. And who wouldn't? They fled the house in a panic. They were probably looking for a place to hide, like Mia and Carter.

The clouds parted, and an almost full moon peeked out. Having been so dark before, the cottage practically glowed. Ally glanced back. She needed to warn them about Philip. If he saw the flashlight and came there, and they still believed Gary was the killer, they might let Philip in...

Ally rushed back down the trail and to the cottage's back door. Through the window, she watched Ziad open a hatch in the closet floor. It must lead to a crawlspace beneath the house. A wave of guilt washed over her. Had Ally known about the crawlspace, she could have hidden Kim there. If she had done that, Kim would still be alive. Pushing her regret aside, she opened the back door.

Ziad gasped. He held his arms over his head. "Don't kill us! Please. I always liked you, Mrs. Hawthorne."

"Me, too!" Nashwa cried.

"Quiet!" Ally whispered, slipping inside.

"You're not going to kill us?" Ziad asked. "Then come with us. We're hiding!"

"I can't. There isn't time to explain, so listen. Gary is dead, and he wasn't the killer. Philip might be. He's chasing me with a shotgun. I have to warn the others, too. You hide."

"Okay! I hide." Nashwa disappeared without another word.

"Philip? Mrs. Hawthorne's brother?" Ziad crouched beside the hole in the floor, shaking his head. "He was a foul man, but a murderer?"

A sob echoed out of the hole. Nashwa gasped for air and choked on her tears, the sound filling the kitchen.

"You need to keep Nashwa quiet. Philip is out there hunting for me. If I saw your flashlight, he may have too. I don't know what's going on, so stay hidden."

Nashwa's arm popped out of the hole like a gopher. Her fingers snagged the cuff on Ziad's pants. She pulled and whimpered, "Hide, Ziad. We need to hide."

"Thank you for warning us. Thank you," Ziad said.

"Go!" Ally held her finger to her lips as Ziad dropped into the crawl space and pulled the hatch closed. Ally slipped out the back door into the night, praying Ziad could keep Nashwa silent.

Hurrying back to the path, Ally started jogging again. With the light from the moon, it was easier to see her way. She ran up the hill and glanced back. Down below, a shadow moved on the path approaching the cottage. Short and broad-shouldered, Philip's bear-like silhouette was easy to differentiate between Tim and Scott, the only other men out on the island.

Philip stopped and watched the guest house.

Ally's heart thundered in her chest as her own voice screamed in her head, *There's nothing else you can do for them. Run! You warned Ziad and Nashwa. If she cries and Philip hears her, that's on her, not you. Run!*

Somewhere, deep inside, a calmer voice whispered, *Is that the right thing to do?*

Philip crept forward. He turned at the walkway and headed toward the cottage's front door.

Her instinct for self-preservation shouted all the louder, but she listened to the soft, calm voice and drew her gun. She had to try to save Ziad and Nashwa.

Ally planted her feet, raised the pistol, and aimed at the shadow. She exhaled slowly. Once all of the air was out of her lungs, she pulled the trigger. The gun kicked like a mule, slamming her arms back and almost striking her in the face.

Philip's shotgun roared. Pellets blasted the brush around her, and something punched into her thigh.

Screaming, she stumbled back but remained on her feet. Her hand touched her leg and came away wet and sticky.

Ally grimaced. For being shot, there was a surprisingly small amount of blood. She turned and limped up the path. Tears poured down her cheeks, but the pain was only a little more than that of a bad charley horse.

Forcing herself to jog, she fled up the hill. It was now a foot race. Could she reach the safety of the house before Philip crested the hill and got a clear shot at her? She had to run. Her life depended on it.

Chapter Thirty

Ally stumbled and limped her way up the winding path, pushing on despite her wounded leg. The pain had become far worse. Her leg cramped and locked. She pitched forward, her cut hands scraping against the gravel as she collapsed onto the path. She stifled a scream. Tears streamed down her muddy cheeks as she lay on the unforgiving ground.

She rose onto her left knee, but when she planted her right foot, the intense jab from the shotgun pellet embedded in her thigh sent her muscles into a spasm.

Ally crashed back to the ground and rolled onto her back. A freezing rain fell. She gazed up at the drops of water reflecting the moonlight. It was hauntingly beautiful, like flying through a star field.

She remembered lying on her back as a little girl, watching the evening sky with her father. She asked him about her greatest fear — what it felt like to die. Technically, he had once. He'd been shot on a mission and declared dead by a medic. A different medic restarted his heart. Ally had finally worked up to the nerve to ask him, and she never forgot his answer.

"Great."

She'd waited for him to continue, but she'd made a face when he didn't. "I asked what it felt like to die!"

"I heard you. And I said it felt great. While the medic was trying to patch all the bullet holes in me, it hurt like nothing I ever felt before. I didn't think someone could live with that much pain. Maybe that's why my heart stopped. Maybe I hurt so bad I shut off. Either way, the pain ended, and it felt wonderful."

"Did you see a bright light?"

He crookedly smiled. "No, but I don't know if I was technically dead-dead. There were other wounded, and the medic had to look at them. Since I didn't have a pulse, he did his job and moved on."

"You didn't see anything?"

"No, but I felt something — peace. All the pain just vanished. It was a really neat feeling."

"I don't want to die, Daddy. I'm afraid."

She felt like she'd punched him in the gut from the expression on his face. He closed his eyes briefly and rolled over to stare directly at her. "I don't want you to either, butterfly. But it's not up to me. The thing is, you've got nothing to be afraid of, right?"

"Mom said that because I accepted Jesus, that when I die, I'll get to see her again in Heaven."

"Are you scared of Heaven?"

"No."

"So what do you have to be afraid of?"

Ally sat up. Her father was right. And maybe today wasn't her day to die. Even if it was, she wasn't going down like a pig in the mud. Snarling, Ally made it to her feet. She hobbled on, gaining some speed as she went. Limping and hopping on her good leg, she crested the hill.

Every light in the house was on. The back yard looked like a sporting field. It was so bright. She hopped down the path, rain, mud, and blood running down her face.

Footsteps sounded behind her.

She'd never reach the door without Philip having a clear shot at her back. A wrought iron bench next to the path was her only cover. She took four more strides and ducked behind it. Resting her wrist on the arm of the bench, she aimed down the gun sight.

Her heartbeat seemed to slow to a crawl until she realized everything had. Rain sparkled in the light as it fell in slow motion. Philip's head crested the hill. The muscles in her back tightened. Her body stiffened, and her forearms turned rigid.

She squeezed the trigger.

The gun roared.

Philip ducked and fired.

Pellets peppered the ground to her right.

Forcing her eyes to stay open, she waited for the muzzle to lower and fired again.

So did Philip.

Behind her, a window shattered.

Ally pulled the trigger. The gun clicked. She pulled again. CLICK.

Philip stood up and aimed.

CLICK.

Philip must have run out of ammo, too.

Ignoring the raging pain, Ally planted her weight on her right leg and sprinted for the house.

The back door swung inward, and Tim raced through the doorway. His eyes were wild, filled with fear and anger. "Stop! Uncle Philip!" he screamed as he dashed toward her. "STOP!"

Ally grabbed her husband as she reached him. Her legs buckled. She was falling.

Tim wrapped an arm around her waist. Jerking

her off her feet, he carried her through the open door. He kicked the door closed.

BLAM!

A small hole blasted through the wood.

Philip must have a pistol, too!

Tim ran into the kitchen, carrying her in his arms.

BLAM!

Wood splintered. Tim groaned and stumbled.

They rounded the corner toward the foyer.

Several more shots broke through the door. Scattered bullet holes stippled the kitchen wall.

Tim set Ally on her feet.

She gasped when her foot touched the tile.

"Are you hurt?" Tim asked, his brown eyes filled with concern.

BLAM! BLAM! BLAM! BLAM! BLAM! BLAM!

Six more rapid shots were fired outside.

The door slammed open. Philip charged into the kitchen. He glared at Ally and Tim. Blood poured from his mouth and nose. His hands balled into fists at his sides. "Rotten bitch." He stumbled forward and crashed face-first to the tile floor.

Philip's back was peppered with six bullet holes. Blood spread out beneath him like an upside-down spider. The acrid stench of gunpowder and blood filled the air.

Tim let go of Ally. "Wait here." He pressed his back against the kitchen wall and peered around the corner. "Scott? Is that you?"

No one answered.

Ally stared down at Philip, horror and confusion growing inside her.

"Gary must be outside. You need to run." Tim took a step toward her and drew a ragged breath. His lips pulled back, revealing his teeth. Blood ran down the wall he had leaned against.

Ally's eyes rounded in fear. "Are you shot?"

Tim nodded. "You need to run. Gary's coming."

Ally shook her head, trying to find the words. "Gary is dead. I found him on the beach. He'd been dead for days. He couldn't have killed the others, and he couldn't have shot Philip." Ally stared into her husband's eyes. Frank thought the killer was Tim's son, but he was wrong about it being Gary. Could it be Scott? The young policeman was the right age, and he had a gun.

Tim grabbed hold of the corner of the wall. His arm shook. "None of this makes sense. I'm sorry I got you mixed up in all of this."

"We need to get out of here." Ally limped over to him. Blood stained Tim's shirt in the back. She reached for him, but he shook his head.

"I can't walk. You go."

Ally grit her teeth. She wasn't leaving her husband to die. She scanned the room and hobbled over to the panty. She grabbed Nashwa's silver serving cart and wheeled it over to Tim. "Lie down."

Tim managed to collapse stomach first onto the cart. His arms dangled, and his feet dragged on the floor, but she could still push it.

"Hang on, babe. I know where we can hide."

Chapter Thirty-One

Ally wheeled Tim down the hallway to Tom's room. She kept glancing back, but no one followed them. Ally knocked on the door and whispered, "Tom. It's Ally."

Wood scraped against the floor, and Tom opened the door a moment later. He recoiled in horror.

"What happened? You're both hurt!"

Ally pushed Tim inside. "Lock the door and move the bureau back against it."

Ally carted Tim over to the bed. She managed to roll him off the cart and onto the mattress. She pulled his shirt up. Blood seeped from a bullet wound in his back. She tore the pillowcase off and bundled it up. Then she wrapped everything into place and pulled it tight using the sheet.

Tim gritted his teeth and swore.

"Bad word," Tom said.

"Sorry, Tom." Tim looked at Ally and flashed a crooked grin that immediately faded. "You need to take Tom out of here and hide."

"I'm not leaving you."

"I think you may not have much say in that matter," Tim grimaced. "I swear I never..."

"Shut up." Ally laid a pillow underneath his head. "I believe you. Don't die on me."

Tom gasped. "Die? Is Tim going to die?"

"Not if we can help it, Tom. We need to hide here. We'll be safe."

"But what about Momma?" Tom's eyes filled with tears. "Momma is in her room!" He rushed toward the hallway door and grabbed the bureau.

Ally pushed against it, but Tom was far too strong. "You can't go out there, Tom!"

"I have to get Momma!"

Ally shook her head. "You need to stay here and protect Tim."

"I can go!" Tom said. "I'm a superhero." He puffed out his chest and pointed at the red, white, and blue shield on his chest.

"You are. But your job is to keep my husband safe. I'll get Victoria." Ally limped over to the cellar door and pointed at the bookcase. "I'll sneak through the basement. Help me move this."

Tom rushed over and pushed it out of the way.

Ally unlocked the door. "Stay with Tim. You need to guard him and keep him safe. Don't answer the door."

Tom nodded.

"It's too dangerous." Tim tried to rise but fell back onto the bed. "You can't go, Ally."

"I have to do this. I love you." Ally locked the door and pulled it closed behind her. She awkwardly hobbled down the steps.

The basement light was still on. The silence was so deep that the ticking of the electric air dampeners seemed loud. She limped across the cellar, supporting her weight by holding onto different objects. Stopping at the shelves at the base of the kitchen stairs, she grabbed a roll of duct tape and clamped her mouth shut. She wrapped the tape around the wound in her thigh four times.

When she put weight on her leg, the muscles still burned, but at least it would support her somewhat. She climbed the stairs, stopping in the doorway to listen. The room was silent. She peeked out. Philip's body lay on the tiles in a pool of blood. Outside, she could hear the ocean and the patter of the rain. A cold breeze swept into the room. Ally hurried around Philip's body and crept into the foyer.

The tick of the grandfather clock sounded like a sledgehammer in the silence. Limping across the marble floor, she grabbed the railing and started upstairs. Even with the support of the banister, the climb up the staircase was agonizing. She paused at the top to catch her breath, then hobbled forward. She held onto the wall until she reached Victoria's bedroom and shoved open the door.

The room's splendor would have taken her breath away if Ally hadn't been running for her life. She'd never seen it before. The bed, draped in crimson silk and golden embroidered bedsheets, was the centerpiece of a room fit for royalty. The chandelier hanging above it was made of dozens of faux candles, each flickering, casting a warm glow across the walls and furniture. The collection of priceless antiques, each encased in glass cabinets, looked like they were worth more than Ally would make in a lifetime.

Victoria stood beside the window, staring out at the darkness.

"You need to come with me now!" Ally panted. "Philip is dead, and Tim has been shot."

"Unfortunately, that is not possible," Victoria crossed her arms.

The door slammed shut behind Ally. Scott stood next to the wall with his gun drawn. "You are the one person I'm sorry got mixed up in all this. Please move over next to your mother-in-law," he said.

Ally held up her shaking hands. "Victoria didn't kill your mother, Scott. Philip did. You killed him. You've got your revenge. This has to stop."

"I'm not going to ask again." Scott pointed his gun at her chest. "Move over next to Victoria."

"Come stand beside me, Ally." Victoria's voice was level and calm. "I think it's time that we have a little family chat."

Ally limped over to stand beside Victoria.

"My daughter-in-law is injured. You, of course, will permit her to sit down?"

Scott nodded.

Victoria pulled up a chair, and Ally gratefully collapsed onto it. Victoria turned toward the desk.

"Don't move." Scott took one step forward.

"Oh, please." Victoria rolled her eyes. "It is clear that you want to have a conversation, or else you would have simply shot me. Why don't we have that talk over bourbon? I'm sure Ally needs a drink, and I certainly do. Would you like one?"

"No."

Victoria strode over to the table next to the window and poured two long-stemmed snifter bowls of bourbon with a steady hand.

Ally wondered how she could have such liquid steel running through her veins to act so cool. But drinking wasn't going to get them out of this situation. Ally had to try something. "I found Jane's body. It's in the cellar. You can give her a proper burial. Philip killed her."

"No, he didn't," Scott said. "Victoria did. We

bugged the house. When Philip came up here after I broke the hole in the boat, he and Victoria got into a big fight at breakfast. I heard every word when they argued. Philip didn't kill my mother. He only buried her. She's the one who killed her, and now she's going to pay."

Victoria laughed. It was light and airy. The kind of laugh someone makes when they're having wine with a dear old friend, not staring down the barrel of a gun held by someone who just accused you of killing their mother. "Oh, good. You're not the Boy Scout I thought you were. Name a price to start the negotiations."

Ally shook her head. "He isn't talking about you paying with money!"

"Of course he is. He's a Hawthorne, after all. The love of money is in his DNA. It's what drives us."

Ally stared at Scott. He didn't deny what Victoria said. He studied Victoria like a poker player, trying to figure out the cards in her hand.

"You have several offshore accounts," Scott said. "I'm going to give you a few of my own, and you will transfer that money into them."

Ally's mouth twisted in horror. "Is that what this is all about? Money? You don't care about what happened to your mother?"

"Do try not to antagonize the man with the gun," Victoria said, handing the drink to Ally. "I must say, I'm disappointed in this part of your plan, Scott. You didn't think this through. I can't access my funds with the cell tower disabled."

Scott smirked. "I can turn the tower back on with the press of a button. You have the bank information?"

"Of course." Victoria sipped her drink.

"You're nothing but a thief!" Ally shouted, ready to throw the drink in his face.

Scott glared and pointed the gun at Ally's head. "Nothing is going to bring my mother back. Do you have any idea what kind of life I've had while these people lived like kings? Now it's my turn!"

"Spoken like a true Hawthorne." Victoria toasted him. "But you still have a lot to learn. You're begging for scraps when you could share the spoils."

"I'm not going to fall for your games." He scoffed. "Like you'd really welcome me to the family with open arms."

"You are my grandson. Blood of my blood and heir to my name and fortune."

"I killed your brother and your lover. You would never forgive me for that."

"Not for killing Philip. No, I couldn't forgive you for that. I do, however, understand why you did it. So, I'm negotiating a truce. I have two hundred thousand dollars in the wall safe. Along with several jewels. You can take those, plus the overseas accounts, for letting us live."

"And then what? I walk away?"

"No. You disappear, and I help you do that. I have the means. You see, you have the proof I am a killer. What would I do, go to the police? I think not. So, I will transfer..." Victoria's voice trailed off. Her hand shook as she took another sip from her drink. She spilled some liquid on her lip, and it ran down her chin. She covered her mouth with her other hand. "My apologies. Please give me a moment to catch my breath."

Ally's eyes widened. For the first time since she'd known her mother-in-law, she worried this was a real medical emergency. "Sit down, Victoria."

"That's not a bad idea," Victoria gasped. She reached for the chair next to Ally and stumbled. The bowl of her long-stemmed glass shattered against the armrest.

Scott rushed forward. "Don't die before you give me those numbers, you old —"

Victoria reeled up and plunged the broken end of the long-stemmed glass into the middle of his throat.

Scott clutched at his neck, the gun tumbling from his hand. It bounced on the carpet and lay at Ally's feet.

Victoria snatched the gun off the ground and rose with a victorious smirk on her lips. "You, my stupid bastard of a child, are no Hawthorne." She aimed the gun at his head and pulled the trigger.

Ally sat there with her mouth hanging open. Her hand touched the side of her face, now splattered with Scott's blood. She'd never witnessed anything so brutal. She stared at Victoria in horror. Her mother-in-law had slaughtered her grandson and now stood there grinning with pride.

Victoria's smile slowly faded. She took a deep breath and turned to gaze at Ally. "There aren't many things in my life that I regret. This, I fear, will be one of them." She raised the gun and pointed it at Ally's chest.

Chapter Thirty-Two

The drink in Ally's hand tumbled from her fingers. She stared up at her mother-in-law, holding Scott's gun pointed at her chest. Anger and disgust rose within her. "Why are you going to kill me?"

Victoria's chin tilted down, and she frowned. The disappointment in her voice was evident when she spoke. "I had such hopes for you, Ally. I thought Tim would never get over Jane. He was absolutely devastated when she abandoned him. And then you came into his life and bandaged up all his wounds. Even the guilt he bore regarding Tom, you healed."

"He still feels responsible."

"As he should. If he had obeyed, his brother wouldn't be damaged goods."

Ally regretted dropping her drink. She would have loved to have thrown it in Victoria's face. "Scott was telling the truth. You killed Jane."

"I did. And that is why you can't leave this room. If Tim ever found out, he would never forgive me, and with your Christian conscience always shining through, I wouldn't sleep well letting you walk away."

Ally eyed the door. With her leg, she'd never escape without getting shot first. "You won't get away with it."

Victoria laughed. She tilted the pistol in her hand. "You forget, my dear, what a wonderful storyteller I am. I will simply explain to the police that to save my life, you stabbed Scott, and he shot you. I hope you're appreciative I'm painting your death so heroically."

"The police will keep looking for the motive. Once they realize that Scott came here to get revenge for his mother's murder, they'll keep digging. They'll discover that Scott was Tim's son."

"You are prone to drama, but my explanation will be simple greed. Scott was a thief. It was an elaborate robbery gone bad. No one will know about Scott's lineage or connection to Jane. And since all of us will be seen as victims, me especially, considering the dual loss of my daughter-in-law and twin brother, the investigation will close swiftly, I assure you."

Ally went absolutely still. She couldn't move. It was as if she'd turned to stone. Victoria kept talking, but it was little more than a buzzing in Ally's ears. She imagined a puzzle piece tumbling through the air and landing in the center of this elaborate scheme, filling in the last part of the mystery.

We bugged the house. That's what Scott said. *We.*

Victoria lost her twin brother, Philip. Twins ran in the Hawthorne family.

Jane didn't have one baby. She had two.

"Are you listening to me?" Victoria shouted.

Ally raised her head and smiled.

"You thought of something. I can see it in your face. What?" Victoria's eyes hardened. "What did I miss?"

The door to the hallway swung open. A gunshot rang out.

Victoria screamed and dropped her pistol. Blood stained her blouse at the shoulder.

Kim stepped into the room, a smoking pistol in her hand. The shackles were missing from her wrists. "Sit down next to Ally or the next shot will be in your knee."

Victoria straightened up and, to Ally's amazement, flashed a pained grin. "Oh, well played. And here I thought the helpless mistress died aboard the fishing boat. My son even tried to rescue you."

Kim stared down at Scott's body. Her eyes welled with tears.

"I'm so sorry that she killed your boyfriend." Victoria pointed at Ally as she sat down.

Ally raised her hand, ready to backhand her mother-in-law across the face for trying to pin Scott's murder on her.

"Don't move, Ally." Still wearing the dirty red dress, Kim kept the gun trained on Victoria. "I know Victoria killed Scott. I listened to the whole thing. And he wasn't my boyfriend. He was my brother."

Victoria's mouth opened and closed. For the first time, Ally watched her mother-in-law truly at a loss for words.

"You killed Jane Nelson, and you're going to tell me every detail," Kim said.

Victoria crossed her arms. "Why would I do that?"

Kim took one step closer, aimed the gun at Victoria's leg, and closed one eye.

Victoria raised her hand. "You made your point. You said you bugged my home. Then you must know all the details. Why have me repeat them?"

"I want to know why."

"Oh, you are a Hawthorne —" Victoria began to

say, but Kim fired over her head. The bullet shattered glass somewhere behind them.

"Save it. My brother was greedy. I'm not. I don't want your blood money. All I want is the truth."

Victoria took a deep breath. "Are you sure? We are talking about an awful lot of money."

Kim fired again, and Victoria screamed as the bullet struck her calf.

Victoria's hands turned to white claws as she squeezed the arms of her chair.

"Kim, please stop," Ally begged.

"Tell me!" Kim aimed the gun at Victoria's other leg.

"You win. I will tell you the truth, but before I do, promise me that before you kill me, you'll listen to my very generous offer."

"You still think you can buy your way out of this?"

"Of course I do. Money is the universal lifesaver. And I have lots of it."

"Talk."

Victoria took a deep breath. Her bottom lip quivered. "My son, Tom, was very fond of Tim's new girlfriend. I tried to keep him away from her, but —"

BLAM!

Victoria shrieked as another bullet tore into her left leg.

"Don't lie to me," Kim said. "I know that you killed my mother. I want to know why."

Ally slapped Victoria across the face. "How dare you try to say Tom was responsible!"

Victoria's hand went to her bleeding lip. She stared daggers at Ally. "I was trying to save your life."

"Ha!" Kim laughed. "You only ever thought about yourself. Start talking, or I will go to work on the other leg. And remember, I already know most of the story."

Victoria grimaced as she leaned back in her chair. The fire inside her blazed in her eyes. Her lip curled, and when she spoke, her voice was low and gravelly, filled with hate. "When my son started high school, he fell in love with a girl named Jane Nelson, your mother. Jane showed up on my doorstep one day with a sob story about being pregnant. She claimed it was Tim's, but I didn't believe her. I doubt she even knew who the father was."

Ally swallowed down the bile rising in her throat.

"I gave Jane a plane ticket and a check to cover the abortion and provided more money than a lifetime of welfare benefits. She left, and I thought the matter was settled."

"But she came back," Kim said.

Ally watched as the polished mask Victoria always wore seemed to crack and fall off her face.

Victoria sat up straighter. She lifted her chin and peered down her nose at this cleaning woman who held her at gunpoint and dared threaten her.

"Yes. Jane said she had to tell Tim about the pregnancy. She didn't get the abortion. She thought he had a right to know. It would have destroyed my relationship with my son. I reminded her of my payment. Jane tore up my check in front of me and threw the pieces in my face. Then she had the audacity to turn her back to me! She wanted to push my buttons and see if she got away with it. So I waited until she reached the top of the stairs and gave her a little push. I didn't intend for her to break her neck, but accidents do happen."

Kim's hand shook with rage.

Victoria's cheeks blazed. Gone was the cold, calculating manipulator. Her eyes were glossy and filled with wrath, and she let her hate do the thinking, "Do you know the one mistake I made in all of this?"

"Killing my mother?"

Victoria smiled cruelly. "Not killing her when she was pregnant with you." Victoria lunged forward but didn't make it out of the chair.

Kim fired four shots into Victoria's chest.

Ally's mother-in-law fell silently back onto the seat. Her head flopped to the side, and her chest lay unmoving.

Kim fired two more rounds into Victoria's body.

Ally flinched.

Kim aimed the gun at Ally.

Ally slowly raised her hands. "Please don't."

Kim swallowed. She pulled at her left ear.

"I found your mother," Ally blurted out. "In the alcove where I met you in the wine cellar."

Fresh tears fell from Kim's eyes. "You're a good person, Ally."

"There's been enough killing. There doesn't have to be any more." Tears rolled down Ally's cheeks. "Tim didn't know about you and your brother. He thought your mother broke up with him and moved away."

Kim stared down at Scott. "I never really got a chance to know Scott. We were adopted separately. I found him three years ago. I thought he was as obsessed as I was in finding the truth, but he only wanted the money."

Ally tried calming her breathing and forced herself to shut her mouth. Kim was talking, and that was a lot better than shooting.

"I discovered who my birth mother was," Kim continued, "and went looking for her. When we found out she was last seen on this island, we came up with a plan to uncover the truth. I didn't want to kill anyone innocent. That wouldn't be right. Scott thought we should kidnap one of them and make them talk, but you heard her." Kim pointed at Victoria. "She would have said anything to get us to let her go. I moved here and got a job as a house cleaner. It provided me with full access to the home."

"You planted cameras and microphones," Ally said.

Kim nodded. "But no one ever discussed anything about my mom. Scott was a cop already and transferred here. He got the original police reports, but they weren't proof. I needed a way to get them all talking about it. I thought if they believed that history was repeating itself, someone would start talking."

Ally's stomach churned. Kim had been searching for answers for years. "Tim didn't have an affair?"

Kim cringed. "No. I'm sorry, but that ruse was necessary. I hired Gary and staged the photo in the restaurant. Then Gary got greedy and demanded more money from Scott."

"He killed Gary and Dennis?"

"Dennis deserved it. He saw my mother that night but changed his story. If he hadn't, the police might have solved my mother's murder. Everyone else that Scott killed was involved in Jane's death. Dr. Bradley kept his mouth shut because of his affair with Victoria. They were lovers. Philip buried my mother, and Frank took a bribe to look the other way."

Ally hung her head. "You've avenged your mother."

"No. There's one more person who needs to die."

Ally's chest tightened. She stared at Kim. "No one

else was involved in your mother's killing. They're all dead."

"I'm sorry, Ally. But Tim must pay for his part."

"What?" Ally grabbed the arms of the chair and froze when Kim aimed the gun at her. "Tim had nothing to do with Jane's murder. He didn't even know she came here. You bugged the house. You know that!"

"I do. But he confessed his other crime to you."

Ally's mouth opened, but no words came out. Her eyebrows pinched together, but Kim wasn't making any sense. "Tim never confessed to me about anything. He's always denied involvement."

"Tim told you. Jane asked him to run away with her, but he refused."

"Tim didn't know she was pregnant. They were still in high school. He told her to wait."

"It doesn't matter. If Tim had gone with Jane, my mother would have lived. And I'm sorry, but if Tom tries to stop me, I'll have to kill him too."

Ally's mind raced. She couldn't let Kim go to Tom's room, but there wasn't any way to stop her without winding up as dead as Victoria. "Tom is the sweetest soul you'll ever meet. He has truly never done anything to hurt anyone. Your mother liked him. He was nice to her. You can't go..." Ally's voice trailed off. Tom had barricaded himself and Tim in the room. Kim could never get inside with the bureau in the way. Ally forced herself to sit back in the chair and shut up.

Kim's cold eyes met Ally's, and she spoke as if she'd read Ally's thoughts. "Barricading the doors to Tom's room was a good idea. But it won't do them any good." Kim sighed. "You forgot. Tom's bedroom was the summer kitchen, so it has a dumbwaiter."

"No!"

Ally charged her.

Kim fired.

The bullet tore into Ally's thigh. She screamed and fell forward, sprawling on the carpet. "Don't do this!" Ally pleaded.

"I'm sorry. But your husband has to die." Kim shut the door.

The sound of something heavy being pushed in front of it rumbled into the room. Ally was trapped, but it didn't matter. With a bullet wound in each leg, she'd never get to Tom's room in time. Kim was right.

Her husband was going to die.

Chapter Thirty-Three

Ally lay helpless on the floor of Victoria's bedroom. Kim was on her way to Tom's room to murder her husband, and there was nothing Ally could do to stop her. Ally clasped her bloody hands together. If there was ever a time to call out to God...

Ally's eyes widened. She grabbed the carpet and crawled over to the window. Pulling herself up by the window frame, she shoved the window open.

"TOM! TOM!" She screamed.

On the first floor, Tom opened his window.

"She's coming! She's going to use the dumbwaiter. She's coming!"

Tom held his hands up and out. Even from this distance, she could tell he didn't understand.

"The bad guy is coming! She's coming to kill Tim!"

Tom darted back into the room. If he didn't understand her, what was he going to do?

It was up to her. She had to try something.

Ally grabbed the heavy curtain and gritted her teeth. Hand over hand, she pulled herself upright. She pushed the curtain through the window. It wouldn't be that far of a drop if she could hold on to it.

Climbing out the window, she clung to the fabric. The ground beneath her looked further away than only one story. She started to slide down. Metal snapped, the curtain rod folded in half, and she plummeted.

The glass above her broke as the curtain rod slammed into the panes. The top of the curtain held fast against the frame. Ally's arms jerked up, and she fell a few yards to the bushes below. The shrubs cushioned the impact, but the pain that shot up her legs made her shriek in agony. She rolled onto the gravel, barely able to breathe.

But she couldn't stop. Kim was going to kill Tim. Tom would try to protect him, and Kim would kill him, too.

Ally crawled. Hand over hand, she pulled herself across the front walkway.

Inside the house, someone yelled her name. She shook her head. It wasn't possible. Her mind was playing tricks on her. It sounded like Tim.

A gunshot rang out.

From inside, Tim yelled again, "Ally!"

On the far side of the house, a door smashed open.

Ally's eyes widened when Tim appeared wearing jeans and a white dress shirt. He raced across the grass, running toward the dock. "ALLY!" he shouted.

Ally's hope rose, but how could it be? Tim was too hurt. He couldn't walk, let alone run. It couldn't be him. She gasped.

It wasn't Tim. Tom was acting as a distraction. He was leading Kim away to save his brother.

"ALLY!" Tom screamed again as he sprinted toward the ocean.

The side door banged open, and Kim ran into view. She screamed — a guttural, rage-filled cry at the sky and heavens above.

The rain dampened Tom's white shirt. The red, white, and blue shield was now visible underneath.

"Stop, Kim! It isn't Tim. It's Tom! Please don't!"

BLAM!

Kim fired.

Tom stumbled. He slipped on the grass and crashed to the ground.

"NO!!" Ally crawled toward him, dragging her legs behind.

Kim ran over and stood over Tom.

Tom tried to get up but fell onto his knees.

"He didn't do anything!" Ally begged. "He's innocent. He's innocent!"

Kim lifted the gun.

Tom rolled onto his back. He raised his trembling hands and stared into Kim's face.

BLAM!

Ally screamed.

Kim stared out to the ocean. The hate had left her face. She looked so young. Her eyes rounded in confusion. A red spot on Kim's chest appeared and grew larger.

BLAM!

Another gunshot was fired, but it wasn't Kim shooting. Ally's eyes followed the noise. It had come from the sea. A boat sat in the harbor, close to the dock.

The gun tumbled from Kim's hand. She pitched backward, crashing to the ground.

Ally crawled over to Tom. From the docks, a police siren blared to life, and lights flashed on top of the boat.

Tom lay faceup on the grass.

Ally reached his side.

He gazed at her. "Did I do it?"

Ally nodded, the tears streaming down her face. "Don't talk. Just hold on. Help's coming. The police are here."

Tom's eyebrows rose. "I'm okay. I'm not hurt. I don't feel any pain."

Ally pressed her hand against the wound in his side, blood seeping between her fingers. "You're my superhero."

Tom smiled and closed his eyes.

Chapter Thirty-Four

Ally sat in her wheelchair next to Tim's hospital bed. She held his hand and lightly stroked his arm as he stared at the sealed letter in his hand. She hadn't been far from his side during the last three weeks.

"You don't have to do this," Ally said.

"I need to know." He opened the flap of the envelope and removed the paper. His eyes scanned the page, and he hung his head.

Ally gently took the letter from his hand. It was the result of the paternity test. She read through the legal mumbo-jumbo and reached the conclusion of the lab. Kim and Scott were fraternal twins. Jane Nelson was their mother. Tim was not their father.

Ally covered her mouth with her hand. In some way, she felt horrible for Kim and Scott, yet she couldn't condone the monsters they became. She closed her eyes. All she and Tim had done since being rescued was cry and apologize to each other. She was out of tears, and he seemed to be as well.

Tim took a deep breath. "I think I'm going to need a lot of therapy to deal with this." He looked at her and crookedly smiled. "They have couples therapy, right?"

Ally nodded. "I've got a feeling we'll have frequent flyer miles in the therapy department." She squeezed his hand. "That's not a bad thing."

"I'm sure it will be fun." Tim rolled his eyes.

"What's gonna be fun?" Tom yelled from the other bed. "Can I do it too?"

"I don't know if you need to, buddy." Tim smiled. "You're the most well-adjusted of all of us. I've got a question for you," Tim said. "When we get out of here, how'd you like to come live with us?"

"Back on the island?" Tom made a horrified face.

"No. And not in California either." Tim squeezed Ally's hand and said, "Why don't you tell him."

"My father lives in Kansas. The people are very nice, and we'd both like to have a little distance away from the ocean. It's a small city but it has a funny name — Manhattan. "

Tom's mouth fell open. "No!"

Tim exchanged a puzzled glance with Ally, "You wouldn't like to live there?"

"I'd love to!" Tom raised both hands over his head. "Superman lives in Kansas, and the Avenger's headquarters is in Manhattan!"

Ally smiled. Tom was so happy; she didn't have the heart to correct him.

"Can I make my room look like a superhero base?" Tom asked.

"Of course you can, Buddy," Tim said.

Ally took Tim's hand. "I think I'm the happiest girl in the world. I'm going to have two superheroes watching over me."

They all laughed.

THE END

Join the FREE Preferred Reader Program

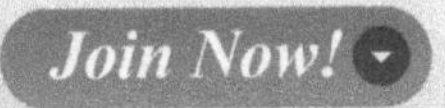

Visit ChristopherGreyson.com to sign-up!

<u>ONE LITTLE LIE</u>

A LIE IS A WELCOME MAT FOR THE DEVIL...

Kate had high hopes when she moved to her husband's hometown, but her domestic bliss was short-lived. Blindsided by her spouse's public affair with his high school sweetheart, everything she worked for begins to unravel, along with her sanity. Confused, alone, and afraid, can Kate untangle the web of lies and unmask her stalker, or will she lose everything—including her life?

One Little Lie is a riveting suspense novel set in an idyllic town where money talks, gossip flows, and the court of public opinion rules. Jump on for a fun, fast-paced ride with a book you can't put down!

The Detective Jack Stratton Mystery-Thriller Series

The Detective Jack Stratton Mystery-Thriller Series, authored by *Wall Street Journal* bestselling writer Christopher Greyson, has 5,000+ five-star reviews and over a million readers and counting. If you'd love to read another page-turning thriller with mystery, humor, and a dash of romance, pick up the next book in the highly acclaimed series today:

<u>And Then She Was GONE</u>

A hometown hero with a heart of gold, Jack Stratton was raised in a whorehouse by his prostitute mother. When his foster mother asks him to look into a missing girl's disappearance, Jack quickly gets drawn into a baffling mystery. As Jack digs deeper, everyone becomes a suspect—including himself.

<u>GIRL JACKED</u>

They say a dangerous man is the one who had it all and lost it. But they're wrong, it's the one who lost everything but has a chance to get it back...

Guilt has driven a wedge between Jack and the family he loves. When Jack, now a police officer, hears the news that his foster sister Michelle is missing, it cuts straight to his core. The police think she just took off, but Jack knows Michelle would never leave her loved ones behind—like he did. Forced to confront the demons from his past, Jack must take action, find Michelle, and bring her home... or die trying.

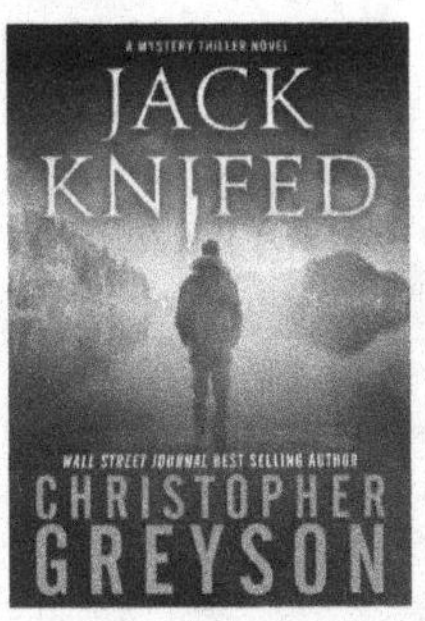

JACK KNIFED

How far would you go to uncover the truth of your past?

Constant nightmares have forced Jack to seek answers about his rough childhood and the dark secrets hidden there. The mystery surrounding Jack's birth father leads Jack to investigate the twenty-seven-year-old murder case in Hope Falls.

A heart-rending mystery-thriller about lost love, betrayal, and murder that will keep you on the edge of your seat.

JACKS ARE WILD

As the body count rises, the stakes are life and death—with no rules except one—Jacks are Wild.

When Jack's sexy old flame disappears, no one thinks it's suspicious except Jack and one unbalanced witness. Jack feels in his gut that something is wrong. He knows that Marisa has a past, and if it ever caught up with her—it would be deadly. The trail leads him into all sorts of trouble—landing him smack in the middle of an all-out mob war between the Italian Mafia and the Japanese Yakuza.

A strong hero, smart women sleuths, and more twists and turns than a piece of licorice.

JACK AND THE GIANT KILLER

A serial killer is stalking Jack's town--and no one's safe. But they don't know Jack.

Rogue hero Jack Stratton is back in another action-packed, thrilling adventure. While recovering from a gunshot wound, Jack gets a seemingly harmless private investigation job—locate the owner of a lost dog—Jack begrudgingly assists. Little does he know it will place him directly in the crosshairs of a merciless serial killer.

An action-packed thrill ride until the very end!

<u>DATA JACK</u>

Can Jack and Alice stop a pack of ruthless criminals before they can Data Jack?

Jack Stratton's back is up against the wall. He's broke, kicked off the force, and his new bounty hunting business has slowed to a trickle. He thinks things are turning around when Alice gets a lucrative job setting up a home data network.When the computer program the CEO invented becomes the key tool in an international data heist, things turn deadly. In this digital age of hackers, spyware, and cyber terrorism-- data is more valuable than gold. The thieves plan to steal the keys to the digital kingdom and with this much money at stake, they'll kill for it. Can Jack and Alice stop the pack of ruthless criminals before they can *Data Jack?*

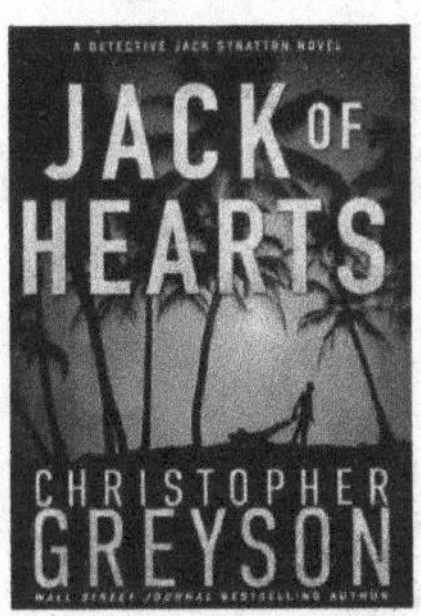

JACK OF HEARTS

Jack Stratton is heading south for some fun in the sun. Already nervous about introducing his girlfriend, Alice, to his parents, the last thing Jack needed was for the dog-sitter to cancel, forcing him to bring Lady, their 120-pound King Shepherd, on the plane with them. The dog holds Jack responsible and wants payback. On top of everything, Jack is still waiting for Alice's answer to his marriage proposal.

When his mother and the members of her neighborhood book club ask him to catch the "Orange Blossom Cove Bandit," a small-time thief who's stealing garden gnomes and peace of mind from their quiet retirement community, how can Jack refuse?

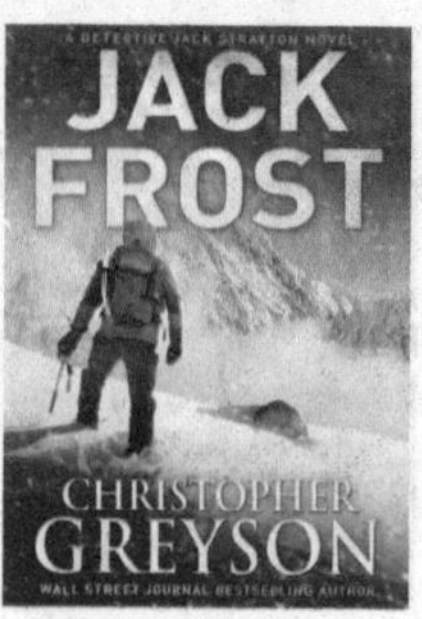

<u>JACK FROST</u>

What do you get when you mix the block-buster television show Survivor with Agatha Christie's masterpiece And Then There Were None…

Jack has a new assignment: to investigate the suspicious death of a soundman on the hit TV show *Planet Survival*. Jack goes undercover as a security agent where the show is filming on nearby Mount Minuit. Soon trapped on the treacherous peak by a blizzard, a mysterious killer continues to stalk the cast and crew of *Planet Survival*. What started out as a game is now a deadly competition for survival. As the temperature drops and the body count rises, what will get them first? The mountain or the killer?

JACK OF DIAMONDS

All Jack Stratton wants to do is get married to the woman he loves—and make it through the wedding. It seems like he is finally getting his wish until he responds to a police distress call and discovers his old partner unconscious in an abandoned house. Investigators insist it was just an accident, but Jack fears there may be more to it. Sketches of women cover the walls, and among them is one sketch that makes Jack's blood run cold—a sketch of Alice, pinned up beside an invitation to a very special wedding—his own.

This time, "till death do us part" might just be a bit too accurate!

CAPTAIN JACK

Looking forward to some fun in the surf and sand, newlyweds Jack and Alice Stratton are determined not to let something like a hurricane upset their honeymoon plans. But the storm's winds and churning tides unearthed a secret long hidden beneath the turquoise waters of the island paradise.

A local tour boat captain discovers a lost submarine and offers to sell the location to a man known only as the Dyab—the Devil. When the captain is murdered, the police suspect Jack and Alice and confiscate their passports. Trapped between the Devil and the deep blue sea, the handsome young detective and his blushing bride have nowhere to turn and everything to lose as they set out to prove their innocence and find the real killer.

JACK OF SPADES

The most dangerous killer is the one you don't see...

When a distraught man calls 911 to report a murder that hasn't even happened, police think it's a hoax or a crackpot until the caller turns out to be a highly respected Doctor. After his warning comes violently true, the killing thrusts Jack Stratton into his first official case as a new detective. Money, sex, and drugs are all motives. Still, these aren't your usual suspects: a tenured professor, a tech CEO, a mathematical genius, and a convicted felon have a million reasons to kill, but who did it? Can Jack follow the trail of victims and catch the mastermind, or will his first case be his last?

Hear your favorite characters
come to life in audio versions of
the Detective Jack Stratton
Mystery-Thriller Series!
Audio Books now available on Audible!
Listen Now

Novels featuring Jack Stratton in order:
<u>AND THEN SHE WAS GONE</u>
<u>GIRL JACKED</u>
<u>JACK KNIFED</u>
<u>JACKS ARE WILD</u>
<u>JACK AND THE GIANT KILLER</u>
<u>DATA JACK</u>
<u>JACK OF HEARTS</u>
<u>JACK FROST</u>
<u>JACK OF DIAMONDS</u>
<u>CAPTAIN JACK</u>

Fantasy Adventure
PURE OF HEART

Orphaned and alone, rogue-teen Dean Walker has learned how to take care of himself on the rough city streets. Unjustly wanted by the police, he takes refuge within the shadows of the city. When Dean stumbles upon an old man being mugged, he tries to help—only to discover that the victim is anything but helpless and far more than he appears. Together with three friends, he sets out on an epic quest where only the pure of heart will prevail.

A BEAUTIFUL PLACE TO DIE

When you wound an angel, you unleash a demon.

It was supposed to be a simple assignment, get a DNA sample from a young boy, but it turns into a deadly trap. With a price on the boy's head and a target on her back, Kiku must not only shield him from the ruthless Russian mafia but also from a traitor within the Yakuza itself. Torn between love and honor, duty and scorn, Kiku must decide where her loyalties lie before it's too late.

KINDLE THE FIRES OF WAR

She's outnumbered 100 to 1.
They're going to need more men.

Kiku has gone rogue. Now hunted by the Russian mob and the Yakuza, Kiku heads to Hong Kong's underbelly to rescue her lover. Faced with impossible odds, Kiku must outwit, outfight, and outrun everyone trying to capture her and collect the two-million-dollar bounty. Rats fueled by greed or vengeance, driven by ruthless leaders, run rampant, all hoping to score. The mob, Yakuza, and Hong Kong's black market—they all wanted to fight. Kiku started a war.

DANCE OF DEATH

To save the one she loves, she'll kill them all.

Kiku's quest to rescue her lover has gone disastrously wrong. With the odds stacked against her, her enemies think she'll run and hide to save herself. They're wrong—dead wrong. Kiku decides to take the fight to them instead. Now the hunter, Kiku, will stop at nothing to protect those she loves.

The Adventures of Finn & Annie — MiniMystery Series

In these heartwarming short stories, join Finn and Annie as they investigate their way through murder, arson, theft, embezzlement, and maybe even love, seeking to distinguish between truth and lies, scammers and victims. A MiniMystery series that will touch your heart and leave you craving more!

Acknowledgments

I would like to thank all the wonderful readers out there. It is you who make the literary world what it is today—a place of dreams filled with tales of adventure! Word of mouth is crucial for any author to succeed. If you enjoyed the novel, please consider leaving a review at Amazon, even if it is only a line or two; it would make all the difference and I would appreciate it very much.

I would also like to thank my amazing wife for standing beside me every step of the way on this journey. My thanks also go out to Laura and Christopher, my two awesome kids, and my dear mother and the rest of my family.

ABOUT THE AUTHOR

My name is Christopher Greyson, and I am a storyteller. Since I was a little boy, I have dreamt of what mystery was around the next corner, or what quest lay over the hill. If I couldn't find an adventure, one usually found me, and now I weave those tales into my stories.

My love for tales of mystery and adventure began with my grandfather, a decorated World War I hero. I will never forget being introduced to his friend, a WWI pilot who flew across the skies at the same time as the feared, legendary Red Baron. I love to hear from my readers. Please go to Christopher-Greyson.com and sign up for my mailing list to receive periodic updates on new book releases. Thank you for reading my novels. I hope my stories have brightened your day.

Sincerely,

THE WOMAN BENEATH THE STAIRS
Copyright: Christopher Greyson
Published: February 7th 2024

The right of Christopher Greyson to be identified as author of this
Work has been asserted by him in accordance with sections 77
and 78 of the Copyright, Designs and Patents Act 1988.

All rights reserved. No part of this publication may be
reproduced, distributed, or transmitted in any form or by any
means, including photocopying, recording, or other electronic or
mechanical methods, without the prior written permission of the
publisher.

Any references to historical events, real people, or real places are
used fictitiously. Names, characters, and places are products of
the author's imagination.

Find out more about the author and upcoming books online at
www.ChristopherGreyson.com.